"Have you some h... that makes you co...

For one brief moment ... words that he simply sta... ... his head and burst out laughi... ...er life as a novice had not dulled her w... ...r tongue. There was nothing he liked more in the world than to laugh— well, *almost* nothing—and in his experience few women had a talent for amusement. Not this one, however. She annoyed him and challenged him, yet did not fail to keep him entertained.

Robin was tempted to tell her that the problem with his clothes lay in the fact that he was wearing too many.

"Indeed, you have guessed it aright, and well I could use with some help with a certain itch that needs to be scratched," Robin drawled. He saw her eyes widen and her cheeks grow pink....

Praise for Deborah Simmons's previous titles

My Lord de Burgh
"…a luminous novel…a love story not to be missed."
—*Romantic Times Magazine*

The Gentleman Thief
"Ms. Simmons has a delightful flair for comedy."
—*Romantic Times Magazine*

Robber Bride
"…totally captivating, Ms. Simmons' powerful characters do magical things with this excellent plot."
—*Affaire de Coeur*

Deborah Simmons

My Lady de Burgh

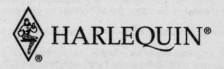

HARLEQUIN®

TORONTO • NEW YORK • LONDON
AMSTERDAM • PARIS • SYDNEY • HAMBURG
STOCKHOLM • ATHENS • TOKYO • MILAN • MADRID
PRAGUE • WARSAW • BUDAPEST • AUCKLAND

ISBN 0-373-29184-1

MY LADY DE BURGH

Copyright © 2001 by Deborah Siegenthal

Visit us at www.eHarlequin.com

Printed in U.S.A.

**Available from Harlequin Historicals and
DEBORAH SIMMONS**

Fortune Hunter #132
Silent Heart #185
The Squire's Daughter #208
The Devil's Lady #241
The Vicar's Daughter #258
*Taming the Wolf #284
The Devil Earl #317
Maiden Bride #332
Tempting Kate #371
The Knights of Christmas #387
*"A Wish for Noel"
*The de Burgh Bride #399
The Last Rogue #427
*Robber Bride #455
The Gentleman Thief #495
*My Lord de Burgh #533
*My Lady de Burgh #584

*The de Burghs

Please address questions and book requests to:
Harlequin Reader Service
U.S.: 3010 Walden Ave., P.O. Box 1325, Buffalo, NY 14269
Canadian: P.O. Box 609, Fort Erie, Ont. L2A 5X3

For all my wonderful readers in Japan,
with thanks for all your generosity,
support and enthusiasm

Chapter One

The de Burghs had been cursed.

Robin was certain of it. Although the family continued to be prosperous and powerful, all of its members seemingly healthy and strong, there was an insidious force at work that was gradually weakening its ranks and scattering the de Burghs across the countryside. And Robin knew well its name. *Marriage.*

Just four years ago the seven sons of the Earl of Campion had been bachelors and determined to remain so. Then, as if directed by some unseen hand, one by one, Dunstan, Geoffrey and Simon had taken wives. Even the earl himself had wed again at Christmastide! And now Robin had been called home to the celebration of his brother Stephen's nuptials.

As he glanced around the great hall of Campion Castle, Robin was not cheered by the sight of the many couples. Instead of tendering congratulations, he wanted to howl in outrage. Not only did he protest the fate of his siblings, but of the three de Burghs yet unmarried, he was the oldest, a knowledge that made him decidedly tense. And with good reason. Robin had no idea how the other two felt about it, but he was starting to sweat.

It was not that he had anything against women. They provided a welcome diversion at times, some more than others, of course, but even the most comely or entertaining did not tempt him in the slightest toward a lasting union. The very thought of being shackled to one of them forever made Robin lift a finger to loosen his suddenly tight neckline. Already, he felt the noose closing around him, collaring him forever to some unknown, unnamed female.

Although usually the most lighthearted member of the family, Robin was becoming downright surly as he contemplated his future. As both a man and a knight, he resented the feeling of helplessness that assailed him. He wanted to strike out, but what use was his skill with a sword against a phantom? Robin gritted his teeth even as he wondered how much time he had left. Although his brothers appeared to have succumbed without a fight, he refused to accept his fate so easily.

Surely there was some way to prevent what lay ahead! Robin had been taught that reasoning could extricate him from most situations, and normally he would have asked his father for advice, but the earl had already been felled by the curse. In this instance, whatever wisdom he offered would be suspect. And there was no sense in approaching his married brothers.

Robin's options were dwindling, and he felt the cold, clammy press of desperation. He had always thought the de Burghs invincible, for they were powerful men, strong warriors, learned in varying degrees and skillful at running a vast demesne. Wealth and privilege and capability had resulted in an inbred arrogance that continued to show itself, even in those who now called themselves husbands, but Robin felt his own confidence faltering. Only three de Burgh bachelors remained; perhaps it was time they put their heads together.

Having made his decision, Robin moved into action swiftly, seeking Reynold among those who crowded the vast, vaulted hall. He found the younger de Burgh seated on a bench, his back against the wall and his bad leg stretched out before him. Normally glum, Reynold appeared even more grim than ever, and Robin wondered if he was counting his last hours of freedom, as well.

Flashing Reynold what he hoped was an encouraging grin, Robin sank down beside his brother and tried to think of what to say. No one had openly broached the subject of this sudden alarming propensity for marriage, and Robin was not sure how to begin. Luckily, Reynold spoke first.

"Can you believe it?" he asked, shaking his head as he gazed at Stephen. "After all the women he has dallied with, I never thought to see him settle down. Or give up his taste for wine."

"Nor did I," Robin agreed. He studied Reynold carefully, but his brother's expression was unreadable, as usual. However, he was determined to plunge onward. Although the de Burghs would rather die than admit a weakness, clearly honesty was called for in this instance, and time was running out. Perhaps together they could somehow bring about an end to the weddings. Hopefully, before his own.

"I never expected to see any of our brothers wed," Robin said, slanting a glance toward his sibling.

"Don't you think it odd that they are all doing it? And so quickly?"

Reynold shrugged stiffly. He was never talkative, so Robin wasn't particularly disheartened by his lack of comment. And there was no point in waiting any longer. "Well, I do. I think it damned odd," Robin said. He leaned closer, to speak in a low undertone. "In fact, I think 'tis the work of a curse."

Reynold swung round to stare at him, but Robin was undeterred by the scrutiny. "How else would you account for it?" he demanded. "Just a few years ago we were all bachelors and liking it well enough. Now, as if manipulated by some mysterious force, the de Burghs are being shackled to females, one by one, even Father!" Robin shuddered. "I tell you, we must do something before we are next!"

Robin followed Reynold's glance down to the cup in his hand and frowned. He had been drinking a bit much of the freely flowing wine, but who wouldn't, when faced with his sentence for the future? Surely, even the implacable Reynold must be worried. "Aren't you concerned?" he asked.

His brother's stoic expression changed not a whit. "About what?"

"About being snared by some woman!" Robin said, waving a hand toward their once-carefree brothers, who now hovered near their respective wives, smitten and witless. "About becoming one of *them!*"

Reynold snorted. "I should be so lucky."

"Lucky? I tell you, they've been cursed!" Robin protested.

Reynold eyed him as if he had lost his mind. "Look at them, Robin," he said. "Do you think they're unhappy?"

Robin obediently glanced toward the sibling who stood closest in their line of sight. It was Stephen, and Robin had to admit that his charming brother looked even better than ever, but that was probably because he had quit drinking. Of course, he was grinning like a fool, as they all were, even surly Simon. As for Geoffrey, the scholar, he was crowing over the infant in his arms, just as if he had personally given birth to it, and Robin felt a stab of something alien.

"Of course, they all *appear* happy, otherwise they wouldn't have gone through with it, would they?" he said. "I tell you, it's all part of some blight upon the family."

"Most men would trade their souls for such a blight," Reynold murmured. Something stark and wistful passed over his face, only to be replaced by a scowl. "There's no curse," he muttered.

"And just how can you be sure of that?" Robin asked, annoyed by Reynold's skepticism.

"Because I will never marry," he said, and rising to his feet, Reynold stalked away, limping slightly.

Robin frowned. Was it his imagination or had his always moody brother become even more surly? It was probably because he alone of the seven de Burgh brothers remained at Campion. Robin wondered if he ought to stay on after the celebration instead of returning to Baddersly, a demesne he had been holding for Dunstan. But the thought of all the changes that had been wrought here in his absence, especially the addition of a new lady of the castle, a stepmother, made him wince. He wanted to go back to the Campion of old, not this new, unfamiliar place.

It seemed just yesterday he and his brothers had all lived here together, playing tricks on one another, relying strictly on each other, confiding only in each other, sometimes including their sire and sometimes not, though little enough got past the Earl of Campion. Oh, there were squabbles, of course, but they had been one, big, boisterous clan.

Now everything was different. His brothers were scattered all over the kingdom, living with their wives, returning for Christmas or an unusual occasion such as this one. It just wasn't right. Robin grunted in dismay at the emptiness that yawned before him whenever he considered his family. Although his wasn't a bitter nature, he felt betrayed somehow.

Yet he was loathe to blame his brothers. They obviously were befuddled or under some kind of enchantment. How else to explain their sudden perplexing behavior? Robin had grown up with them in a household of men, lived now among the knights of Baddersly, and he just couldn't comprehend this abrupt penchant for taking wives.

It had started with Dunstan, the eldest, and the man Robin most admired in the world. Having served the king as a knight, Dunstan had won a demesne of his own, Wessex, and was now known as the Wolf of Wessex. When he wed Marion, a woman whom all the de Burghs held in affectionate regard, Robin had been startled. But the marriage had been forced by circumstance, Marion's guardian having threatened her. And since Dunstan lived apart anyway, the new arrangement had little altered things at home.

Poor Geoffrey had been forced to wed by king's decree, in a union designed to end the warring between Dunstan and his neighbor. At the time Robin had been thankful for his own escape, though sorry enough for Geoff, whose bride was a horrifying creature. She had since become more agreeable, but Robin still retained his sympathy for his brother, although Geoff seemed as devoted to her as Dunstan was to Marion. Still, the circumstances surrounding both couples were so unusual that Robin's suspicions hadn't been aroused.

It was Simon's nuptials that had shaken him.

Simon, the fiercest of them all, a warrior through and through, had, *of his own volition,* fallen for the woman who had bested him in battle! By the time Robin and his siblings had reached Simon, he was too far gone to help. Geoffrey had even insisted on matchmaking between the two, an act Robin considered tantamount to betrayal of his own flesh and blood.

It was at that point that Robin began to think of Dunstan, Geoffrey and Simon as possessed. And this celebration for Stephen, who was known for sampling the charms of women far and wide, had just confirmed his opinion. If Stephen could marry, then the rest of them were doomed. His once strong brothers had been felled, weakened and ensnared, and Robin had no intention of being the next to surrender.

Not that he particularly disliked women. He had dallied with a few, and they had provided him with most pleasant divertissement. Most pleasant. But outside the bedchamber, their appeal waned. For the most part, Robin found them to be petulant and demanding creatures, and he was not going to be saddled with a lifetime of that, no matter how happy his brothers appeared!

Perhaps Reynold yearned for such a fate, but Robin did not, and he would be taken for a fool before he would just sit around waiting for his own ruin. The more he thought about it, the more determined he became. With or without help, he was going to try to discover whatever bedeviled the de Burghs before it was too late. Drawing a deep breath, Robin knew a powerful surge of resolution, only to feel it flag as he came to a disappointing realization.

Unfortunately, he didn't know a thing about curses or how to remove them. The earl had raised his sons to be educated and enlightened, and they scoffed at witches, sorcery and the like. Although Robin had always been more inclined than the others toward the power of charms and talismans and relics, he had no idea where to find a totem to ward off weddings. As far as he knew, there was no patron saint of bachelors, unless one counted monks, and Robin had no desire to take a vow of chastity.

Quickly, he dismissed the Church as a source of aid in this matter, for its views on marriage were well known. No, he needed someone who possessed expertise of a more mystical nature. Robin racked his brain, but the only people he suspected might be familiar with such things were the l'Estranges, Stephen's new wife and her relatives. The hall had been buzzing with vague gossip about them ever since Robin had arrived. But somehow he didn't think the bride would appreciate it if he accused her, however obliquely, of being part of a scourge upon the de Burghs.

Robin frowned thoughtfully. Although he couldn't approach Brighid, she did have aunts, and they were rumored to have a knowledge of healing and other unusual skills. Perhaps, if he didn't seek to redress the wrongs of his older brothers, already lost to their wives, but sought strictly to prevent his own impending doom, Robin could coax them into helping him.

Taking a fortifying drink, he rose to his feet, immediately regretting his abrupt movement as he became slightly light-headed. With a grimace, he set his empty cup down, unwilling to replace Stephen as the drunkard of the family. He had always been his own man, neither envious nor imitative of his brothers, and he was not about to start now. Drawing a bracing breath, he headed through the festive crowd in search of the Mistresses l'Estrange.

They were not hard to find, for they wore very colorful costumes that stood out in the throng. The shorter, plump aunt even had some kind of little bells sewn on her sleeves, an obvious sign of eccentricity, if not otherworldly abilities. Robin grinned, feeling a renewing surge of his innate confidence. Surely, she could help him.

"Mistress l'Estrange?" he asked, and was rewarded by a jingling as the small, white-haired woman turned to greet him, a welcoming smile upon her face.

"My lord!"

"Please call me Robin, Mistress," he said, inclining his head graciously.

"Of course! And I am Cafell. Have you met my sister Armes?" she said, gesturing toward a taller, more taciturn woman.

Robin nodded again. "Mistress." He had intended to begin with the less dour one. Although not possessed of Stephen's reputation, he could play the charmer as well as any other de Burgh, and she looked more agreeable than her sister. But having gone this far, he didn't want to wait. It seemed imperative, suddenly, that he take some action.

He flashed them one of his best grins. "May I say what a pleasure it is to welcome you into our family."

"Why, thank you, my lord Robin," Cafell said, preening happily.

"Robin will do," he said, inclining his head once more as he subtly tried to maneuver the older woman to the side. Unfortunately, her sister followed, so he was forced to address them both.

"Indeed, I count your arrival as a stroke of good fortune for myself since I am in dire need of your special talents," he said smoothly.

Cafell's brow furrowed. "You have an injury that requires healing?"

Robin laughed. "No. My problem is a bit more unusual than that." He lowered his voice. "A most delicate matter, really—"

Armes cut him off with a sharp look. "This wouldn't have anything to do with the heritage of the l'Estranges, would it?" she asked.

Robin drew up short. Perhaps there was some sort of protocol involved here that he knew nothing about. "Well, yes—"

"Oh, good!" Cafell said, clapping her hands with glee, despite her sister's admonishing look. Robin glanced from one to the other in question. Although Cafell appeared delighted by his request, Armes remained rather forbidding. He wondered just what abilities she had and whether he was going to end up with even more trouble. He was already fending off one curse; he did not care to have another laid upon him.

"Tell us! What can we do for you?" Cafell said, interrupting his gloomy thoughts.

"Sister, I hardly think—" Armes began.

Cafell waved her arm in an airy gesture that produced little jingling sounds. "Oh, Brighid can hardly complain when she—"

"But he is a de Burgh!" Armes protested, while Robin swung his gaze from one sister to the other, trying to follow the conversation.

"All the better!" Cafell said, rubbing her hands together in a manner that began to alarm Robin. He started to reconsider his plan and stepped back a pace, only to feel the little woman's touch upon his arm. "Don't go, Lord Robin!" she admonished before turning to her sister.

"Armes, we must at least hear him out, for the sake of common courtesy, if nothing else. We are related now, after all," she added, which didn't hearten Robin one bit. She turned back to him brightly. "Come, now, tell us what troubles you."

"Well," Robin began. He eyed Armes warily, but she finally gave him a stiff nod, which he interpreted as a gesture to proceed.

"Go on, dear," Cafell urged.

"Well, I was thinking about all these weddings," Robin said. Warming to his subject, he drew a deep breath and plunged onward. "I find them all odd, following so closely on one another, when just a few years ago, we de Burghs were all bachelors."

Armes frowned. "What's so odd about it? Seven healthy young men of marriageable age are bound to seek out spouses, especially lords from such an important family."

"To carry on the dynasty!" Cafell noted, gleefully.

"Perhaps," Robin admitted, though privately he didn't accept that explanation. His brothers had never seemed intent upon reproducing until *after* they were wed. And why all of them at once? Dunstan had married late, but the others were doing so younger and younger. "Could it be that someone has put some kind of, ah, spell on us all?"

"Probably your own sire," Armes muttered, and Robin blinked, wondering if he had heard her aright.

"Oh, he's jesting, aren't you, Robin?" Cafell said, playfully striking his chest. "Your brother warned us that you were a trickster."

Robin felt his hopes ebb. Perhaps he was known for a few pranks here and there, but he was deadly serious, and he didn't know how to impress his urgency upon the eccentric l'Estranges.

"*I* think he means it," Armes said, and they both studied him with renewed interest.

"Why, Sister, I do believe you're right! But, why would you want to—"

"He's worried about himself," Armes said in a rather disgusted tone that made Robin straighten, though he could hardly take offense at what was the truth.

"Oh, you poor boy!" Cafell exclaimed, patting his arm, which produced more little bell sounds. He glanced around, uncomfortably, but she only leaned closer, as if to impart some secret. "I wish we could look into your future, to reassure you, but Brighid frowns upon those things, you see. Although I admit she is growing more open-minded of late." Cafell looked a question at her sister, who firmly shook her head.

"I do not think she would appreciate that sort of interference with her new family," Armes said.

Robin felt his shoulders droop in disappointment. He didn't want a bit of soothsaying; he needed a curse lifted. And even if these two were willing to help, it didn't appear they had the necessary skills. Abruptly, he brightened as a new course struck him. "Perhaps there is someone else you know, in the same line of trade, so to speak, who might be able to consider the problem?" he asked hopefully.

Armes sniffed. "'Tis not as though we belong to a guild, young man!"

"We really know of no others with such talents beyond our own family," Cafell explained gently. At Robin's crestfallen expression, she patted him again. "Now, don't despair. We shall think of something!"

The two women exchanged glances, then Cafell frowned pensively. Finally, she said, "Well, there is Cousin Anfri."

"A complete charlatan!" Armes sniffed.

"How about Mali?"

"Dead," Armes replied. "The l'Estranges are not blessed with many progeny."

Robin wondered if the union with Stephen would change that, but Cafell suddenly yelped, startling him. "What about Vala?" she said.

"Oh, poor Vala, she was quite the beauty, and so gifted," Armes said.

"Didn't she marry one of the Welsh princes?" Cafell asked.

"Yes," Armes replied. "What was his name?"

"Owain ap Ednyfed?"

"I believe so," Armes said with a nod. "But I understood that she died not long afterwards."

"Did she? I was of the opinion that was not certain, but it is possible," Cafell said. "So much fighting over there through the years, you understand, one prince against another or Llewelyn himself, and, of course, against the king. We were lucky to be well away from it all." She paused. "But I thought there was a daughter."

Armes frowned. "I don't recall. That was a long time ago, and there was only hearsay—"

"Perhaps, Lord Robin could go and see!" Cafell suggested. She leaned forward, whispering confidentially, once more. "Vala was very gifted."

Robin perked up at this news. "Where would I find her?" he asked.

"Why, in Wales, of course. That's where most of the l'Estranges are, except us, of course."

Robin stared at the two women, who were smiling benignly, and stifled a groan. Stephen and his bride had returned from Wales with rumors of war at their heels, the Welsh princes seizing lands and rousing the people against Edward. Were these two gentlewomen trying to get him killed? Having no intention of marching into a country in the midst of battle, Robin eyed them askance.

The l'Estranges seemed to be oblivious to such danger, however, and they waited expectantly for his answer, so he choked out a polite thank you and excused himself with a nod. As he walked away, Robin realized he had reached an impasse in his efforts to lift the curse.

But his lack of success was hard to accept, for if he did nothing, then surely he would find himself wed. *And soon.*

* * *

Robin watched his host raise a cup in salute to the de Burghs and wondered, not for the first time, what on earth he was doing on the Marches while unrest was abroad in the land. Whether prompted by concern for his way of life or drunk on too much wine or just eager to escape the press of people at Campion, he had left his family home in search of the mysterious Vala, against all tenets of good sense.

Arriving unannounced, he had nonetheless been welcomed by the lord and lady, who proceeded to hold a feast in his honor, a celebration with which Robin was vaguely uncomfortable. From the veiled hints, he gathered that they thought his unexpected arrival, coming so soon after Stephen's, meant that he and his brothers were engaged in some sort of covert mission for the crown. Robin would have laughed aloud, if it were not for the tense atmosphere that hung thick over the castle.

It wasn't until late, after he had been regaled with the transgressions of Llewelyn and his brother David and their followers that Robin finally approached the topic that had sent him recklessly to the boundary between England and Wales. He leaned back in a casual pose and tapped the edge of the table.

"So, tell me, do you know anything of a prince named Owain ap Ednyfed or his wife, Vala?" Robin asked.

The lord and lady exchanged glances. "What of them?"

Robin smiled benignly. "Relatives in England were asking about her."

The lord frowned. "She died long ago."

Something about his curt reply made Robin alert, and he shook his head as a servant offered him more

wine, for he needed his wits about him. "Was there
a child?" he asked.

Again, the surreptitious looks were exchanged, and
he could feel the lord's eyes boring into him, probing
him for secrets. No doubt, they thought him privy to
knowledge of an uprising or the fate of their holdings.
Little did they guess that his query had more to do
with a dotty pair of so-called soothsayers than any
questions of Welsh independence.

Somehow Robin didn't think they would find his
quest amusing, and so he gracefully retired early. He
was no warmonger like his brother Simon, and this
visit had made him determined to turn around and hie
himself back to safer ground as soon as possible.

Unfortunately for the remaining de Burgh bachelors, it appeared that he had met not just an impasse,
but the end of his road. Idly, Robin wondered what
the lord would say should he ask the direction of a
local wise woman, perhaps some ancient Celtic prac-
titioner, and he snorted to himself. The whole idea of
finding someone to lift a curse seemed absurd now
that he was well away from Campion Castle and the
l'Estrange aunts.

He was too easily swayed. How often had his
brothers traded on that trait, especially Stephen, who
had sold him plenty of counterfeit religious relics in
his youth? And, apparently, age had made him no
wiser. Desperate to avoid the same fate as his siblings,
he had latched on to the first scheme presented to him,
no matter how foolhardy, when he would do better to
pursue more traditional avenues.

A true relic might counteract the curse, Robin
mused. Perhaps he should approach a priest or even
make a pilgrimage to some shrine, though he had no

idea which one. Saint Agnes was the patron saint of purity, but since it wasn't really purity he craved, Robin dismissed that idea with a grunt.

The sound, followed swiftly by another, echoed off the castle walls and Robin slowed his steps. Although full of rich food and wine, his de Burgh senses were still as sharp as ever, and as he reached the dark passage before his assigned chamber, he felt the presence of another.

The local situation being what it was, Robin slipped a hand to the dagger he kept tucked at his waist. Larger and more lethal than the usual dining knife, it could be silent and deadly when wielded with his skill. His fingers closing around it, Robin turned slightly, just in case a cudgel was poised behind him, a distinct possibility considering that everyone here thought him a spy.

But when he pivoted to glance around, Robin saw that no assassin stood there, only the man who had served him at table. Still, the fellow had a furtive air about him that kept Robin alert. "My lord," he whispered, looking back over his shoulder as if he would speak in secrecy.

"Aye?" Robin answered, though he had no wish to be further embroiled in the problems of the Marches.

"She did not die, but fled," he said.

"Who? Vala?" Robin asked.

The man gave a stealthy nod. "And there was issue, a daughter who lived, though all would deny it now. I saw her myself!"

Intrigued, Robin stepped closer. "Where are they now?"

But footsteps rang out in the passageway behind,

and the man grew wild-eyed, edging past Robin hurriedly.

"Wait!" Robin called after him.

"Look to a refuge for women in your own land, my lord, one for those burdened by sorrows!" he said. Then he disappeared into the darkness, leaving Robin to contemplate the whole curious episode with a jaundiced eye. Just when he thought the road had ended, instead it opened up in all directions.

But did he care to follow?

Robin moved restlessly atop his massive destrier and wondered what on earth he was doing poised outside a nunnery. And not just any nunnery, but Our Lady of All Sorrows.

It had been a long, strange ride. Although he had seen no further sign of the servant who had spoken to him so clandestinely, Robin had bid goodbye to his host, determined to forget all about the woman who had married a Welsh prince. But somehow, once he left the border, Robin had ended up at the nearest abbey, the only place he would deem a refuge for women, and there he had inquired about other such houses. And when he heard the name of Our Lady of All Sorrows, he knew a sudden urge to travel there.

Robin told himself that simple curiosity drove him, for the conflicting tales of Vala's fate would interest anyone. And he had always loved a good puzzle. In addition, he might well provide a service for Stephen's wife's family, who, no doubt, would be happy to learn their kin still lived. Perhaps even a reunion could be arranged.

Yet, despite these smug assurances, Robin was aware of some other, deeper compulsion urging him

onward. Whether it was concern for his own future
or a simple desire to put the matter to rest, he wasn't
sure. But when he discovered that the nunnery lay not
far from Baddersly, he returned to his brother's demesne in good time. There he left behind his men-at-
arms, so that he might continue alone on the last
stretch of a journey that even he was beginning to
view as bizarre.

And so he found himself on this bright early-spring
day looking upon the gatehouse to a small abbey surrounded by groves of tall elms. And faced with his
destination at last, Robin felt a twinge of shame at
what had brought him here. His selfish desires to
avoid marriage, which the Church so encouraged,
seemed a blaspheme upon this sacred house.

Our Lady of All Sorrows obviously was a place of
peace, of quiet women, pure of soul and body, de-
voting their life to worship. And, for a long moment,
Robin remained where he was, hesitant to enter the
sanctuary that lay within, to disturb the stillness, broken only by the soft call of birds among the branches
above him.

It was while he was considering his course that the
cry went up, rising from within the walls to drift upon
the wind and reach his ears, faint and frantic. At first,
Robin could hardly think he heard aright, but soon
the words came to him loud and clear. Although he
had never imagined such issuing from a holy house,
he could no longer ignore the astonishing plea.

Robin charged through the gates even as *"Help!
Murder!"* rang in his ears.

Chapter Two

Robin barely paused to tether his horse before rushing toward the heavy doors of the abbey. Inside he found absolute chaos as nuns and servants ran either toward the screams or away from them. Brushing past the others, he strode ahead, hand upon the hilt of his sword, until he burst outside once more, into some sort of walled garden.

He surveyed the area quickly, taking in the small group of women standing in a circle. To one side of them, a nun was seated on a stone bench, making loud gasping noises, a less shrill version of the shrieking he had heard, while two others tried to comfort her. The lone man, probably some sort of servant, appeared to be as horrified as the women, and detecting no threat from him, Robin relaxed slightly.

Still, he kept his weapon at the ready as he stepped toward the small knot of females. Several of them fell back as he approached until at last he could see what held their attention and had caused the furor. In the center of the group a young woman lay prone on the grass, obviously dead.

As Robin took in this sad sight, the nuns seemed

suddenly to become aware of his presence, for those nearest him squeaked and quailed, gathering together in a trembling huddle, leaving two others who remained apart, apparently unafraid. Robin's eyes went to the closest of the duo, an imposing figure whose eyes brimmed with intelligence and concern. Assuming she was the abbess, Robin opened his mouth to introduce himself, but a voice stopped him.

"Come to finish off the rest of us, have you?"

Robin started, stunned that someone would accuse him, a de Burgh, of doing murder, and he glanced down to where the second fearless female crouched near the deceased. Again, he prepared to speak, intending to deliver a scathing denial, but when he took a good look at her, his mouth stopped working. In fact, for a long, helpless moment, every one of Robin's bodily functions shut down, and all he could do was stare. At *her*.

Like the others, she wore a wimple that left little of her face showing, but what he could see was distinctive. Beautiful, in fact. Her forehead was smooth and pale, her brows delicate, tipped at the corners and an intriguing reddish color, like summer sunlight or autumn harvest. They hovered over eyes a lovely shade of blue that fascinated him. Though he could see nothing of her hair, her face was oval, ending in a stubborn little chin topped by lips set, too, in a stubborn manner. Oh, but what lips! Gently curved, they held a hint of color that reminded him of exotic berries or ripe fruit.

And suddenly, he was desperately hungry. Robin felt the world spinning around him as he gaped, rushing from beneath his feet to hurl him headlong into a future for which he was unprepared, but at the very last moment, he gulped, his fingers clinging tenaciously to the life he had known. And in that instant, he recognized her.

She was *the One,* the female who would destroy his existence as he knew it, enslave his mind, ensnare his body and suck all the fun out of everything. Well, it wasn't going to happen. Robin felt his mouth begin to work again, and it turned down into a fierce scowl. Curse or no curse, he was not going to marry this woman. Ever. And it was impossible anyway, he realized, as a sudden dizziness claimed him.

Day of God, he was destined for a *nun!*

"If blood makes you queasy, you had better sit down." Robin heard the voice, rife with disdain, and realized that *she* was speaking. Obviously, she no longer deemed him the murderer, but now she thought he might faint at the mere sight of death. Robin wasn't sure which presumption was more insulting.

He glared at her. "I am not a killer, but neither am I likely to swoon at a little blood," he said, injecting a healthy dose of contempt into his voice. Then, in a gesture of dismissal, he flicked his gaze to the abbess. "I am Robin de Burgh of Baddersly, where I stand in stead of my brother, Baron of Wessex," he explained with the innate confidence of his family.

Even if *she* had no idea who he was, the abbess ought to recognize his name. At the very least, she would be familiar with the surrounding holdings, especially one as large as Baddersly. "I was outside and heard the cries for help and came directly," Robin added.

"My lord," the abbess said, inclining her head graciously. "I am the abbess here. We are honored by your presence, though you find us in a quandary, for it appears that one of our fold has met with an accident, or worse.''

"No accident this,'' *she* said, drawing his attention once again. "But murder most foul.''

"Ah. So it was you I heard shrieking,'' Robin said. Although he suspected it was the other nun who continued to sniff and moan upon the bench, he could not help mocking this one in return for the taunts she had tendered him.

"Not I!'' she answered, her eyes flashing, and Robin smiled smugly, pleased to get back some of his own.

"'Twas Catherine you heard, and we are grateful to her for sending up the alarm,'' the abbess said, halting the argument that Robin sensed was forthcoming from the younger woman who eyed him so rebelliously.

"In fact, it appears that her cries served us well since they summoned you, my lord. 'Tis most fortuitous that you were passing by at this moment,'' the abbess said, and Robin made no move to contradict her. After what had happened on the Marches, he thought it wise to be more discreet concerning his interest in the former Vala l'Estrange. And this unfortunate business might provide the perfect opportunity to make subtle inquiries without revealing his true purpose.

"Has the coroner been summoned?'' he asked.

"Actually, I think he has just arrived,'' the abbess replied. When Robin looked around, she smiled slightly. "I believe you are the coroner, my lord. The man who holds Baddersly has always taken that office, though there has been little enough need for him in recent years, thank the Lord.''

"But his sudden appearance here might be no coincidence," *she* said, rising to her feet, and Robin's outrage at her accusation was tempered by curiosity as she stood. She was taller than he had expected, but still the top of her head would barely reach his chin. She appeared slender, yet shapely, allowing Robin's imagination to wander until he told himself it was most unseemly to speculate on what a nun might look like naked.

"Sybil!" the abbess scolded. "You have no reason to speak so of Lord de Burgh, whose aid will be most welcome."

So her name was Sybil. Robin rolled it around in his mind, and, again, he felt that fierce sense of recognition. *Sybil.* Her name spoke of ancient mysteries, oracles and exotic lures tendered to unsuspecting men. Robin frowned. Luckily, he could not be counted among them, for he distrusted her on sight.

"As penance for your speech, you will work with Lord de Burgh on his investigation into the sad death of Elisa, providing him whatever assistance he might require," the abbess said.

Horrified at her words, Robin opened his mouth to protest, but Sybil was quicker. "But he might be the murderer!" she exclaimed.

Robin felt his face flush. "As well could *she* be!" he countered. If Sybil was the One, why did he feel like thrashing her? Surely, his brothers had not suffered this odd reaction to their intended spouses!

"I hardly think either one of you is responsible, but you may keep an eye upon each other, if you are so uneasy," the abbess said. "That is, if you will be gracious enough to aid us, my lord? I could send a message to the bishop, of course, but since you are already here…''

Robin tore his attention away from Sybil and back to the abbess, knowing full well that the older woman had neatly maneuvered him. But it little mattered in this case, for he had his own reasons for agreeing.

''Certainly, Reverend Abbess, I would be most happy to help you in any way I can,'' Robin said, firmly ignoring Sybil's complaints. She made a noise that sounded awfully like a snort of contempt, but stepped back to gesture toward the prone body in invitation, as if daring him to investigate. Did she think he would fall faint at the sight? Robin nearly laughed aloud, for he had been in battle. He was a de Burgh.

''Who found her?'' Robin asked as he knelt beside the dead woman.

''Catherine and I,'' Sybil answered in a belligerent tone, and Robin pondered what she could possibly have against him. Perhaps she was one of those nuns who held a grudge against men. Or mayhap she simply resented his intrusion into her ordered existence. Still, she seemed too sharp-tongued for a holy woman. And too beautiful. And too shapely.

Robin glanced down at the body, the dead one, in an effort to tear his thoughts away from the live one that was claiming far too much of his interest. ''Did you touch her?''

''Of course, we checked to see if she still lived!'' Sybil replied, her answer sending the nun Catherine into a new fit of wailing. Robin glanced up at the One sharply in reprimand, and her mutinous expression made him wonder if all that bravado covered up her own fears. Or her own guilt.

Wonderful. Not only was he was destined for a nun,

an abomination in itself, but a *murdering* nun. That
made her worse than his brother Geoffrey's wife, who
had killed her first husband defending herself, but at
least belonged to no holy order. Nay, Robin told himself, quite firmly, this woman was not meant for him,
no matter that she seemed for all the world to be the
One. She was a woman of God, and he would do well
to remember as much.

Robin shook his head and tried to concentrate upon
the matter at hand. "Did you move her or was she
exactly like this when you found her?" he asked. The
dead woman's form was twisted, the upper portion
lying mostly on her back, while the lower rested on
her side. Blood had seeped from a wound to the back
of her head, but was no longer fresh. Dark, thick and
drying, its condition told Robin that she probably had
died during the night, certainly not within the last
hour.

"I only turned her slightly," Sybil said, her voice
still ringing with animosity.

Robin ignored it to continue his study of the deceased. Nearby lay a large rock with blood upon its
surface that appeared to correspond to the woman's
injury. Indeed, the situation of the body made it appear as if she had fallen and struck her head, though
it would take a mighty tumble to do such damage.
Robin looked around, his gaze lighting upon the
nearby stone wall, and he mentally judged the distance from its top to the ground. If Elisa had been
climbing over the top during the night and had
slipped, she might well have met her death.

"Perhaps 'tis no murder, after all," Robin said,
"But an unfortunate accident." Although he didn't
want to speculate on the nun's reason for clambering

over the high stone barrier, Robin knew that she would likely not be the first member of her order to engage in clandestine meetings.

"Nay! Elisa would not have been on the wall," Sybil said, following his thoughts as easily as if he had spoken them aloud. He glanced up to see that she had crossed her arms in front of her in a stance so belligerent that Robin didn't know whether to laugh or growl in exasperation. "Besides, 'tis too convenient," she added. "More likely, the murderer arranged all in a effort to appease the gullible."

Robin bristled at the insult, but, instead of arguing, he lifted the dead woman's head, carefully inspecting the wound to see if it matched the marks on the stone. Long ago, he had learned the secret of concentration from his father and his brother Geoffrey, and so he tried to focus solely upon what he was doing, despite the sound of the abbess herding the nuns from the scene.

All of them, that is, except for Sybil. She remained, continuing her complaints, and even though Robin heeded not her words, she definitely was a distraction. How on earth had she come to be a nun? Obviously, this order did not hold to the tenets of silence, Robin decided, even as he heard her voice on the edges of his awareness, tempting him to stop her mouth, preferably with his own.

Loosing a low oath that he hoped might offend a woman of God, or at least make her be quiet, Robin assessed the injury before him. During the studies of his younger years, he had taken an interest in medicine, so the sight did not disturb him. Nor was he likely to faint away as Sybil had suggested. But he did find something interesting.

"You're right," he said suddenly, finally putting a stop to the incessant flow of speech from Sybil's lips. "She was murdered," he said into the blessed silence. The peace was brief, however.

"What? How do you know?" Sybil asked, and he gently turned Elisa's upper body onto her side.

"Look here," he said. When Sybil gamely knelt beside him, Robin tried to ignore the pleasant waft of her scent. She was too near, but there was no help for it. Gritting his teeth, he pointed to a spot on the back of the dead woman's head. "Another blow."

Sybil looked at him then, her eyes wide, and he saw that they weren't just blue, but a light, lovely color surrounded by a rim of darker blue. He felt himself swaying, nearly falling, before he caught himself. Drawing a deep breath, he looked at the dead woman.

"She was struck twice," he explained in a strained voice. "Obviously, the smaller injury did not kill her, and your murderer was forced to render another blow. If she had simply fallen, she would have been hurt only once."

"I knew it," Sybil said beside him, her tone so rife with excitement that it roused an answering clamor within his traitorous body. Against his will, Robin felt alive, as if every humor within him was cavorting and screaming, *She's the One!* He had to struggle for breath, taking in a deep draught to steady himself. And although his fingers itched to reach for her, instead he wiped them on the grass and rose to his feet, greeting the returning abbess with no little relief.

"I am sorry, Reverend Abbess, but I fear your worst suspicions were correct. She was killed," Robin said.

The abbess shook her head sadly, her gaze resting

for a long moment upon the dead woman before she returned her attention to Robin. "Then I must trust you to discover who did this foul deed, for we cannot have someone preying upon the good women here."

Robin nodded his agreement, and the abbess once more inclined her head toward the body. "Now, let us allow the infirmaress to attend Elisa."

"As you wish," Robin answered. "I have examined the wounds, but I would like to look around here a bit," he added, though the garden area was well trampled by those who had come before him. Walking slowly about the body, Robin knelt to inspect the ground several times, and found nothing unusual for his efforts. His keen-eyed brother Dunstan might have been able to make something of the tracks in the grass, but the comings and goings of onlookers had obscured whatever slight impressions might have been here earlier, leaving Robin no trail. Of course, the knowledge that Sybil's blue gaze followed his every move didn't help.

Did she feel the attraction between them, or was a nun oblivious to such things? More likely, this one was too shrewish to notice, Robin thought. And he was saddled with her for the duration of his stay here! Suddenly, Robin wondered if he could solve the murder while avoiding Sybil and keeping to his original mission to find out about Vala l'Estrange. It seemed a complex assignment, but Robin was too much of a de Burgh to give in to doubt. He had never failed at anything yet.

Although he had learned nothing in his search, Robin was determined to continue it outside the nearby walls. Rising to his feet, he turned to the ab-

bess. "I would inspect the area on the other side, and
I will need to speak with all of the nuns," he said.

"We will make arrangements to have them meet
with you in the hall," the abbess replied. "And, of
course, we will provide you with chambers in the
guest house. Sybil can show you to a set of rooms."

The thought of being alone with the One made
Robin's entire being rouse to alertness again. His gaze
immediately transferred to Sybil, though against his
will. It was an altogether unsettling sensation. He had
always been the master of his fate, but now he sensed
an ominous sway in his command. Is this how his
brothers had felt, helpless victims of an overpowering
something beyond their control? Although seized by
lust, more was involved here than mere sex, though
how could that be when he hardly knew her, and what
he did know of her, he heartily disliked? And yet, he
was drawn to her, yearning to discover everything
about her, her history, her facets, her *secrets*.

Robin shook his head to clear it and told himself
in a firm, manly, decisive way that this woman held
no power over him. But somehow he was still studying her as she hovered over the dead woman, presumably awaiting the approach of the infirmaress and
other nuns...*other nuns*. That knowledge brought
Robin a certain comfort, for no matter what her unusual effect upon him, Sybil could not be meant for
him.

Obviously, something had gone awry this time, allowing him to escape the curse, for his intended already had answered a higher calling. Safe in that assurance, Robin donned a smug smile as he watched
her take charge of the removal of the body, issuing
directions that were the province of the infirmaress.

Apparently, Sybil made no discrimination, but alienated everyone with whom she came in contact.

Robin might have laughed, if he hadn't been so exasperated. He turned to the abbess, who now stood beside him. "Rather forceful for a nun, isn't she?" he commented in a dry tone that did not hide his opinion.

The abbess lifted her brows. "Oh, Sybil is not a member of our order, though she has long dwelt with us. She remains a novice, having never taken her vows. I sometimes fear she is destined for the outside world, with all of its heartaches," the abbess said, and Robin felt his complacency drop away, along with his grin. Not *his* world, he thought, with something akin to panic.

Seemingly oblivious to his reaction, the abbess left him to speak with one of the other women, while Robin reached up to tug at the suddenly constricting neck of his tunic. With a scowl, he glared at Sibyl, outraged at what he considered her duplicity. Perhaps she was not a nun, but that didn't mean he was going to turn around and marry her. It was not as though she could make him, he thought mutinously, for how could she? Hold a knife to his throat? Lure him into a compromising situation? Robin grunted in amusement.

In truth, there was naught she could do, for he was prepared for any tricks. Already, he was one step ahead of his brothers in that he knew what was afoot. Seizing upon that small advantage, Robin felt his innate confidence returning. After all, forewarned was forearmed, and Robin was a master of weapons.

As Sybil stood watching the nuns take away Elise, she clenched her hands at her sides to prevent herself

from following. The grief she had set aside momentarily returned, fresh and sharp, making her want to
put herself between Elisa and the women who would
prepare her for burial, as if she might, by dint of her
own fierce will, somehow delay the inevitable or
change the events that had transpired.

Swift upon the heels of those thoughts came a
shocking rage, directed at a religious existence that
somehow had allowed this abomination, at the world
in general and, finally, at Sybil herself, where it
turned into a gnawing guilt that threatened to eat
away at her very being. The words *if only, if only,*
beat so loudly in her head as to drive her mad.

If only she had gone to the abbess when she had
first suspected that Elisa had taken an unhealthy interest in someone outside the nunnery walls. If only
she had pressed her friend to give up the relationship.
But Elisa had never admitted she was seeing anyone,
and Sybil, well aware of the punishments awaiting a
nun who strayed from her vows, had said nothing. At
the time, Sybil had thought she was keeping a confidence. Now, she saw things differently, for banish-
ment or excommunication would have been a better
fate for Elisa than death.

If only she had done *something!* But Sybil had
never dreamed that Elisa's preoccupation had gone so
far. She had been behaving strangely, yet who would
have thought such an innocent would tryst right
within the convent walls? Or that the lover she was
meeting would do her in? Sybil shuddered, her intrin-
sic courage at odds with the frightening reality of the
outside.

It was an old conflict. Having abided at Our Lady

of All Sorrows since her childhood, Sybil knew no other existence, yet she had always possessed a healthy curiosity about the world. That sense of wonder had tugged at her, keeping her from her vows even when others urged her to take them. Those nuns who had lived outside the walls had impressed upon both she and Elisa the dangers to be found there.

If only Elisa had heeded the warnings. Guilt rose to swamp Sybil again, for hadn't she, too, been stricken with a restlessness that the nunnery could not satisfy? A harsh, bleak winter had left her eager for spring, anticipating some change in the air instead of the same deadly dull march of days. As had happened often before, she felt stifled, as if she were choking on her very existence, but what else was there for her?

She had no family, no entrée into a venue she knew nothing about. How would she manage, even if she arranged to leave? The Church liked to keep those who had once entered these walls within them always, and Sybil felt the heavy burden of her duty, of promises made to nuns now dead. Then she would try to be pious and worthy, but her unruly nature always was at odds with her good intentions. And eventually, the monotony would begin to slowly constrict her again until she felt she couldn't breathe, that her life here was no better than bondage.

Then she would turn her head toward the west and wonder what lay beyond the orchard and the fields and even the village itself…. As if through no will of her own, Sybil turned her head, but this time she saw a sight that had never greeted her before: Robin de Burgh.

He looked strange in the little herb garden, though others of his sex had been here before on occasion—

servants usually. He was different somehow. Larger, more masculine, he seemed to fill the small space with his strength and his maleness, as out of place as a bull among the delicate early-blooming violets. No, not a bull, with its rage and clumsiness, but something else wholly beyond her experience.

Sybil's brow furrowed at that puzzle. She didn't care to be caught at a loss, and her reaction came swiftly and automatically, outrage pushing aside her guilt and pain. How could the abbess ask her to work with this, this *man?* Not only was he a member of the outside world, but he was a male! He had no business involving himself in the affairs of the nuns. He was an intruder into this sheltered place, a reminder of what existed outside, bold and untamed and *unknown.*

Sybil seethed. She had taken exception to him the moment he strode into the garden, free and strong and confident, his clothes boldly declaring his station and the set of his wide jaw bespeaking his arrogance. He represented all that she was not, and Sybil was honest enough to admit that she resented his power and his sex. But there was more to her rancor than simple envy.

What she most disliked about Robin de Burgh was the way he made her feel, for he affected her as no one ever had before. It was apparent the instant she laid eyes upon him. She had been kneeling over Elise, shocked and stunned, Catherine's screams ringing in her ears, when she lifted her head. And there he had been, bigger than life, bigger than anything she had ever seen. She had noticed men before, monks and clerks and laborers from the home farm, even villagers, but never had she seen anyone like Robin de Burgh.

His chest was broad, his shoulders massive, his arms and legs thick with muscle, and yet he moved with a grace that belied his form. A knight, the abbess had called him, which explained the strength of his body, but not the reaction of her own. Sybil felt as though she had taken a blow to the chest, her heart pumping, her lungs struggling for breath, and then she had looked upon his face....

He was beautiful.

Sybil had slipped back upon her heels, dumbstruck that a mere man could exhibit such perfection: thick, dark hair, a comely brow over wide cheeks, tanned and unmarked, and eyes that reminded her of burnt sugar, rich and clear and sweet. As if they weren't bad enough, then there was his mouth, which made her own feel dry and wanting. Indeed, her entire being seemed seized by unruly desires, and, not one to meekly accept such disturbing sensations, Sybil had spoken, drawing his ire, eager for it, in the hope that his hold over her would be broken.

But it wasn't. Even now she burned with an odd sort of need for this man, and this man only, a feeling that made her even more resentful of his presence here and the task the abbess had laid before her, to work with him. It was intolerable, Sybil vowed, and would soon be put to an end. He might be coroner, but she would find Elise's murderer herself and be rid of Robin de Burgh and the havoc he wrought.

Just thinking of him had quickened her heartbeat, and Sybil glared across the small expanse of the garden at him, but that did little to ease her distress. Indeed, her gaze was caught by the shift of his wide shoulders as he began to move, and she trembled like a weakling as her attention drifted down his tall back to the narrow hips that were hidden beneath his mail coat. Cheeks flaming, Sybil drew a deep breath and shook off this unhealthy preoccupation with a male form, quickly transforming her dismay into anger.

"Where are you going?" she demanded even as she hurried after him.

He didn't bother to stop and acknowledge her, but spoke over one of those massive shoulders of his. "Outside to have a look about the grounds."

Sybil hesitated a moment, seized by a cowardly urge to quit his company, but it was swiftly overwhelmed by curiosity. And determination. Should this knight find something, she refused to remain ignorant of it. Besides, she was to keep an eye upon him. Although her instincts told her he was not a killer, still she owed it to the abbess to do her duty. And right now her duty was Robin de Burgh.

And so she followed. He did not wait for her, and she cursed his long legs that seemed to eat up the ground as he strode through the passage to the great hall. Oblivious to the stares of those around him, he continued out the main doors and around the building, unerringly heading toward the walls of the herb garden, which looked out over the orchard.

There she found him pacing along the stone barrier, head bent, as if he expected the murderer to have left his mark upon the grass. He paused, here and there, just as he had in the garden, kneeling to inspect the ground, though Sybil could see nothing. Finally, he lifted his head and looked at her, his eyes so beautiful that Sybil nearly swallowed her tongue.

"There's nothing here," he said, with a grimace.

Sybil could do no more than stare stupidly at him while she tried to control the sudden trembling in her limbs.

"Have there been any strangers about?" he asked.

Sybil shook her head. She found it difficult to concentrate on his words when his mouth moved. She had torn her attention away from his eyes only to find it engaged by his lips. Out here in the vast expanse of the grounds, he seemed more approachable, more real, as the sunlight dappled his features, and somehow the notion made her heart pound erratically.

Then his mouth moved again. "No one unusual?" he prompted, and his questioning look made Sybil wrest control of herself from whatever forces were affecting her.

"No. None that I am aware of beyond the occasional cleric, but I deal mostly with boarders, not travelers. We should check with Elizabeth, who handles lodging for the poor, pilgrims and others seeking but a night's stay. And the abbess would have more contact with visitors."

"And the servants knowledge of packmen and the sort," Robin mused. Rising to his feet in one graceful motion that almost stopped her breath, he glanced toward Sybil again, and she felt his attention clear down to her toes. He seemed to study her with a wary sort of animosity, that had Sybil wondering just what his complaint was before she realized he probably disliked being paired with a woman.

"If you're to help, then let us be about questioning these people while their memories are fresh," he snapped, confirming her suspicions.

Well, she didn't care to be stuck with him either, Sybil thought, lifting her chin, but the abbess had decreed that they must work together, so she would obey. She could only hope that the killer would be found soon, for once the murder was solved, Robin de Burgh would be on his way.

And Sybil would be glad of it.

Chapter Three

Although Robin didn't like spending any more time than necessary with the One, she appeared to be not only his assistant as coroner, but his sole contact within the nunnery—unless he wanted to go chasing after the abbess. Striding away from the orchard after an especially long, unsettling glance at her, Robin had to slow his steps for her to catch up with him, even as he tried to avoid looking upon her. It was a nearly impossible task, but he managed it while barking out a request for a messenger.

After all, he couldn't remain here indefinitely, when no one at Baddersly knew his exact where-abouts. He had promised the solicitous steward there that he would not hare off without a word, as his brother Simon had done before him. God knows he didn't want Florian to think he was entangled with a female, as Simon had been. And anyway, he needed some clothes and personal effects, more than the few he had brought with him, for he had no idea how long he would be staying.

That thought made him frown. For the sake of the residents here and his own peace of mind, Robin hoped that he could soon find the murderer, ask about Vala, and be on his way—*far* away from Sybil. In the meantime, however, he had to suffer her to show him a chamber in the guest house; simply following her into the building was an exercise in both restraint and agitation.

Watching the subtle sway of her hips, Robin gritted his teeth in an effort to control his baser impulses, even while he wondered what the abbess was thinking to put someone like Sybil in charge of tenants. No wonder the old woman thought her destined for the world! A beautiful young novice like his One had no business being anywhere near the guests, let alone taking them to their rooms.

If he were running things, Sybil would find herself cloistered as far as she could be from outsiders. Why, he could just imagine some lecherous old nobleman leering at her, or worse, and the thought wrought havoc with his temper. Although he usually took a lighthearted view of nearly everything, Robin suddenly found himself struggling against a fierce surge of possessiveness.

Sybil ought to be protected instead of flaunted before the eyes of any stray man, whether tenants, clergy, servants or whoever. And Robin certainly didn't trust the nunnery walls to secure her. Indeed, he was surprised that she wasn't the one lying dead, murdered by some jealous admirer or unwanted suitor. The thought made him suck in a harsh breath, as if someone had kicked him in the gut, and it was all he could do not to reach out and grab her to him, just to keep her safe.

Robin shook his head, struggling to gather his straying wits. In all probability, if he were to touch her, the One would scream her head off, and then she wouldn't be the only one suspecting him of murder! Deliberately, he backed away, though his whole body seemed to rebel against such a course. Robin tried to reason with it.

Just because he felt this odd sense of recognition in connection with Sybil did not mean that she was his responsibility. Why should it matter to him what happened to her, if she got herself in some kind of trouble or even was involved somehow in the death of the nun? She was *not* his concern, Robin told himself. Still, he felt atypically disoriented as she led him through the guest house to a private chamber, as if his mind was at war with the rest of him. *And losing.*

Robin took a deep breath and looked around. It was a well-appointed room, better than the average wayfarer could expect, and he nodded in approval as he dropped his pack upon a low stool. The bed was larger than he had anticipated, and he stared at it long and hard before his gaze swung back toward Sybil. Although the door remained open, the knowledge that they were alone together sent his blood rushing to nether regions.

Along with the surge of lust, Robin felt that curious sense of familiarity, as if he had known this woman forever, that despite her black looks and tart tongue, they were made for one another. For a long moment, he even had the notion that should he hold out his hand, she would take it, joining him eagerly. But instead of extending his fingers toward her, Robin lifted them to the neck of his tunic, where he tugged hard. Tempted as he was by the sight of that bed, he knew that such urges led to madness, *or at least to marriage.* And with a groan of panic, he hurried from the premises so swiftly that his companion was forced to run after him.

Once back in the main building, they were met by a grim-looking older nun with a coarse complexion. A forbidding creature, she nodded stiffly at them and without a word, led them down the corridor once more to what she called "the day room of the novices," a spare chamber with little more than a narrow table and benches.

It hardly seemed a cozy place, and for the first time, Robin wondered what kind of life these nuns, even the novices like Sybil, must have. As a de Burgh born into wealth and privilege, he was well used to his comforts, but what comforts did Sybil have? The question disturbed him, and he sank down onto a bench irritably. What did it matter to him how she lived?

"Although the order is gathering in the chapel to say prayers for the dead, as is only proper, the Reverend Abbess has decreed that each must leave, one at a time, to speak with you," the old nun said, her fierce expression leaving no doubt of her disapproval.

"As for you, Sybil—" her voice a venomous hiss, the nun turned her bulky figure toward the smaller novice in a vaguely menacing fashion that made Robin half rise from his seat, "I assume that you will find some time to appear in the chapel and pray for the one who has left us, especially since you *claimed* to be her friend."

Sybil blanched, and Robin stood, immediately taking exception to this harridan who was harrying his...whatever. He had to struggle against the urge to knock the old woman down, although his brain told him that attacking a nun might not be the best way to begin his duties here. Drawing a deep breath, he launched an entirely different type of offense.

"Thank you for your most gracious assistance," he said, giving the bully his best de Burgh smile, the one with the dimple. After all, he had not grown up around Stephen without learning a few of his older brother's tricks. "Would you care to be the first to join us?"

The old woman blinked, the only sign that his wiles had dented her rigid facade, but drew herself up stiffly. "I certainly would not! I have other responsibilities that require my attention, along with religious duties that must be observed, though some of us neglect them!" she added, with a cold glance at Sybil.

"Later, then," Robin said, bowing slightly in a show of graciousness. But his eyes narrowed as he watched her go, putting her to memory, just in case she did not return. Her attitude, though perhaps normal for her, made him wonder if she were avoiding the questions he was bound to ask in pursing the killer.

Turning back to Sybil, Robin was relieved to note that she had regained her color. "What ails her?" he asked, inclining his head toward the doorway.

Sybil shook her head. "That is Maud. She often gets her tail puffy."

"Her tail puffy?" Robin echoed, bemused.

"Like one of the cats that prowl the gardens and fields when met with another," Sybil explained.

"She doesn't seem overly fond of you," Robin commented.

Sybil shrugged. "She likes very much to be in

charge, and considers herself second only to the abbess. No doubt, she resents my assignment.''

''Ah. She would assist me herself,'' Robin said, thoughtfully.

Sybil pursed her lovely lips. ''Don't flatter yourself. Maud would rather draw her own conclusions, without answering to anyone. Right now, she probably is put out because she thinks I have the abbess's favor, which she is always currying. But she is mistaken, for this assignment is a *penance*,'' Sybil noted, making her disdain for his company very clear.

Why did she dislike him so? Robin swallowed the prick to his pride and studied her, but she swiftly turned her face away. Had she something to hide? He wondered once again if her odd behavior stemmed from guilt, but felt a swift, fierce resistance to that notion. Although he had no intention of marrying her, Robin would not care to see her hang for murder. His protective instincts rose to the fore, but he promptly squashed them, reminding himself that Sybil's troubles were none of his business. As coroner, he would do his best to see justice done, whether the intriguing novice was involved or not.

Robin's grim musings were interrupted by a faint knock upon the door. Striding forward, he pulled it open, only to hear a gasp as a slight nun eyed him fearfully. It was Catherine, the screamer, so he drew a deep, steadying breath and put on his best de Burgh manners.

''I beg your pardon,'' he said. ''Please come in.'' He tried to put the nun at ease, for he needed whatever information these women could provide him. His suspicions about Sybil aside, Robin guessed that the killer was someone known to the deceased, probably a man to strike such a blow, though a strong woman like Maud might do such damage as well. And if she got her tail puffy enough, she just might attack, Robin mused.

Still, Elisa's killer had most likely been a man and one with whom she had had close, perhaps even intimate, contact. Most murders were the result of too much drink or overwrought passions, and since the nun could hardly have been carousing at an alehouse, that left one probability, Robin thought grimly. He hoped that someone at the nunnery knew the identity of the fellow.

Catherine, however, was *not* that someone. When questioned, she alternated between moaning, crying and useless babbling about a vengeful God. Since Robin was fairly certain that a more earthly being had been involved, he finally let the nun return to the chapel. Although mindful of her mourning, he nonetheless was relieved to be rid of the weepy woman. He had to admit he preferred Sybil's contempt; it was better than caterwauling.

Robin's eyes narrowed. For someone who had given him a running argument earlier, the One was being awfully quiet. He slanted her a glance, wondering what was going on in that lovely little head of hers, but she only returned his curious look with a mutinous expression. Obviously, there was no use in pursuing that line of inquiry. He could only guess that she was not speaking to him now that they were alone.

Robin would have been amused, if he hadn't been so concerned about his investigation. He'd better have more success with the next nun, or he was going to be here forever. That notion made him glance surreptitiously back at the One even as he tugged at his neckline.

"Is there a problem with your clothing?"

Robin blinked, surprised at the sound of her voice, but not by the scornful tone of it. What was she asking? Something about his *clothes?* He felt heat surge through him even as he lifted his brows in mute question.

She sent him a pointed look. "It just seems to me that your tunic is too tight since you are always pulling at the neck of it. Or have you some bodily rash that makes you constantly itch and rub yourself?"

For one brief moment, Robin was so stunned by her words that he simply stared, then he threw back his head and burst out laughing. Obviously, her life as a novice had not dulled her wits or her tongue, and Robin couldn't help but feel a rush of pleasure. There was nothing he liked more in the world than to laugh, well, *almost* nothing, and in his experience few women had a talent for amusement. Not this one, however. She annoyed him and challenged him, yet did not fail to keep him entertained.

Robin was tempted to tell her that the problem with his clothes lay in the fact that he was wearing too many, but that hardly seemed appropriate banter for these surroundings. Instead, he assumed a sober expression and stepped toward where she sat on the bench watching him warily.

"Indeed, you have guessed it aright, and well I could use some help with a certain itch that needs be scratched," Robin drawled. He saw her eyes widen and her cheeks grow pink, but his own face betrayed nothing as he turned and pointed behind him.

"There's a spot on my back that I can't quite reach....
If you wouldn't mind?"

Robin heard her snort and bit back a grin. "What?
Are you not sworn to tend to the ailing and unfortunate?" he asked over his shoulder. "I assure you that
it is not contagious, at least I do not think so, though
I cannot quite be sure, of course."

He lifted his brows at Sybil, who, by now, was
actually sputtering, and decided that she was not well
versed in jests, which made her a perfect foil for him.
It was almost if he were young again and tormenting
his brothers—only better. He turned around to face
her once more.

"Perhaps this spot suits you better?" he asked. "If
you could just rub my chest." *Or lower.* Robin put a
hand over his heart to indicate his need, but his grin
faded as wide blue eyes met his own and held. For
one, long breathless moment, they stared at each
other, aware of an underlying attraction so powerful
that it seemed the very air around them conspired to
force them together. Indeed, Robin nearly took a step
forward, but the door opened, echoing loudly in the
silence.

He whirled around, with a combination of irritation
and relief, to face the new arrival. She was older and
shy and quiet, just the kind of female Robin thought
of as suiting her vocation. Glancing at Sybil, he lifted
his brows slightly. Now here was someone she ought
to emulate. Not surprisingly, she appeared to be in
disagreement, for she gave him a mulish frown that
made his lips twitch.

Robin couldn't help it; he was beginning to find
her indefatigable scorn amusing. After all, how many
women disdained a de Burgh? Of course, this one was

a novice, and could be excused on that score, even if she didn't act a bit like a religious woman. And that probably was just as well, Robin decided, as he began questioning the new arrival, for Sybil was far more interesting.

The decorous nun was just *too* quiet, shaking her head in answer to every one of his queries. Robin was beginning to wonder if she could speak at all when she finally lifted her head. "Elisa was the treasuress, and I am the sacrist, so we did not have reason for speech," she said. Privately, Robin revised his original opinion of her, for what kind of woman required a reason to talk to another? Aloud he echoed, "Sacrist?"

"I care for the church fabric and plate," she said, lowering her head demurely.

"So you don't have much contact with outsiders or strangers?" Robin asked.

She shook her head.

"What about those within the order? Have there been any quarrels recently?"

She looked horrified, as if he had suggested some kind of sacrilege, and Robin decided that he *definitely* preferred Sybil's plain speaking to this female's delicate sensibilities.

After a few more useless questions, he let the paragon go and leaned back against the wall, brooding, as he once again considered what kind of life these women had. He had known that some orders didn't encourage conversation, but knowing and seeing for himself were two different things, and the discovery unsettled him.

He had never given much thought to the religious world, none of the de Burghs having the least inclination for that sort of calling. They didn't have the temperament for it, but then, neither did Sybil. How had she ended up here? Holy houses offered a home for those who were devoted, a haven for those who had not the money or prospects for marriage, and a possible route to power for those without their own. Which had brought Sybil here? Robin was inclined to think the latter, but then, why hadn't she taken her vows?

She was a curious conundrum, he thought, letting his gaze slide back to her once more, and though he had always been attracted to puzzles, never before had he met the female kind. Evidently intending to rebuff his interest, Sybil gave him a glare that only sparked it further. Robin wondered what had happened to her infamous contempt when they had stared at one another, for he had seen no sign of it then.

Before he could pursue that intriguing line of thought, the next nun appeared. Although not as quiet as the previous member of the order, she appeared to be even more timid. She was older than Sybil, but kept darting glances at the novice, especially when Robin asked about Elisa's personal life and possible quarrels within the order. Was she loathe to speak in front of Sybil?

"Have you seen any strangers about?" he asked, but the woman only appeared shocked by the idea. And afraid. Her fear struck Robin with new resolve, for holy women should not have to suffer such fright within the very cloister walls. "Very well. Thank you. And I promise you that I shall see to it that no one here is harmed," he said.

She nodded, a tiny movement of her head, but it was that small motion that made Robin realize she was not just frightened by a nameless murderer, but by himself. And he was taken aback by the discovery. No man had cause to fear the de Burghs except their enemies, and women...well, women had always been thrilled by the presence of his family members and grateful for the protection they offered.

Never had he incited anyone to horror, and Robin didn't like the feeling. He frowned. Was it because he was a man inside the sheltered world of the nunnery, or was something else involved? With a curt word, he excused her, and as she scurried away, he wondered how the devil he was going to find out anything from women like these.

"They are not accustomed to...knights," Sybil told him, spitting out the last word as if he were some kind of monster. He was tempted to ask her if he would be more acceptable if he were unable to defend himself and them, but he kept his mouth shut as he mulled over this disturbing development.

He was still lost in thought when Sybil stood to greet the woman at the door. This nun was quite elderly, to the point of deafness, so Robin was forced to nearly shout into her ear. He repeated his questions over and over until Sybil saw fit to point out that the old woman had her own room from which she rarely ventured forth, so saw little of others. Upon receipt of that information, Robin ushered the elderly nun out, while casting a dubious glance over his shoulder at his companion. As he suspected, Sybil appeared to be fighting back her amusement at his discomfiture.

With a scowl, Robin turned his attention back to the nun who was leaning on him and called to a servant passing in the corridor. He asked the girl to escort the elderly woman back to the chapel and to fetch him some paper and quill, so that he might better record the names of those he had already seen. His scholarly brother Geoffrey had often made notes when he was studying, and Robin equated this tedious investigation to a learning experience.

When he again entered the room, Sybil was wearing a look of surprise instead of her usual surly glare. "You can write?" she asked.

"Of course, I can write," Robin said. "My father, the Earl of Campion, sets great store by learning. Can you not?"

"Of course, I can write! I have been schooled by the nuns since I was very young," Sybil said.

"Too bad they couldn't teach you better manners," Robin observed dryly. When she looked as though she was going to make a sharp retort, he spoke again. "I thought you religious women were supposed to be humble," he added, his expression all innocence. *Was that a tic in her cheek?* Robin decided that goading her was far better than fighting with her, and that jesting was better than both. "About that itch…" he began, only to whoop in laughter when she threw something at him.

Luckily, he was blessed with quick reflexes and she with poor aim. He ducked, though it proved unnecessary as her toss went wide. As it sailed by him, Robin saw 'twas only a wooden cup that had been abandoned in the corner, and he watched it fall to the floor, where it rolled across the tiles. His blood up, Robin glanced back at his foe, in anticipation of a lively exchange, but the shocked look on her face told him there would be no more missiles, at least not immediately.

Obviously, such outbursts were new to her, as well as frowned upon in the nunnery, but Robin found himself wanting to hand her another cup, to stand

before her and egg her on to release some of whatever
it was remained pent up inside her. Robin sensed that
behind those novice's clothes lay a passionate
woman, stifled by her surroundings. And suddenly,
he wanted to release all that tension in quite another
manner entirely.

With a grunt of denial, Robin tugged at the neck
of his tunic, caught himself and grimaced. He was
becoming far too cozy with the One for his own good.
It was none of his business what kind of temperament
she possessed or what kind of life she led here or
anything else about her. He was better off sparring
with her than making such speculations or worse, *enjoying* himself with her. Robin blanched, the arrival
of a servant with his quill the only thing that saved
him from incipient panic.

He had just mumbled his thanks when another nun
arrived, one who, he soon discovered, disapproved of
the whole questioning process. Although she gave
him no rebuke, she answered him as shortly as possible, until Robin sat back and ran a hand through his
hair in exasperation.

"I'm just trying to find out who killed Elisa, so
that no further blood is shed," he said, his patience
already tested this day.

"I hardly think anyone else here will meet such an
end," the nun replied, with a sniff. Robin studied her
carefully. Was her disapprobation meant for him or
the deceased?

"And why do you say that?" he asked. "Was there
some reason why Elisa was targeted when others were
not?" The question probed as close to his own sup-
positions as he dared without revealing them outright.
Unfortunately, it resulted in a squawk of protest from
Sybil and a demure look from the nun. Sending his

companion a caustic glance, Robin wondered whether her presence was a help or a hindrance to him.

Definitely a hindrance, he soon decided, for the nun would say nothing further, finally excusing herself huffily. After she left, Robin pointedly closed the door behind her. "Just what are you doing?" he asked, advancing on the One with nothing but menace on his mind.

"What do you mean?" she asked, rising to her feet, in fearless, foolish challenge. Although he had to admire her pluck, he was in no mood for her posturing.

"You know very well what I mean!" Robin said, his voice silky yet threatening. "If you plan to interfere with my work, then I shall have you removed from the room."

"You cannot!" she answered. "The abbess told me to—"

Robin cut her off. "The abbess told you to *assist* me, not impede me!"

"I will not let you speak ill of the dead!" she answered, that tiny tic in her cheek the only evidence that she was not as composed as she would have him believe. Nor as brave. Robin felt the bluster seep out of him.

"Sybil," he said in a gentler tone. Stepping forward once more, he reached for her, but she winced, seemingly as wary of him as he was of her. However, Robin doubted that it was rooted in the same cause, for she gave no indication that she recognized him as anything other than a boorish knight who was disrupting her existence and maligning her friend. With a sigh, Robin dropped his hand and moved back, wondering how he was going to find out who Elisa's lover was if he was not allowed to allude to the possibility of there being one.

Another puzzle, perhaps unsolvable, Robin thought, before the moment was shattered by the entrance of one of the nuns. Taking a deep breath, he turned away from Sybil and tried to focus on the task ahead. Graciously seating the woman, he poured on the de Burgh charm, while sending a warning glance to his companion.

To her credit, she did not protest again, but neither did he make any headway. The older nuns claimed to have had little contact with Elisa, while the younger ones professed ignorance of her personal life. Surely, within the small confines of this community, someone must have heard something! Although Sybil informed him that gossip was proscribed by the bishop, Robin did not believe that the good women, no matter how devoted, had given it up entirely.

He was so frustrated by the end of the day that he began to wonder if he was going to have to begin the questioning all over again—alone. Obviously, Sybil had been a friend to the deceased, and, as such, put a damper on any revelations the other women might provide about her. With mixed feelings, Robin considered asking the abbess to assign Sybil some other task. It would be better for him, too, if he were rid of her, he thought, quelling an unruly objection somewhere in his body. Presumably, it lodged in his nether regions, yet it seemed to be higher up in his chest, which held his yearning for the family life he had no more.

With a frown, Robin realized that despite her tart tongue and surly behavior, he was going to miss the One, not just immediately, but maybe forever.

Chapter Four

Despite his feelings, or perhaps because of them, Robin abruptly rose to his feet, determined to leave the room and seek out the abbess. Indeed, he went so far as to open the door, only to be faced with the formidable Maud, who stood just outside the threshold. Had she been listening or spying? Robin didn't see how she could learn much through the nunnery's thick walls and doors, yet who knew what kind of intrigues went on in the cloister? Certainly, these women had little enough to entertain them.

Recovering quickly, Robin greeted the nun with feigned warmth. Although he might have denied it, he was only too eager to postpone—mayhap indefinitely—his plans to dismiss Sybil and latch on to Maud. After all, here was someone who wasn't afraid to speak her mind or gossip malevolently. Indeed, Maud looked as if she had made plenty of enemies and would be happy to add more to her collection. Ushering her inside, Robin donned his best smile, though it appeared to have little effect. Maud soon made it obvious that she had returned only under duress.

"The abbess insisted that I come, though I have no idea why since I know nothing of this business," she said, with a pinched expression that dared Robin to argue with her.

"Although pleased as I am, as always, to do the Reverend Abbess's bidding, I do not see what right *she* has to be here," Maud added, looking pointedly at Sybil. "I hardly think I can speak freely when I know that my words might be misconstrued or bandied about later by others. Perhaps, if she were to leave the room..." Maud suggested.

Although Robin had just considered the same course, he found he didn't care for the notion quite so well when Maud proposed it. Logic warred with unfounded emotion for an instant, until reason prevailed and he bowed his head graciously toward the harridan. "If you would feel more comfortable—" he began, only to be cut off by Sybil's protest.

"The abbess told me to remain with Lord de Burgh," she said, in a voice that brooked no dispute, and Robin couldn't help admiring her courage.

"Indeed?" Maud replied, lifting one eyebrow in a manner that managed to insinuate all sorts of things, none of them complimentary, especially to a novice. Robin felt his blood churn in response, urging him to Sybil's defense, but he kept his face expressionless.

"Indeed," Sybil replied firmly, giving no indication that the barbs had struck her at all.

Whether Maud sensed his annoyance or Sybil's stubbornness or only had been issuing an idle threat, Robin didn't know, but she conceded with a scowl. "Very well, then, but I warn you not to interfere with my speech or repeat anything that I say," she said, glaring at the younger woman.

Sybil dropped her head in a gesture of submission that didn't fool Robin one bit, and he wondered if Maud had planned to speak in front of her all along, perhaps even to taunt her with gossip. The older woman reminded him of a spider, hatching plots and tossing webs around the hapless nuns. Whatever she might say, Robin knew he must keep the focus on Elisa and not worry about Sybil, who seemed more than capable of holding her own anyway.

"I assure you that you may speak freely," Robin said, smiling at Maud. "Indeed, I was hoping that you would do so as I fear that the other nuns have not been of any assistance to me at all, but you…" Robin trailed off, inclining his head respectfully. "You appear to be far more knowledgeable and observant. Surely, you must have an idea as to the culprit."

Ignoring a choked sound from Sybil, Robin gave the harridan an encouraging smile, and she acknowledged his flattery with a lofty look. "Naturally, I am more perceptive than most of these flibbertigibbets who neglect their duties," Maud said, raising her bulky body until she sat arrow-straight upon the bench. "However, 'tis not really my place to comment."

"Ah, but I cannot finish my work here until I have come to some sort of conclusion," Robin pointed out.

"Well," Maud said, making a show of hesitation. "I refuse to pass judgment upon the organization of the order, but in my opinion Elisa was far too young for such a responsible position as treasuress," Maud said, her jealousy obvious. "Such a post required her to have more contact with the outside world than is wise, what with the submission of bills from tradesmen and servants and clerics and who knows who, let alone all that fraternizing with the bailiff.''

Maud sniffed haughtily. ''So I, for one, am not surprised that she came to a bad end.'' At her caustic words, Robin shot a glance toward Sybil and nearly groaned. Not only was the tic working in her cheek, but her hands were fisted at her sides, as though she might strike Maud at any moment. However, she was valiantly keeping her mouth shut, and, for that Robin was grateful.

Tearing his gaze away from Sybil, he returned it firmly to Maud. ''Go on,'' he urged. Obviously pleased at gaining his ear while at the same time thwarting her rival, the older woman nodded.

''Well, as we all know, only evil can come of too much association with outsiders,'' she said, again looking at Sybil, as if to accuse her of misbehavior or even of being a bad influence upon Elisa.

Robin quickly reclaimed her attention. ''Did you notice any strangers about or anyone who might mean Elisa harm?''

Maud lifted her chin imperiously. ''Unlike some, I do not have much contact with those who are not of the order. And, as I said, *she* dealt with all sorts of questionable persons, from those men who work the home farm to the bailiff. I heard that she had a certain male acquaintance in whom she showed an unseemly amount of interest, but not being privy to her personal associations, I cannot tell you more. Perhaps *Sybil* can elaborate,'' Maud suggested, her mouth twisting with the gibe.

Robin was out of his seat, putting himself between the two women before Maud realized how close she had come to reaping the results of her taunts. ''Thank you,'' he said, while Sybil made incoherent noises behind him. "You have been most helpful." He led the nun to the door, pouring on the de Burgh charm and promising to seek her out if he thought of any further questions. And when at last she left, as regally as she had entered, Robin shut the door and turned to face Sybil.

One look at her face told him why she had never taken her vows. Although she tried hard to suppress the truth, she was far too volatile for a life of humble devotion. Indeed, she was brimming with life and passion—and fury, which was now directed at him.

"Why did you stop me?" she cried, rushing toward Robin with fists flying. "'Tis long past time someone gave that horrible woman her due!" She struck out at him, raining blows upon his wide chest. Robin let her rage and rant, mostly about the horrible Maud and the poor defamed Elisa, until finally he caught her wrists and held them fast. Then, as if the wind suddenly had turned, letting out her sails, she collapsed against him in a fit of weeping that Robin found far more painful than her fists.

Releasing her hands, he put his arms around her, drawing her close. She buried her face in his tunic, and he held her tightly, trying his best to give the comfort she needed. All thoughts of his position as coroner or hers as novice or even as the One, slipped away, as she released her grief. The most glib of the de Burghs, Robin had no words to give her, only the strength of his body, and despite his initial wariness, he found himself offering it up to her easily.

And when her sobs subsided, Robin became aware of other things, namely, the way she seemed to fit perfectly against him, her head tucked under his chin.

Swift on the heels of that discovery came awareness
of the press of her form, her soft breasts, the curve
of her waist and the heat that warmed him wherever
they touched. Drawing a deep breath, Robin felt himself stiffen, his masculine form growing into a telltale
bulge against her belly.

Sybil lifted her head, as if startled, and Robin could
have cursed himself, but when he looked into those
blue eyes, wide and teary, his tongue cleaved to the
roof of his mouth. A stray curl had popped free of
her wimple, and he saw that it was red, a lively color
fit for this woman. Entranced, Robin lifted his fingers
to tuck it back into place, but that brought his thumb
in contact with the softness of her skin, and he stroked
the delicate curve of her cheek in wonder.

He had to taste her. The urge came over him so
violently that Robin shuddered with the force of it.
He wanted to, *needed* to kiss her, right here, right
now. He felt as if his future, his very life, depended
on it. And Sybil gave no demur. Indeed, she stared
up silently, her luscious lips parted in a tempting
pose, just as though she were as enraptured as he.

Desire rose like a tide, thrumming through his
blood, and for long moments, Robin struggled vainly
against it, grasping at the wits that seemed to have
deserted him. Try though he might to resist, he was
weakening fast, and well he might have given in, had
it not been for the sound of a knock upon the door
jolting him into awareness of his surroundings.

Suddenly, Robin realized that he was embracing
the One, and he swallowed in panic even as Sybil
gasped, as if she, too, were flustered, or even horrified. They broke apart, backing from each other, and
just in time, for they had barely separated when the

door opened. It was the abbess who entered, and Robin eyed the good woman with no little alarm. Then, finding the bench against the back of his legs, he sat down hard, while a flush that had nothing to do with his still-excited body rose in his cheeks.

Luckily, the unsuspecting abbess had her head bent, and did not seem to be aware of the undercurrents around her. Of course, the poor woman was mourning in addition to performing the duties of her office, and Robin immediately felt guilty for his misbehavior in her holy house, though he hadn't really done anything. Yet.

"Has all of the order been here, Sybil?" she asked, turning to the novice. Robin's gaze followed, and he saw that Sybil appeared strained, her hands clasped before her and her face pale and tearstained. At the sight, Robin felt even more the cur, as if he had failed her somehow, though he knew he had given her comfort as best he could. It was what had nearly happened afterward that bothered him, both the wanting and the wishing her well away, a perverse combination, to be sure.

"And have you learned anything?" the abbess asked, swinging her gaze to Robin. He stared at her stupidly, the only lessons he could recall were those in desire and restraint, and how the blue of Sybil's eyes remained undimmed by weeping.

She appeared to be recovering more swiftly, however. "Reverend Abbess," she said, drawing the nun's attention back to herself, an action for which Robin was inordinately grateful. "Isn't it true that Maud has long thought herself your closest assistant, perhaps even your favorite?"

The question brought Robin back to his senses

quickly enough, for he could see where she was going with that line of inquiry, and he rolled his eyes in frustration. As much as he disliked old Maud, he couldn't quite picture her killing off her rivals. Why bother when she could torture them indefinitely with her slurs?

The abbess smiled gently. "Maud is very eager, but I can hardly appreciate one of my flock more than another."

Robin recognized a diplomatically worded answer when he heard it, but Sybil would not be placated. Obviously, her feud with Maud was a long-standing one. "But suppose that someone, believing herself to be in a coveted position, wielded power over others of the order, going so far as to sabotage those who stood in her way?"

The abbess's expression reflected her concern. "Surely, you are not suggesting that one of our own murdered Elisa?" she asked.

Robin rose to his feet. "We are simply exploring all possibilities, Reverend Abbess," he explained. "And although we might deem it unlikely, we must remember that not all nuns are as devoted as you are. Although we might wish otherwise, they are afflicted with the same jealousies and passions as laywomen," he said, with a sidelong glance toward a certain passionate novice.

The abbess frowned, obviously dismayed by his words, but Robin persisted. "Think carefully, and if you can remember any quarrels or suspicious incidents occurring among the residents here, please let me know," he said.

"I will," the abbess promised, though she appeared none too pleased by the prospect.

"We appreciate your cooperation," Robin said to smooth things over. "I would also ask you if you have noticed any strangers about, anyone Elisa would have come in contact with?"

The abbess paused thoughtfully before answering. "I have met with the usual clerics and freemen and travelers." She shook her head, as if frustrated. "I fear that we have fallen into lax habits here. The nuns are often asked to make trips to the village and conduct business with those in the area. As I'm sure you realize, although we are a small order, the home farm requires much organization and employs many of the local people."

"Are there any who might hold a grudge against the nuns or Elisa in particular? Was there someone that she might have seen more of than was usual?" Robin asked, ignoring the low hiss of Sybil's indrawn breath. But the abbess could only shake her head, uncomprehending of such violence or any lapses on the part of her flock.

Robin spoke gently, hiding his frustration, but he had hoped that the abbess might be able to give him a hint, at least, as to the identity of the killer. So far, none but Maud would even admit that Elisa had had a relationship with a man, and all she could do was refer him to Sybil.

Robin's eyes narrowed. He had thought Maud's bitter words a result of the rivalry between them, but he had heard more than once that Sybil and Elisa had been close, had seen it himself, as evidenced by her wild display of grief. And now he glared at the One with new suspicion. All along, he had suffered her presence, allowed her to stifle his questions, to keep the name of her dear departed friend from being sullied, and all along, she probably knew more about the death than anyone.

Biting back a scowl, Robin turned his attention once more to the abbess, but it soon became clear that she could shed no further light upon the murder. Before dismissing her entirely, he asked if he might meet with the servants and people who worked on the lands owned by the nunnery, and she consented. It would be more than he could accomplish this day, of course, but right now Robin wasn't concerned with the lay residents of the area. His gaze slid to the other occupant of the room in grim anticipation.

First, he had a certain novice to question.

Sybil watched the abbess preparing to leave and had to bite her tongue to stop herself from begging the nun to stay. And when the abbess actually stepped out the door, Sybil felt like running after her. It didn't matter where she went as long as it was away—far away—from this man who so disturbed her. Sybil took a deep breath, her heart pounding with the revelations of the last hours. To her shame, few had anything to do with Elisa's death. They had to do with *him.*

He had a dimple.

It was tucked into his left cheek, and appeared when he smiled just so, Sybil remembered with a kind of stunned surprise. And, not only that, he laughed! And not just any kind of laugh, mind you, but one so rich and deep and joyous that it seemed to melt something inside her. Sybil's face flamed as she recalled just what this man was capable of doing to her insides, and the rest of her, as well.

She wasn't sure what was worse, the fact that she

had stared up at him like a besotted ninny while he held her in his arms, or that she had willingly gone into them in the first place, pouring out her grief as if a dam had burst. The memory made Sybil feel ashamed, embarrassed, a fool, and yet, she knew she hadn't thought so at the time. Tucked against that big, hard body, she had felt safe and warm for the first time in her life, as if she were home at last…. Sybil drew a ragged breath and shut her eyes against such nonsensical thoughts, but still the discoveries dismayed her.

He smelled like wood smoke and leather and something indefinable, something that was singularly his, and it was the most wonderful scent Sybil had ever encountered. She wanted to bury her face in his tunic again and just *breathe*. And this time, she wouldn't cry, she would wrap her arms around his strong body and…what? Sybil shook her head. She knew even less about men than she knew about murder, but she was learning.

She had learned that this one possessed compassion. Despite all their heated exchanges, snapping at each other like dogs vying for the bone of the killer, when she had lost her composure entirely, he had enfolded her with his body, treated her to a gruff tenderness that made her weep all the more for the lack of it in her life.

Oh, she had vague memories of sweet nuns, of being held in gentle arms, but who here would have helped her this day? The abbess and most of the nuns would have been appalled by her outburst. Some would have been frightened, some pitying, and a few might have stepped forward to try to aid her. But none could have given her what this strange man had offered: his arms and his strength and his comfort.

When he had first arrived, Sybil had resented what Robin de Burgh could do to her; now she was heartily afraid of it. Before, she had had no idea what was lacking in her life, but now she knew, and she yearned for more with a fierceness that made her tremble. 'Twas a most dangerous desire, for comfort was not all that he gave her with his body. To Sybil's horror, he also had roused in her a certain curiosity for something else in that hushed moment when all the world seemed to dim in the brightness of his being.

His eyes, like some kind of sweet and heady syrup, had held her spellbound, while against her belly she had felt something hard. Sybil had recognized that it was a part of him, and the knowledge had thrilled her, filling her with a power she never knew existed. Her fingers had spread upon the hard expanse of his chest, and she had wanted to rise upon her toes, to somehow make herself closer…

"Perhaps you would allow me the benefit of your knowledge?"

The sound of that deep, harsh, intensely *male* voice nearly made her jump. *"What?"* Sybil said, swinging round to face him in stunned surprise. Surely, she had not heard him right! Could he tell what she was thinking?

But the look upon his face was not one to lure her. Indeed, he wore a hard scowl that marred his beautiful features, hiding his dimple and his laughter, but that nevertheless could not mask the goodness in him. "Who was the man Elisa took an unseemly interest in?" he demanded.

Sybil glared at him, revising her opinion, and not

to the good. She refused to listen to any slurs upon Elisa's name, especially an echo of Maud's horrible slanders! But before she could protest, he stalked across the tiles and grasped her by the shoulders.

"What are you hiding?" he asked, and Sybil knew she ought to spit in his face, but he was touching her, and the heat from his fingers blazed up and down her arms and all through her body until she felt unnaturally weak. Her anger at his insinuations faded away, replaced by a bizarre fascination with his lips. Considering the hard, wide planes of the rest of his face, they appeared soft and a shade lighter than his tanned face. From there her gaze drifted to his cheek, and when she found the spot where his dimple lay hidden, Sybil had to fight against a sudden urge to seek it out with her fingers—or her mouth.

With a low moan that sounded suspiciously like an oath, Robin released her abruptly and turned his head away. "Were you meeting him, too? Is that why you conceal his identity?"

He seemed unaccountably angry, but Sybil could only stare at him dumbfounded. He thought she was seeing a man? She didn't know whether to laugh or to slap him in outrage.

"I don't even know who he was!" she cried.

Robin swung round to her again, his eyes dark and intent, and Sybil cursed her unguarded tongue.

"So there *was* a man," he said, seizing upon her words.

"I don't know!" Sybil protested. "I just know that Elisa had been acting differently, secretively." Wrapping her arms against her suddenly chill form, Sybil turned away from him.

"And why would a man cause that behavior?" Robin asked.

Sybil laughed without humor. "In here? There are few enough reasons for secrecy in the nunnery, but that is one of them. Elisa was a beautiful young woman who readily took her vows, perhaps without much consideration," Sybil said, remembering her own envy of Elisa's easy decision. In deceptively simple terms, Elisa had claimed there was no choice for either of them, and yet Sybil had hesitated.

Sybil drew a deep breath. "Recently, she appeared restless, distracted, and she took more trouble with her appearance, so I just assumed…" she trailed off, unwilling to admit to her own rash conclusion, which might prove groundless. Hugging herself tighter, she glared at Robin. "Perhaps there was no man. Perhaps Maud killed her."

This time it was Robin who snorted in laughter. "And where are all the bodies of her other rivals? I realize that would solve everything to your satisfaction, but it just doesn't ring true."

Sybil felt a rush of anger at his easy dismissal of her suspicion, as well as his disgusting flattery of Maud. "Why are you so intent on believing her?" she demanded.

Robin grinned. "Jealous, sweetheart?"

Sybil felt her face flame. "I am *not* your sweetheart," she snapped.

To her surprise, Robin de Burgh's smug smile faltered a little. "I'm not sure *what* you are to me," he muttered, running a hand through his hair. "But just for a moment, let's suppose Elisa was seeing a man. The abbess said she had contact with a lot of them, considering she was a nun. Who would she be most likely to develop an interest in, this bailiff with whom she spent so much time?''

Sybil gaped at him wide-eyed and then started sputtering in outrage. ''Certainly not!'' she said. ''Farnfold is a big, fat idiot!''

She saw his dimple make a brief appearance, but was too distraught to admire it. ''All right, but what if Elisa didn't think so?'' he asked.

''Of course, she thought so. She complained about him all the time!'' Sybil said.

Robin's eyes focused on her intently. ''Complained? About what? Did he try to molest her?''

Sybil snorted. ''No! She said he was lazy and stupid and she didn't understand why the abbess had given him the position in the first place. She was going to try to get him replaced when—'' Sybil didn't finish her sentence, only lifted her gaze to Robin's in horror. ''You don't think he found out she was going to talk to the abbess and killed her to keep her from it, do you?''

He shrugged. ''I don't know, but I would certainly like to talk to the man.''

Sybil tilted her head. ''There's the bell for vespers. Supper will follow, and he eats in the guest hall, for he lodges in a room there.''

Robin shook his head. ''''Tis late. Better that we talk to him first thing upon the morrow.''

Sybil frowned, unwilling to delay. ''Somehow I doubt that he will rise at two o'clock to say matins,'' she said. She felt a sudden urgency now that Robin had brought that fool Farnfold to her attention, and she silently berated herself for not thinking of him sooner. The bailiff had always seemed to be a big, stupid buffoon, but appearances could deceive. And desperate men could commit desperate acts.

"Perhaps later in the morning, then, sometime after dawn," Robin was saying, and Sybil nodded absently, even as she was forming her own plans. If he wanted to wait until a full day had passed, that was fine, but she had no intention of letting Farnfold destroy whatever evidence of his misdeed that might remain.

"You had better go on to the guest hall, or you will miss your supper," Sybil said abruptly. "Shall I escort you there, or do you remember the way?" Robin eyed her oddly, and Sybil schooled her tempestuous emotions, so as to give nothing away.

"I can find it myself," he said, moving toward the door. He stood for a long a moment on the threshold, his solid masculine form filling the doorway, his gaze searching Sybil's until she was forced to look away. She had the suspicion that when he willed it, Robin de Burgh could see all too clearly.

"Tomorrow then?" she asked, her voice sounding odd even to her ears. But when she dared to glance his way again, he only nodded curtly. And then he was gone.

Seized by a sudden, unexpected pang at his departure, Sybil nearly called him back. But her strong will prevailed, along with a healthy dose of common sense. Robin de Burgh was dangerous, and the less time she spent in his company the better. If what she suspected was correct, then his duties as coroner would be at an end on the morrow, and he would be gone for good.

The thought, meant to cheer her, somehow had the opposite effect, and Sybil felt more alone than ever before as she watched him disappear down the corridor.

Chapter Five

Robin hadn't said much in front of Sybil, but he was taking her suspicions about the bailiff seriously. Very seriously. As the man in charge of the finances of the nunnery, he would take care of most of the business of the place, including collecting rents from tenants, supervising the home farm, selling extra produce and making major purchases such as winter stock.

That kind of position presented a man with a lot of responsibility, as well as plenty of temptation to pocket some of that income himself. And human nature being what it was, Robin felt a distinct unease, along with a growing anger. It was one thing for a lovers' quarrel to end badly, quite another for a man to kill in order to cover up his incompetence—or corruption. In that case, anyone who harbored suspicions about the bailiff was vulnerable, *even Sybil.*

Suddenly, Robin wished he were housed inside the walls of the cloister, or at least closer to where the novices slept, and not so far away in the guest quarters. A fierce sense of protectiveness seized him, making him want to charge right back into the nunnery and haul Sybil away. But how and to where? Swearing softly, Robin tried to gather his scattered wits, but his de Burgh blood was thrumming with the demand that he safeguard her. If he could just lie outside her door or inside, by her bed, *or with her in the bed.*

Robin ran a hand through his hair and blew out an exasperated breath. Such thoughts would get him nowhere. But still his heart thundered with a panic that had nothing to do with Sybil being the One, and everything to do with a possible threat to her. Finally, he decided that the best way to protect Sybil was to find out more about this bailiff. And if Farnfold were in the hall eating, then his room would be empty....

It did not take Robin long to discover where the man slept or that he usually lingered after supper in the hall, drinking ale or wine, if it was available. So when the sun began to sink, Robin crept outside, counting the windows along the west wall until he reached the one that marked the bailiff's quarters. The nunnery itself was not built for defense, especially the guest building, so he managed to scale the side of it without too much trouble. When his hands met the lower edge of the arched opening, he pulled himself up, and with a low grunt, went over the stone ledge.

Once inside, it was easy to find evidence of the man's misdeeds. In addition to the regular account books, which were displayed prominently on a small table, Robin found another hidden away. Sales of sheep and grain, unnoted in the nunnery's records, were listed in the slender volume, making it obvious that the man who had been entrusted to oversee the business of the nunnery was stealing from its inhabitants.

Robin took no pleasure in the confirmation of his suspicions, for he could think of nothing lower, except perhaps murder. And, just as that grim thought struck him, he heard footsteps outside the chamber door. With a glance toward the window, Robin realized that it was too far away, and his gaze swept the room for a hiding place, but there was little furniture. Finally, he ducked beside the bed, draping the hangings over him as best he could as the door opened.

If he had been certain it was the bailiff, Robin might simply have waited for the man, dagger drawn, but his de Burgh blood made him react instinctively, and he soon realized why. The door moved too stealthily, and the footfalls were too light for a man, especially one presumed to be a big idiot, or however Sybil had described him. So Robin lay still, listening carefully, only to hear the swish of skirts.

A nun? Here? Was there no end to the clandestine doings in this house? Robin was not about to lie prone during some tryst, but the woman did not move toward the bed. Indeed, she seemed to be heading toward the records, and he wondered if she were involved in the bailiff's schemes, perhaps even the killing itself. Robin put a hand to his weapon, but then he caught a whiff of scent, delicate yet potent, and he knew without a doubt just who was sneaking around the bailiff's room in the near darkness.

She had not seen him beneath the bed hangings, but when he peeked out, he could see her, a slender figure illuminated by the last of the twilight from the window. Indeed, she was so close that he could nearly reach out and touch her, and with a grim twist of his lips, Robin inched forward, stretched out his arm and grasped her ankle. Luckily, she didn't scream, but she did turn and try to smite him with a record book. It was a heavy volume and might have done some serious damage to his face had he not rolled out of the way quickly, dragging her down with him.

The accounts fell to the floor with a thump, and Sybil tumbled on top of him. She struggled valiantly, even going so far as to bite one of the hands that he used to try to restrain her. But he outweighed her by at least five stone, and she was hampered by her skirts, so he finally managed to roll her beneath him, holding her down with his body as he glared into her face.

"You!" she said, when at last she recognized him.

"You were expecting someone else?" he asked.

"What are you doing here?" she demanded, as if she were in some position to question him, and Robin felt his temper rise.

"I might ask the same of you. What kind of fool are you to be running around the guest quarters in the night? Have you any idea what could happen to you? Or is that why you're here?" Robin heard himself say, though he was fairly sure the same suspicions that had lured him to Farnfold's room had brought Sybil, as well.

But he couldn't think clearly. He was far too angry with her for coming here alone, without his knowledge, despite the abbess's admonition that they work together. His presence here was something else entirely. After all, he was the coroner and a man, a knight who could protect himself, while Sybil was a very desirable woman, a supposed innocent, who had endangered herself needlessly.

Robin wanted to punish her, to teach her a lesson that she wouldn't soon forget. "If you are looking for my chamber, you were misdirected," he taunted, but the words came out rough and hoarse as he realized that he was lying on the rushes with her slender body beneath his own.

He could feel every inch of her, the soft press of her breasts against his chest and the juncture of her thighs below. Whatever blood remained in his head rushed downward, and he grew hard with dizzying speed. The desire came upon him with the same fierce urgency as before, only this time they weren't standing in the novices' day room. They were lying together in the fading twilight, so close that he could feel the rise and fall of her breasts, and he couldn't even remember why he wasn't supposed to touch her.

Dragging in a harsh breath, Robin stared down at her face with stunned lust only to find the same kind of horrified awareness in her expression. It was not exactly agreement, but it was close enough for him. Without pausing a moment to figure out why he shouldn't, Robin lowered his head and took her mouth with his own.

When he was a boy, Robin had tormented his brothers by rubbing his feet along the thick surface of his father's Eastern carpet and then poking them with a jolt. Now, after all these years, he experienced the same sort of sudden, shocking sensation simply from meeting Sybil's lips. It was as if his whole body had come alive, every nerve buzzing and popping with excitement.

Rearing back in surprise, Robin paused only an instant to assimilate that amazing discovery before going back for more. Her lips were soft and smooth and delicious, and he took his time, savoring each one until at last he touched his tongue to the seam between them, begging entrance. He felt her start of surprise, but it only inflamed her further, as if she had been waiting for him. *Only him.*

"Open for me," he whispered. "Open your mouth." Whether she complied or simply parted her lips on a gasp, Robin didn't know, but he seized his chance and entered the moist heat of her. His heart hammered and everything inside him clamored to attention once more as another fierce jolt surged through him. Surely there had never been anything like it, Robin thought, even as he reveled in the sensation.

He sucked on her tongue, and when it retreated, he sent his own roving after it, searching, seeking, meeting with more than mouths. Releasing the arm he had been pinning to the floor, Robin cupped her face, angling her toward him as he deepened the kiss. The skin of her cheek was fine and smooth, and his fingers trembled as he bent her to his will.

He rubbed against her breasts, thrust himself against her thighs and held her face to his, but no matter how closely they touched, it wasn't close enough. He wanted her naked beneath him, naked and writhing and releasing that pent-up passion. *Only for him.* She wasn't fighting him, but neither was she returning his ardor, and Robin groaned in frustration, wanting, *needing* all of her. When he felt her hand lift to his head, her fingers sinking into his hair, he growled his satisfaction. *Yes! This was more like it,* he thought as they entwined in his locks—and then yanked hard.

Again, Robin reared back in stunned surprise. He blinked stupidly, only to find Sybil staring up at him with a look of dazed panic. "Robin! Stop!" she said. "We must stop."

He shook his head, both in instinctive disagreement and to clear it. He had never been so out of control, so lost to himself, and it took him a while to realize the truth of her words. He was lying on the rushes in the room of a man who might enter at any time, a man who might have killed once already, and he was ravishing a prospective nun.

Robin dropped his head, brushing against her forehead. "I'm sorry. You're right. I don't know what came over me. I…"

Her hand was still in his hair, and Robin felt the slow sweep of it down his cheek. He turned toward it automatically, and he couldn't help but press one last heated kiss to the center of her palm. It fell away as if he had burned her, and with a groan of frustration, Robin rolled from her, stretching an arm over his face. For a long moment he lay upon his back, breathing hard and trying to regain his wits until above the sound of his own harsh exhalations, he heard something else: footsteps outside the door once more.

Leaping to his feet, he drew Sybil up with him. "The book!" he whispered, as he grabbed the damning record and ran to the window. Tossing the account below, he swung himself out and down, then held out his hands automatically, only to wonder if he should have left her alone up there. What if she didn't jump? But just as he was considering climbing the wall again, he saw the flash of skirts and felt her in his arms, a delicious weight.

He slid her slowly down his body, which immediately roused again to her presence, and in the darkness, he heard her indrawn breath. A gasp? A sigh? Robin had no time to wonder. Grabbing up the book, he took her hand, pulling her away from the building until they could hold an impromptu discussion under the trees. As was their wont, it quickly grew heated.

"How dare you?" Sybil demanded, in a voice of righteous indignation that rubbed Robin the wrong way. Maybe she hadn't exactly wrestled him to the ground in there, but she had to have felt that jolt between them—unless she was dead from the toes on up.

"How dare *you* sneak into his room like that?" Robin countered, glaring at her shadowy form. "You're lucky he didn't find you and make you his next victim!" Nothing would have happened between them if she had stayed where she belonged, so he wasn't going to take the blame. As far as he was concerned, she was diverting attention from the real issue here: her reckless disregard for her own safety.

For her part, Sybil seemed just as angry as he, though he could see little justification for it. She stood in the darkness under a craggy elm, her arms wrapped around herself, her wimple askew, breathing rapidly, and Robin might have been tempted to take up where he had left off, except for the accusatory look on her face that somehow both shamed and enraged him. After all, it was not as though he had taken her maidenhead, he thought, ignoring the swift, urgent rush of blood that accompanied that notion.

"Do you want to explain what you were doing wandering around a man's room at night?" he demanded, refusing to be sidetracked.

Her chin went up. "Unless you are a total idiot, you know very well what I was doing. And my whereabouts are not your concern!"

For some reason that last declaration annoyed him

further, and Robin nearly reached for her. But the heat between them was still running high, despite their differences, and he did not quite trust himself to touch her. "They are my concern when your abbess sets me to watch over you!"

She made a choked sound of disagreement he well recognized. "She told you to work with me, not watch over me!"

"With a killer loose, how can I do anything else?" It was the truth; Robin knew it as soon as he spoke the words. For no matter how wary he was of this woman or how much she infuriated him, he would protect her with his dying breath, and no one, including Sybil herself, could stop him.

"I can take care of myself. I always have," she said, launching a new battle of wills between them. But before Robin could argue she spoke again. "And anyway, it appears your task here is finished. Am I right? Did Farnfold murder Elisa?"

"It would seem so," Robin said. He glanced down at the book in his hands, though he still ached to fight with her. "I found a separate set of accounts. He's been stealing from the nunnery, and as treasuress, she might have found him out. Or, perhaps the two were working together and had a falling out. She might well have been behaving secretively because he was giving her a share of his ill-gotten gains, in exchange for her silence. Or the two might have had a closer relationship."

Before Robin could see what she was about, Sybil balled up a fist and struck him in the arm. Hard. "What? What?" Robin said, flexing his muscle. For a slender novice she was surprisingly strong, and since when did holy women *strike* people?

"Elisa would never have done anything like *that* with Farnfold!"

"You can't be sure," Robin argued.

"I *can* be sure because Farnfold is a big, fat, ugly, sweaty man!" Sybil charged.

Robin gaped at her, then laughed. He didn't suppose that nuns with wandering eyes had too many potential sinners to choose from. "Some women can overlook things like that in return for gold," he said.

At his words, Sybil struck him again, and he reeled in amazement. "Don't say that," she demanded. "Elisa was a good woman, and if she knew about the bailiff's foul doings, then she would not have dallied with him or shared his stolen wealth. She would have exposed him, and that's why he killed her!"

Robin sobered when she reminded him of the nun's fate. No matter what had gone before, the bailiff was responsible for a heinous crime, in the views of both God and man. "You had better see that the abbess is roused," he said. "Once he discovers that his books are missing, he may bolt, or worse. I'll walk with you to the hall."

With a curt nod, Sybil turned, and Robin found himself following behind her, trying to ignore the gentle sway of her skirts and to forget the ecstasy he had known when she lay beneath him. He was all too aware of the blithe words he had used to warn Reynold: *Of course, they all* appear *happy, otherwise they wouldn't have gone through with it, would they?*

If his brothers had experienced anything remotely like what he had felt with Sybil, Robin could see clearly how they had been ensnared into marriage. Even as he decried it, his blood was pounding with the need for more. He had never considered himself a slave to his desires, like Stephen, but what he shared with Sybil could easily turn his mind from other pursuits.

Groaning a protest, Robin stood in the dim hall, while she went to fetch the abbess. And while he awaited her return, he wondered how he was going to manage to linger long enough to inquire about Vala now that the murder had been solved so swiftly. He had not found an opportunity to broach the subject while questioning the nuns, for Sybil had always been present, watching and listening. And all he needed was for the wily One to get wind of his true mission. Then he would never hear the end of it! Of course, it wouldn't matter because he wouldn't be around that long, Robin decided as a certain uneasiness descended.

Just when he was beginning to feel a strange need to go after her, Sybil reappeared to report that the abbess would see them in her personal quarters as soon as she made herself ready. In the candlelight, Robin could see that Sybil's cheeks were flushed, and he wondered if that was a lingering remnant of what had passed between them, or if the abbess had done some questioning of her own, as to why a novice was running around at this time of night.

Although he had been furious at her antics, Robin now found himself ready to defend her to her own abbess, and only the last remaining bit of sense kept him from asking her if she was all right. He ran his hand through his hair in exasperation. He was fast losing his wits.

"I'll fetch the bailiff," he said gruffly, only too glad to be gone and about more manly pursuits, such as the apprehension of criminals. He walked swiftly back to the guest quarters and Farnfold's chamber, where he found the man preparing to retire.

"What is the meaning of this?" the bailiff demanded, his eyes bulging in their sockets. Sybil was right. The man was corpulent and sweaty, his face florid and rather blank. Not exactly a clever one, if Robin was any judge of men.

"Come, bailiff, for your presence is requested by the abbess who employs you," Robin said.

"At this hour? I doubt it very much, my good man. And who might you be?" Farnfold demanded.

"I am Robin de Burgh, lord of Baddersly and coroner in my brother's stead. The reverend abbess has set me to the task of finding the murderer who dared commit so foul a deed within the nunnery walls."

Farnfold paled at Robin's words. "Murderer!" he squeaked. For all his size, his voice seemed more that of a mouse than a man, and he shook his head until his jowls flapped. "See here, my good man. I know nothing of the nun's death! How should I?" When Robin gave him no answer, his eyes bulged even more. "How do I even know you are who you say you are and not some cutthroat here to rob my purse?"

"You don't," Robin said, with a grim smile.

"See here, then, I shall go nowhere with you. Be off!"

"Oh, I'm not going anywhere without you," Robin said, and he drew his dagger.

"Aha!" the bailiff said. "You are a ruffian! Would you brandish a weapon against an unarmed man?" he said, holding out his hands.

"Only when I think he's a killer," Robin said, and he nudged the knife toward the bailiff's rotund figure,

effectively urging him forward and toward the hall of
the nunnery. Farnfold protested all the way that he
doubted Robin's veracity, that he knew nothing of the
murder, and that he could not imagine the abbess
holding any sort of meeting at this hour. Indeed, he
protested until the very instant that he was thrust into
the room before the woman herself.

There, in front of his employer, he became very
solicitous, nodding and bowing in an obnoxious fashion. "Reverend Abbess, I must admit I was a bit
shocked to be rousted from my retirement by
this...fellow," he said, smiling as if some mistake or
jest had occurred.

However, one look at the expression on his employer's face was enough to wipe away his amusement. "Thank you, my Lord de Burgh," the abbess
said, ignoring the bailiff's speech. Then she lifted a
pale, wrinkled hand toward the purloined account
book.

Farnfold's eyes bulged once more, and he swallowed visibly. "Reverend Abbess, I don't know what
this fellow has been telling you, but you surely cannot
believe the lies of a stranger over one of your own,"
he said.

The abbess only eyed him sternly. "It appears,
Master Farnfold, that you have been abusing our trust,
stealing our money, and—"

"I don't know what you're talking about," Farnfold said.

"Do you deny owning this book, then?" the abbess
asked.

Farnfold sputtered, as if unsure how to answer.

"It contains notations written in your own hand,"
the abbess prompted.

"Why, uh, 'tis mine, yes, but meaningless! Just a few notes of transactions that never came about," he said, staring at the accounts, but a telltale bead of sweat ran down his forehead.

"Indeed," the abbess said, with a sad look. She turned toward Robin. "The bishop has often advised that we should order the presentation of accounts before the whole convent annually, perhaps even twice during the year, but I did not want to cast doubt on Elisa's abilities, considering her youth and devotion to duty. And Master Farnfold himself suggested that we save the expense of an auditor by entrusting him to keep all in order."

The abbess sighed. "I can see that I was wrong in all regards to this matter. And I must accept my share of blame for a misjudgment which cost Elisa her life," she said grimly.

At her words, Farnfold suddenly didn't seem quite as full of bravado. Indeed, he blanched and began to shake like a big, pale bowl of jelly. His limbs trembled and he moved his head from side to side in a most unsettling manner that caused Robin to put his hand to his long dagger, lest some sort of fit be imminent, perhaps one such as that which had resulted in Elisa's death.

But Farnfold did not turn violent. Instead, he began to weep like a babe, falling to his knees before the reverend abbess and begging her forgiveness. "I was weak and greedy, and to this I fully admit, but I would never harm anyone, especially not one of the nuns! Surely, you can see that, Reverend Abbess. Come now, you know me! I did nothing but misdirect some coins and will repay you aught that I owe you! But you cannot accuse me of murder," he moaned, crying into his hands in such a sincere fashion that even Robin was wont to doubt his own suspicions.

The abbess, too, seemed to grow more uncertain the longer Farnfold wailed before her, a puddle of repentant humanity. She glanced at Robin, who could give her no reassurance. Admittedly, they had no evidence beyond his theft, none that proved the man guilty of a far more heinous crime.

"Let's lock him up here for the night, then I'll have the reeve put him in Baddersly's dungeon until some kind of judgment is made," Robin said, and with the aid of one of the wide-eyed manservants, he dragged the blubbering bailiff from the room.

Yet, even as he strode away, Robin wondered about the murder, his heart uneasy. For if Farnfold was not responsible, then who was?

Chapter Six

Sybil was uncertain. She lay awake staring at the ceiling, her mind going in circles, though the call for matins would come all too soon. She knew the abbess would readily excuse her, but she hesitated to take more guilt upon all the rest she was suffering, including a new sort of nagging feeling about the bailiff.

It had all happened so fast: finding Elisa, the questioning during the day, her sudden suspicions about Farnfold and her impulsive decision to search his chamber. The condemning accounts and his resulting confession all swam before her, proclaiming an end to the mystery surrounding Elisa's death. And yet, something didn't ring true.

It was not that his wretched performance of weeping and wailing had swayed her, although Sybil had to admit it seemed convincing enough. Nay, 'twas simply that since she sought her bed, she'd had more time to think upon the entire business. And the more she considered it, the more doubtful she became. For, in their hurry to see Farnfold captured, they had not considered several things, the most glaring being the location of the murder itself.

Why the garden? Sybil wondered. Certainly, Farnfold would have avoided his own chamber or other
rooms inside the nunnery, but why commit his crime
outside and in the middle of the night? Perhaps he
intended to make it look like Elisa was meeting a
lover, but Sybil doubted the bailiff was that clever.
His thefts had been clumsy, his record of them easily
found, so she was not impressed by his ingenuity.
And even should he have come up with such a plan,
why would Elisa agree to meet him there at that hour?

It didn't make any sense. Elisa had complained
about the bailiff often enough, and if she had suspected his misdeeds, she would hardly have treated
with him. No matter what Robin de Burgh might say
to provoke her, Sybil knew Elisa would never be involved in any kind of thievery. Nor would she have
taken payment to turn a blind eye to such doings.

Which brought Sybil back to the same haunting
question: was the bailiff really responsible for Elisa's
death, or had he simply been caught in a coil of his
own making? Sybil could not dismiss her own certainty that Elisa had been meeting someone else, but
who? And why? Had some lovers' quarrel ended
badly? Sybil had to admit she knew little of such
things and still less of the kind of passions that
prompted one to kill.

But she was learning.

Sybil shuddered at the memory of what had happened there on the floor of the bailiff's chamber.
Drawing in a ragged breath, she was forced to admit
that one of the reasons she puzzled so fiercely over
Farnfold's guilt or innocence was to avoid thinking
about that other. Unfortunately, it flooded back to her
now in a sweeping tide.

Robin de Burgh had kissed her.

Sybil turned and hid her face in her pillow. No man had ever touched her before, none had dared even approach her, but *he* had. Indeed, she had a suspicion that there wasn't much the man wouldn't dare. And even she, in all her innocence, knew that they had not merely kissed. He had been lying on top of her, and Sybil flushed scarlet at the memory: the press of his weight upon her, the welcome strength, the amazing things he had done with his mouth.

And, at first, instead of putting a stop to it, she had just lain there, letting him do what he would. She, who had always struggled against her independent bent, had given herself up to him with only the most token resistance. And as much as she might like to excuse her lapse as a product of her own curious wild nature, Sybil knew just how close she had been to putting her arms around him, pulling him tighter and doing all the things to him that he was doing to her. Luckily, Robin didn't know. *And he would never know,* she vowed.

Tomorrow he would take Farnfold away, and she would never see him again. Steeling herself against the odd, wrenching sensation that came with that knowledge, Sybil wrested her thoughts back to the bailiff and the questions that nagged at her. She knew only one thing: she remained uncertain of his guilt.

Robin sat in the same small room, the outermost of the abbess's private quarters, where he had confronted the bailiff. Plagued throughout the night with doubts that had led him here early this morning, he found himself pacing the cramped chamber. When the door opened, he whipped around, seized by sharp anticipation, only to feel it fade as he faced the abbess. He had been waiting for her, of course, so why did he feel disappointed?

She greeted him with her usual graciousness, motioning for him to sit, and he did so. "Well, my Lord de Burgh. I assume that you requested this meeting in which to tender your farewell, or might I be mistaken?" she asked.

Robin opened his mouth to speak, but the gleam in her eyes stopped him. He had a suspicion that she knew very well that he was not leaving, and he was reminded not to underestimate the woman. Despite her misguided trust in the bailiff, she was not foolish. Indeed, in some ways, she reminded him of his father. Perhaps it was the authority with which she carried herself or something in that gaze that saw too well.

"With your permission, I would rather stay, Reverend Abbess," Robin said. He tapped his fingers on the carved arm of his chair, his thoughts focused inward. "I am not accustomed to performing the office of coroner, and though your bailiff certainly appears to be guilty, I would not care to have the blood of an innocent man upon my hands. He is a thief, that much is certain, but is he a murderer? I must admit to some lingering concerns."

The abbess did not appear surprised by his words, and Robin was relieved. Some religious leaders, eager for an end to the matter, might have insisted on a swift judgment. But Robin wanted to be sure before putting a man to death. Better to be thorough, even if it takes more time, his brother Geoffrey would say, than to make a hasty decision you might regret later.

Robin wished Geoff were here. He could use the help of an unbiased party. He had even considered calling in his brother Simon, who was fairly close by at Ansquith, but Simon usually reacted first and asked questions later. Meanwhile, methodical Geoffrey was too far away and too busy with a wife and child to aid him. Robin frowned. Instead, he was stuck with a novice who had an infuriating tendency to disregard her own safety, keep her own council and tempt him to…

"In fact, Sybil expressed the same opinion to me earlier this day," the abbess said.

Startled, Robin glanced with some alarm at the abbess, who eyed him with equanimity. He wondered wildly if Sybil had told all to the nun, including what had happened in the bailiff's chamber. "What?" he asked, tugging at the neck of his suddenly tight tunic. *He would not marry her. They could not make him marry her.*

"She, too, feels that Master Farnfold, though he is certainly guilty of theft, might not have been responsible for Elisa's death," the abbess explained.

Robin stared, his mind a bit slow to change tracks. He was still stuck on Sybil, what had happened between them and—if he was going to stay here longer—what must never happen again. Although he told himself that his loss of control last night had been a fault of the darkness, his anger and the bizarre heightening of his senses, Robin really did not care to test his weak resolve again.

"Ah, yes, Sybil," he murmured. "As to our association—"

The abbess cut him off. "It has proved most fruitful, hasn't it? And since you are of the same mind on the matter, I would have you continue to work together to solve this heinous crime."

Robin frowned. Obviously, Sybil hadn't mentioned anything about the bailiff's room. And although he wasn't about to bring it up himself, Robin knew it would be better to do something to end this partnership now, just in case he found himself lying on top of his assistant again. He cleared his throat.

"Reverend Abbess, since this young woman is a novice, I hardly think it right for her to spend so much time with me, an outsider and, well, a man," he said, shifting uncomfortably, as if in apology for his sex.

The abbess's brows lifted ever so slightly. "I thought the de Burghs were famous for their honor. Are you saying that you are not to be trusted?"

Robin felt his cheeks heat. "Of course, not. 'Tis simply that—"

"Good," the abbess said, dismissing his concerns. "For I think that Sybil, as Elisa's closest friend and the most clever member of our order, will prove invaluable to you."

She was invaluable all right, but not in the way the abbess was thinking. She was a once in a lifetime, the One, his destined spouse, only he wasn't interested. Drawing a deep breath, Robin reminded himself of that fact. Again.

The abbess sighed, drawing his attention once more. "I must admit that I was sorely disappointed to learn of our bailiff's perfidy. However, I, too, find it difficult to believe that he is the one who killed Elisa."

Robin nodded, turning attention back to the crime. He had a gut feeling about Farnfold, a strong one, and he had learned not to ignore such instincts. But if not the bailiff, then who? Perhaps the abbess, having time to think upon it, had some new ideas.

"I know I've asked you this before, but was there anyone else who might have wished the treasuress ill?" The abbess shook her head. Robin cleared his throat again. "Do you think she might have been meeting someone? I have no wish to sully her good name, but could there have been a man?" *There. He had said it,* and he ignored the odd sensation that he had somehow betrayed Sybil with his words.

"Not that I am aware of, but there are many in my flock, and the business of running the nunnery is, well—" the abbess paused to eye him sadly. "I am afraid that I cannot give each the attention that I should. But, if there was such a person, then perhaps Sybil might know of him."

Sybil again. *Can we just get away from her?* Robin wanted to scream. Instead he donned a sympathetic expression. "Tell me a little bit about Elisa. How did she come to be here? When did she arrive?"

"Oh, she has been here since she was just a child, an orphan, I gather, who was accepted into the school at a young age. That was before my time. After the good Abbess Magdalen died, the bishop sent me to take over her duties. So you see, I have only served here for nigh on five years and cannot attest to what went on before."

Robin frowned, unable to hide his disappointment. From the abbess's age, he had judged her to have been with the order for a long time and had hoped to question her about Vala. "Elisa was seventeen?" he asked. The abbess nodded. "So she has been here for what? About ten years?"

The abbess's fine brow wrinkled. "I believe she has been here longer, but I cannot say positively."

Robin tapped his fingers absently. She must have

been a child, indeed. "Would anyone else know? Is there a nun still here who might remember when she arrived?"

"I'm not certain. Perhaps Goodeth can help you, though she keeps much to her own room these days. But 'tis Catherine who maintains the records now, so she could find the exact date for you," the abbess said.

Robin nodded. He would like to get a look at those records to check for Vala. In the meantime, it wouldn't hurt to ask the abbess. "Tell me, did you ever have in residence here a nun by the name of Vala?" Robin said.

The abbess considered the question, then shook her head. "Not that I recall, but as I told you, I do not know the early history well."

"She might have had a child with her," Robin said.

"Now, that would be most unusual," the abbess said. "Although we do have little ones at the school, I assure you that none are the progeny of our nuns." She gave Robin a stern look, and he looked suitably chastened. There were always rumors of indiscretions between holy men and women, but he kept those to himself.

"Perhaps a boarder then," he suggested.

"I doubt it, for we usually do not take in families. Those in our guest house are mostly widows, though the bishop would prefer we bar our doors to such worldly women."

To Robin's relief, she did not ask about Vala, so he let her assume his query sprang from the murder. Of course, he could just drop the whole thing. In light of the nun's death, his pursuit of a phantom l'Estrange relative seemed far less important. And since he had already met his doom, uh, Sybil, there seemed little point in finding someone to lift the curse. He simply was resolved not to succumb to it.

"And, now, if that is all, I beg you excuse me," the abbess said, drawing Robin from his thoughts. "The burial will be today, and I have much to do, so I will turn you back over to Sybil."

He nearly groaned.

But Sybil was not waiting for him outside the small chamber, and Robin's initial twinge of disappointment was quickly swamped by relief. He could not deny that the novice was much on his mind, but less dangerously so when he wasn't with her. To his way of thinking, the longer he could stay away from her, the better. And in her absence, he might just do some investigating of his own. With a smug smile, Robin asked one of the servants to lead him to Goodeth's chamber.

Despite her age and infirmities, Goodeth greeted him warmly, shooing away the servant, and Robin immediately recognized her as the deaf nun he had questioned the day before.

"Well, well, what brings you here, boy?" Although Robin was more accustomed to being addressed as my lord, he didn't object. There was a twinkle in the old woman's eyes as she surveyed him, up and down, with what seemed like excessive interest. He supposed the poor thing didn't get many visitors.

As if reading his thoughts, she gave a little crow of laughter. "What is it, boy? I might not be able to hear as well as I used to, but I can see well enough, and you are a sight for sore eyes,'' she said, with a chuckle.

Robin was nonplussed.

"But I expect being one of Campion's boys, you know that, don't you? Too handsome for your own good, I'll warrant. Oh, I might have taken my vows, but that doesn't mean I still can't recognize a good-looking man when I see him. Well, you're wasting all that de Burgh charm in here. Or are you?'' She eyed him shrewdly. "Where's your little novice?''

Robin felt a certain heat climb in his cheeks. "Sybil is otherwise engaged this morning,'' he muttered.

"Eh? What's that?''

"Sybil. I don't know where she is,'' Robin said, more loudly.

"Well, she isn't here, boy! You'd better be off looking for her, or she'll get away from you,'' Goodeth said, crowing again, as if amusing herself.

What? Was everyone here trying to throw him together with a novice? What kind of nunnery was this? Robin narrowed his eyes at the old woman. "I'm here about the murder,'' he said.

"Whatever you say, boy,'' the old nun said, with a chuckle.

Robin ignored it. "Do you remember when Elisa came to Our Lady of All Sorrows?'' he asked, determined to leave Sybil out of this.

"Of course, I remember. She came with Vala.''

For a moment, Robin forgot to breath. "Vala?'' he echoed in a hoarse voice.

"Yes. In fact, I always thought she was Vala's daughter,'' Goodeth said, without mincing words.

Luckily, the old nun appeared lost in thought or she might have noticed the reaction Robin couldn't control. He felt as if someone had struck him, and he struggled for his composure even as Goodeth went on reminiscing.

"She was a baby, you see, and we never take in infants, though there was that one other. She has more the look of Vala, but ah, they were a pair, from the very beginning."

"When was this?" Robin asked, unable to hide his urgency.

Goodeth eyed him closely. "Well, I suppose it was nigh on seventeen years ago. You'd have to ask Sybil—"

Robin cut her off, heartily sick of the endless references to his assistant, especially when he was so close to the answers he had traveled to Wales and back to find. "What happened to Vala?" he nearly shouted.

"No need to scream at me, boy," Goodeth said, giving him a caustic look. "Vala's been dead for many years. She was always melancholic, sickly, lost in her own world, and she didn't take to the life here, though she had sought it out. Some of them don't, you know. 'Tis different, harder in some ways, though with its own rewards."

Robin heard her talking, but he was no longer listening. *Vala was dead.* He felt stricken, as if his idiotic quest actually meant something, when he had known all along it was naught but foolishness. And swift on the heels of his own selfish disappointment came a sharp grief, for the loss of both mother and child. They had fled their heritage, taking refuge here only to fall victim to the cruelties of life that even these walls could not protect against.

"I see," Robin said, though he didn't. Death was

never understandable. He drew several deep draughts of air, trying to banish the desolate feeling that had come over him. 'Twas foolish, for he had known neither woman, and yet, he felt their loss.

Suddenly aware of his surroundings, Robin jerked his attention back to the old nun. "Well, thank you," he said, loosing a breath and placing his hands upon his knees. "You have been very helpful."

"Going so soon, are you?" Goodeth asked. "Well, you had better find out where that novice of yours has run off to, else she get herself into some mischief. There's been a murder, you know," she said.

"I know," Robin said gently, uncertain whether Goodeth was reminding him or herself. But, suddenly, he felt uneasy. Perhaps, he should look for Sybil. Hadn't he sworn just yesterday to protect her? Instead, he was avoiding her, out of his own selfishness.

With a sound of dismay, Robin felt like smacking himself in the head. His only excuse for such a lapse was that he hadn't been thinking clearly since he had arrived at the nunnery, perhaps even earlier.

With a nod to the older nun, he slipped out the door, half hoping that Sybil would be waiting in the corridor. Anticipation sizzled through him at the notion, but the only person he could see was a rather stout nun, walking away from the area. She might have been passing by on her own business, and yet Robin wondered otherwise when he recognized her bulky form.

Maud again? His eyes narrowed for an instant, then he strode to her side. "Ah, Maud, just the person I was looking for," he said, with a gracious smile.

She stopped to give him a pinched look, and he couldn't tell if she had been following him or whether it was merely coincidence that she had appeared outside the old nun's chamber.

"I was just chatting with Goodeth," he said, watching her carefully, but she gave nothing away, her face stiff with disapproval.

"Goodeth," she repeated with a sniff. "I am surprised you were able to conduct a conversation with her. She is most absentminded these days." Then she eyed him shrewdly, as if to judge just what he had learned from the old nun. "I thought you would be gone by now since the abbess said that Master Farnfold confessed."

"To thievery, not murder," Robin said easily. He smiled. "I'm just tying up a few loose ends here."

"Well! I'm sure you know that your continued presence here is hardly conducive to a religious atmosphere."

"I beg your pardon," Robin said, assuming a regretful expression.

"If I were in authority, you can be sure that this matter would be turned over to the bishop, where it rightfully belongs," Maud declared haughtily.

And where it would probably be covered up, Robin thought. As for the rest of her claim, he didn't dare imagine what life would be like for the poor inhabitants, if Maud ruled here.

"Yes, well, that's why I've come to you," Robin said, looking suitably secretive. He glanced up and down the hallway and leaned closer. "I know you didn't want to speak freely before, so I was hoping for a word with you alone," he said, sending Sybil his silent apologies.

Maud preened for a moment in triumph. "Well, I cannot help but feel that a novice has no business poking her head into these matters,'' she said with grim superiority. ''Indeed, this is just how these young women are led astray, with such worldly associations.''

Robin tried not to remember the depth of his own association with Sybil. ''As for Elisa, what makes you think she was carrying on an illicit relationship?'' he asked.

Maud eyed him askance. ''I may be a nun, my lord, but I am not blind. I have lived a long time and seen most everything, and after all these years, I know the signs.''

When Robin lifted his brows in question, Maud frowned. ''She began taking more care with her clothing, adding little decorations, which is forbidden, and she hardly covered her forehead. She was missing from chapel more than once and was outside the walls far more often than errands for her so-called office would require.''

Maud's face hardened. ''The reverend abbess is too lax, of course, and the girl had worked her way into some favor, though from what I gather, her so-called skills with the books were not what they would seem now.'' She puffed up like a laying hen, and Robin decided she probably was the only resident of the nunnery who had been pleased to learn that the accounts were not in order.

''And just where did Elisa go when she left the house?'' Robin asked.

Maud gave him a sour look, as if he was pushing her too far too fast, but he was feeling a certain urgency now, along with his underlying concern for Sybil. He wanted to get this over with and find her.

''To the orchard, like some kind of villein, dragging her skirts through the mud, coming back with grass stains upon her cloak,'' she muttered fiercely, with a real venom that Robin found difficult to interpret. ''Which is what comes from accepting these orphans of unknown antecedents. Both of them act as low as the most common of women!'' As if catching herself, Maud drew herself upward. ''Look out in the fields or among the trees for Elisa's lover,'' she advised.

Robin met her gaze intently and nearly reached out to grasp her arm. She knew, and by faith, she was going to tell him. ''Give me a name,'' he said, with a fierceness that matched her own.

For a moment, he thought she wouldn't, then she sneered at him. ''Tobias. That is what I heard. A simple laborer with nothing beyond a wretched cot to call his own! And that is all I can tell you.''

Was it? Had it been a coincidence that this nun had been outside his questioning chamber twice? And if not, was she spying because she must know everything that happened within the nunnery, whether her business or not? Or was there a more insidious reason?

''I fear this won't reflect well upon the abbess at all,'' Maud noted, though she hardly appeared heartbroken at the knowledge, and Robin considered her aspirations. Obviously, Sybil was correct about the woman's jealousies. She had been passed over for the position of abbess and forced to accept an outsider. Did she now seek to undermine the abbess's regime or simply to establish her own place within it? She harbored no love for the deceased, but had she envied Elisa's growing influence enough to kill her? Was this talk of a lover named Tobias simply a ruse to lead him astray?

Robin frowned, disliking the thought that a nun, no matter how obnoxious, might be responsible. But he realized that Our Lady of All Sorrows was not quite what he had imagined, a hallowed place where those pure of mind and heart and body gathered together. Instead, it contained all types of people, including those who sought power for its own ends and wielded it ruthlessly.

Perhaps he ought to ask Sybil more about Maud, he thought, but the idea caught him up short, as he again wondered where the novice was at this moment. His eyes narrowed at Maud. Robin was aware that the older woman had no great love for Sybil, either. And if the novice got too close to her schemes...

Robin bowed slightly, his graciousness tempered by the gaze he fixed upon her. "Thank you for your help. I appreciate your plain-speaking, and so I shall do the same for you. I will not rest until the killer is caught, and I would have the whole of the nunnery and all of the countryside know that I will be harder to slay than one young nun," Robin warned.

"Let it be known, too, that the novice Sybil and those who dwell here are now under my protection. Should anything happen to her, the wrath of the de Burghs will be called down, and though I believe you when you say you have seen many things, Maud, believe me when I tell you that you have seen nothing of the like in your lifetime. Nor do you wish to."

Apparently, he had managed at last to shake Maud from her haughty pose, for she was gaping at him, an expression of outrage on her pinched face. Satisfied that she had recognized the threat implicit in his words, Robin turned on his heel and strode away from the bitter old woman.

Although he did not really think she would dare move against him, he wanted the word to spread that he would tolerate no further violence, especially against Sybil. The thought brought his underlying concern for her to the forefront. Suddenly, it became imperative that he locate her, not out of any desire for her company, but to assure himself of her safety.

At the very notion, something dormant roared to life within him. She had to be safe. And he must know it. *Now.*

Chapter Seven

By the time someone told him they had seen Sybil heading for the fields, Robin was in a rare mood, fueled by both rage and something that came perilously close to fear, an emotion that he couldn't remember ever feeling before. And he heartily resented it. As the de Burgh who had once been the most carefree, he was assailed now from all sides, short-tempered, fretful and panicked. And it was all *her* fault.

He wasn't heartened when he finally spied her standing beside a small knot of workers, talking to them earnestly. Even though he told himself she was alive and well, all Robin wanted to do was throttle her. Had the woman no sense at all but to march into a band of strange ruffians with a murderer about?

As he strode toward her, Robin watched a stray breeze catch a strand of her hair that had escaped from her wimple. Seeing the color again set off the memory of touching it, *of touching her,* and abruptly his anger and concern changed into something else, until all he wanted to do was tear away the sign of her novice's status and see her hair for himself, then take off her plain garb and see her body for himself.

Robin shuddered, halting his steps in an effort to gain control of himself. It seemed that any strong emotions involving Sybil roused passions that tested the limits of his control. Drawing in several deep breaths, he leaned forward and laid his hands against his thighs, slowly willing away his desire. He was a lighthearted fellow, a prankster, not a primitive like his brother Dunstan, who had been known to toss his wife over his shoulder and carry her off, Robin told himself. And yet, that's exactly what he wanted to do to Sybil.

As he straightened, Robin realized that this was probably how it all started, with a fierce lust impossible to quench. *And it ended in marriage.* But he was made of stronger stuff than his brothers, and he was not going to give in to the thundering in his blood. Neither was he going to give her his name. But he just might give her a piece of his mind.

So he strode over to where she stood, seemingly oblivious to his presence. The men before her were aware of him, however. They had been regarding Sybil with open, friendly expressions, but drew back as he approached, and Robin wondered if they were closing ranks against an intruder or simply had thought better of importuning a young novice.

Although Robin didn't expect her to be grateful at his intercession, he didn't anticipate her fury either. But when had she done anything that made sense? he wondered as she turned toward him, her blue eyes flashing. "What are you doing here?" she demanded.

"I might ask the same of you, *assistant,*" he said.

"I thought we were supposed to be working together."

"I'm not the one who had a *private* audience this morning," she snapped.

Robin scowled, chagrined for a moment before he realized she was again trying to distract him from the real issue. "That's no excuse for you to go running off alone and exposing yourself to myriad dangers!" he said, lifting an arm to encompass the laborers, who were watching him warily. He couldn't recall ever shouting at a woman, but this one deserved it.

Unfortunately, instead of cowering properly, Sybil laughed. The sound so entranced Robin that for a moment he stood dumbfounded by the sound of it. Light, airy and delightful, it sang through him like the tingling of bells. Bells that might very well be tolling his doom. He sobered immediately.

"Do you see bugbears behind every bush?" Sybil asked him. "I have lived here all my life and walked here aplenty before your arrival. I am not about to cower in my room without a big, brave knight to attend me."

Her obvious scorn so enraged him that Robin felt dizzy with it. He didn't trust himself to move, else he might attack her himself, only he wouldn't use a rock, he'd use his bare hands...and enjoy every minute of it.

"You laugh?" he asked through clenched teeth. "Do you think that's what your friend Elisa did? Do you trust these men with your life?" he asked. As he swung toward them, the workers scattered, returning to the oxen waiting in the fields. And far from looking appreciative or even contrite, Sybil turned to him with a fierce expression.

"Now, see what you have done!" she said, pointing to the disappearing laborers. "They are simple people who have worked the nunnery's land for years, as have their fathers before them, not exactly the sort I would call *dangerous*. I was trying to find out some information, but now I will never coax them into confiding in me!"

She knew. Had she known all along? *"You knew,"* Robin breathed, his chest hurting inexplicably at her deception. "You knew, and yet you let me take in the bailiff?" He was no longer shouting, his voice preternaturally calm, but now Sybil's eyes widened, with either fear or confusion.

"What do you mean?"

"Every time I tried to find out if Elisa had a lover, you protested, yet here you are, trying to seek him out!" Robin felt a sudden, painful twist deep inside as he was struck by a new suspicion. "Is he your lover, too?" He couldn't help himself; he reached out and took her by the shoulders as raw fury and pain and something else rushed through him. *"Are you out here to warn him?"*

"No!" Sybil protested. "Robin, no," she said, and just as they had last evening, those simple words seemed to bring him to his senses. Releasing her with an oath, Robin turned and ran his hand through his hair in exasperation. This kind of behavior just wasn't him. He was never struck with violent urges. *What was happening to him?*

"I wouldn't have gone to the bailiff's chamber, if I hadn't thought him guilty," Sybil said in a low, serious tone. "And I was as eager as anyone to have him be so, to put an end to the mystery surrounding Elisa's death. But the more I thought about it, the more it seemed…not right. I spoke to the abbess this morning and would have talked to you, as well, but I wasn't invited to your meeting with her,'' she added.

And somehow Robin actually felt guilty, even though he was the coroner! He shook his head, trying to clear his thoughts amid the mire of his emotions.

''I admit that I didn't want to believe Elisa was doing anything that might be construed as wrong,'' Sybil said, slowly. ''And I'm sorry if that attitude hindered our progress, but this morning I—'' She paused to take a deep breath. ''This morning, I went through her things and I found something. A cherry blossom, nearly fresh and carefully preserved in the pages of her Psalter.''

Robin stared at her numbly for a moment before his wits kicked in. ''A love token?'' he asked.

Sybil shrugged. ''I don't know, but I was wondering, since the orchard is on the other side of the garden…'' Her words trailed off, then she lifted her chin. ''And I was asking those men if they had seen anyone in there with her when you charged up like a bull on a rampage!''

''You might better have asked who *tended* the trees,'' Robin said.

Sybil's blue eyes widened once more, and, for a moment, Robin was hard-pressed to keep his mind upon the murder. He forced himself to concentrate upon their conversation and nothing else. ''I already know who she was meeting. 'Twas a laborer named Tobias,'' he muttered.

Sybil was startled, he could tell, and something else he could not identify. ''When did you find this out?'' she demanded.

''Just now, before coming to look for you,'' Robin

said. And it was the truth, though he hadn't been seeking her out for the purpose of sharing the news with her. However, he knew how often their thoughts turned together, along the same track, at least when it came to the murder. He took a deep breath. "So it seems we are on the trail of someone else."

Although it went against his better judgment to use the word *we* in this instance, Robin fast was becoming convinced that the only safe place for her was under his protection. *Right where he could see her.* And, sure enough, the words had barely left his mouth before Sybil glanced toward the orchard and Robin followed her gaze to where a lone figure was digging out underbrush. He put his hand to the sword he had donned this morning, and they fell into step together as they climbed the gentle slope.

"I know Tobias, or at least who he is," Sybil said. "He seems a quiet, shy sort of fellow, not a killer."

"In the heat of passion, anything can happen," Robin said, gruffly, then he felt his cheeks redden at the accuracy of the statement. He cleared his throat. "We'll know more after we talk to him."

But it was not Tobias in the orchard. The man who was working there was old and gnarled, hardly the kind a pretty young novice would choose for a liaison. Still, they stopped before him, watching as he turned over new earth, perhaps in preparation for additional plantings. When he finished, Sybil called to him by name.

"We are looking for Tobias," she said, once she had gained his attention.

The old man shook his head. "Not here," he said, before returning to his task.

"Do you know where he is?" Robin asked.

"No."

"Have you seen him?" Sybil put in.

"No."

Growing impatient, Robin blew out a breath. "And when, exactly, was the last time you saw him?"

The man paused to lean upon his shovel. "Let me see," he said, squinting as if in thought. "The day before yesterday," he answered, returning once more to his digging without further elaboration. Robin caught Sybil's gaze, and he knew they both were thinking the same thing: *the day before the murder.*

"Where does he live?" Robin asked. The old man told them in his usual short and succinct speech, and they soon were making the short journey to a small cottage.

Hand on the hilt of his sword, Robin stepped inside first, hoping to discover the man hiding out at home, but they found nothing. In fact, the place looked as if it had been stripped of anything worthwhile, leaving only rushes and a ragged pallet behind.

Again, Sybil's gaze swung to his. "Do you think something could have happened to him, too?" she asked.

Robin shook his head. "More likely he's run away," he replied. Once outside, he glanced up at the midday sun and made a decision. "Let's go into the village. I've a thirst for some of their ale," he said. Ignoring Sybil's dumbfounded expression, he strode away, knowing that she would soon hurry to catch up with him.

"You're not going to drink *now,* are you?" she asked in a horrified tone that made Robin's lips twitch in amusement.

"Yes, and you're drinking with me," he said, thoroughly enjoying the shocked expression that traveled across her face.

As he suspected, Sybil argued with him as he headed toward the village, pointing out all the things they should be doing instead of drinking, but Robin noticed that she never actually refused to come with him, and he felt a kind of smug satisfaction at the knowledge. Whether she liked it or not, he was going to protect her—at least until his work here was finished.

Sybil knew that Robin had some ulterior motive for going to the village, some reason that he was keeping to himself, and though it infuriated her, she doggedly stayed with him—just to find out what he was up to. She had thought herself clever for trying to trace Elisa's keepsake, but the obnoxious, overbearing knight obviously had done as well or better than she in ferreting out information. The thought rankled, and Sybil was not about to let him learn more without her.

So she walked along beside him, finally halting her protests to bask in the lovely spring weather. Once she relaxed, Sybil was surprised at how good it felt to be on the road. Her errands had always been few and brief, so she normally treasured such outings, and slowing her steps, she knew a heady sense of freedom. 'Twas a dangerous sensation, and yet, she could not help savoring it.

Suddenly, she felt like stretching out her arms and spinning around, so glad was she to be away from the stifling walls of the nunnery. How wonderful it would be to come and go as she pleased, without obligation to bind her there and without a duty to behave circumspectly whenever she moved without. The thought was sobering, for she realized that despite the giddy pleasure that came over her, she still represented the nunnery. Yet, she continued to feel a certain freedom, for she certainly need fear no danger this afternoon. Doubtless the man beside her could meet any challenge.

Sybil confirmed that belief with one glance, for her companion was armed with a deadly looking dagger as well as a long sword. Yet she suspected the weapons were not so much a deterrent as were the strength and confidence that he exuded. Not only would Robin de Burgh make a ruffian think twice, he would make any female *look* twice, Sybil decided, her heart hurrying its pace.

Sybil herself darted more than one surreptitious peek at the man beside her, and with each glance his way, Sybil admired some new feature, from his gleaming dark hair to his thick lashes to his mobile mouth. Even the column of his throat seemed to claim her interest, especially when she remembered the feel of it beneath her palm as they lay pressed together.

But Sybil would not think of that. All day she had refused to let her mind wander along that path, concentrating instead upon Elisa's killer. Of course, it had helped when she found that Robin was closeted with the abbess this morning. Her ensuing outrage, along with a strange feeling of betrayal, had banished any unwelcome thoughts. And Sybil had kept them at bay right until the moment he had charged up to her, bigger and more potent then ever, scattering the workers and her thoughts in equal measure.

Still, she had clung to her indignation, especially after he had had the gall to shout at her! But now, with the scent of spring in the air and the awareness of him beside her, it was more difficult to recall just why she was angry, just why she resented his male presence, and just why she had put a stop to his kisses.

Drawing in a deep breath, Sybil let the memories rush back, washing over her, filling her with warmth and forbidden pleasures. It had all been incredible, like a dream, only more vivid, more intense than waking life. One would think that the heavy body of such a man would be frightening, overpowering, but it had felt deliciously good, wonderfully solid and safe and tantalizing where it touched.

And that wasn't all that had touched her. All too easily, Sybil remembered the brush of his hands, his mouth and his *tongue*. The texture of his hair, the scent of him, the low rumble in his chest that signified his pleasure: all had been a heady mix that had threatened to drag Sybil under, into the same coil of Elisa's making. And only that knowledge had given her the strength to put a stop to it, to bring them both to their senses.

Oh, she knew that Robin de Burgh would never turn upon her with violence. Despite the temper she had seen him exhibit, he was no murderer, so passion would not be the death of her. Yet it could well bring about her downfall and her disgrace. Sybil never had considered such a possibility, but the pull between a man and a woman was stronger than she had ever imagined.

Of course, she had never imagined anyone like Robin de Burgh. Knight, lord, coroner, leader of men, commander of confidence, he exuded a startling masculine presence, far greater than anything Sybil had ever seen. He was strong and bold and handsome, yet she knew he could be graceful, gentle and amusing. Sybil recalled how that whole business about his alleged rash had left her gaping in wonderment. Had anyone ever teased her before? Certainly not anyone who looked like Robin, and despite her initial dislike of the man, Sybil admitted that she would have to be dead herself not to feel something for him.

But feelings were one thing, while acting upon them quite another. Everything about Robin de Burgh caused her to misbehave grievously, from the anger he inspired to the desire he conjured, and Sybil was well aware that she must restrain all her reckless impulses. Even the apparently innocent act of walking beside him was fraught with all sorts of temptations, from her admiration of his physical form to her longing for freedom, which had grown more intense since his arrival.

And when they reached the outskirts of the village, Sybil found herself enjoying the deference accorded the two of them owing to Robin's title and bearing. It was wrong, she knew, to take pleasure in such worldly things, yet she did. And how could she explain the hot surge of pride she felt when other women eyed him covetously, or her own jealousy when their gazes lingered too long?

Although Sybil repeatedly reminded herself that she was a simple novice intent upon a task, she continued to revel in the afternoon's liberty, delighting in that which she should not and rebelling against the bonds that held her. And when at last they stood in front of the clustered buildings that made up the small community of Wotten, Sybil drew in a deep breath, eager for adventure.

"Where do you intend to do this drinking?" she asked.

"Well, if this one is like most villages I've seen, brewers will dot the road on either side," he said as he eyed the huts and cottages.

Sybil nodded. The people of Wotten often brewed a batch of ale, stuck out a sign, and sold it at the established price of three gallons for a penny until it was gone. And both men and women were known to gather in their neighbors' homes for an evening's imbibing. But the convivial atmosphere sometimes turned ugly, with violence often breaking out between those who had drunk to excess.

At least, that is what Sybil had heard. Those from the nunnery, of course, had no reason to enter such places. *Until now.* Perversely, Sybil felt a start of excitement at the prospect of such forbidden activities, which she tried her best to quell. Naturally, her companion felt no such qualms, she thought, with a glance toward him. Indeed, there was something about Robin de Burgh that simply reeked *forbidden.*

"Do you think most of these places were in business a few days ago?" he asked.

Turning her attention back to the crude signs and branches sticking out at intervals over the doors, Sybil shrugged. "I have no idea."

"Well, let's find out," Robin said. And Sybil felt an idiotic thrill, a swift surge of pleasure that came from being in this man's company when they weren't arguing and he treated her as an equal. Hiding the smile that seemed to come unbidden to her lips, she hurried to keep up with him, following him through the low door into a dark interior.

The place was small, with a noisome smell that

made Sybil wrinkle her nose. They took seats at a bench thrust against a muddy wall, while a large woman in a dirty apron brought them their drinks in cups that appeared none too clean. Cautiously, Sybil took a taste and frowned at the sour brew, which was nothing at all like that served at Our Lady of All Sorrows.

"Why, this woman ought to be fined for selling such a weak and ill-flavored product," Sybil said, but Robin swiftly hushed her. And, instead of complaining to the big, fierce-looking female, Robin began to flatter her, as only the handsome, smooth-tongued lord could do.

Sybil had seen him pour on the charm before, with the undeserving Maud, but she could only sit there gaping while he reduced this ungainly creature to gravelly grunts that she assumed were giggles. There was a reason for all this cajolery, as Sybil soon discovered, for while she sat sipping the dreadful ale, Robin soon was prying all manner of information from the now-voluble woman.

How long had she been in business? What competition did she have? Did she see many travelers? Had there been any strangers about recently? Did she know the people of the abbey? The bailiff? The nuns? The gardeners? And when at last, he seemed to have exhausted his questions, Robin tossed the woman a coin, rose to his feet, and headed outside once more, Sybil on his heels.

And so it went in each place that they visited. Most were the same, dark and dreary and dank and smelly, though after a while, Sybil became inured to the odor. In one of the better places, Robin coaxed some bread and cheese from the owner, but usually, they just drank. The questions, too, were most often the same, as were the answers.

However, at one site, apparently favored by the nunnery's laborers, Robin was able to ferret out information about Tobias, ultimately learning that he had an uncle who lived in another village, less than a day's journey away. Warmed by the ale, Sybil could only watch and marvel at Robin's skill. Had she thought him inept, arrogant, overbearing? Now she could only admire his wit, his intelligence, his cleverness—and the rest of him—as well, from the top of his dark head to the tip of his boots.

By the time they had reached the last alehouse, Sybil was light-headed and finding it more and more difficult to follow the course of Robin's queries. But even she sat up straight when the grizzled old man who called the place home reported that he had seen two strangers just three days ago, travel-stained and curious. Perking up her ears, Sybil swung forward, nearly falling before Robin put out a strong arm to catch her.

"Asked more questions than you, my lord," the old fellow said. "But 'twere all about the abbey and the nuns there. I told them that we didn't serve a lot of holy women in here, but they didn't think it funny. Queer pair they were, all solemn and fierce-looking, and I didn't care for the way they talked. But persistent they were, so when I saw one of the nuns outside, that mean old Maud, I sent them out to her. Figured she was a match for anyone," he said, chuckling.

Sybil blinked in horror. Maud! Hadn't she, like all the other nuns, claimed that she had met with no strangers during the past week? Sybil made some kind of gurgling noise, which finally drew Robin's attention to her. He eyed her with a rather odd expression, then took his leave of the old fellow, dragging her along with him. Robin was a big man, with a long stride, and Sybil had to stumble to keep up with him, so that she felt dizzy and winded when they at last reached the edge of the village. There, finally, he stopped, turning to face her.

"What is the matter with you?" he demanded.

Sybil simply stared at him, unable to form a coherent thought. One lock of dark hair had fallen across his forehead, and she had the irresistible urge to tuck it back in place. Or kiss it. Or kiss him, she thought, her gaze dipping down to his beautiful lips. She swayed forward.

"You're drunk!" he accused.

Sybil's eyes widened.

"You weren't supposed to drink!" he said.

"But you gave me ale!" she protested.

"You were with me, so I had to buy for us both! I thought you'd have the sense to leave it or toss it," Robin said. With a disgusted look, he turned away, muttering under his breath.

Sybil wasn't sure, but she suspected an insult was in there somewhere. "I am not drunk," she said, lifting her chin with great dignity. "'Twas only ale, after all."

"Enough to sink a ship," Robin said. His gaze swung back to hers, and he swore. "How can I take you back to the nunnery like this?" He paused to scowl at her, and Sybil had the inane notion that she ought to lift her fingers to his lips and curve them into a smile instead. She giggled. He swore again.

"Let's head toward the brook," he said, running a hand through his dark hair. But Sybil thought she heard him mutter something about dunking her head in, and she squawked in protest, reeling backward until he stopped her with a well-placed arm.

"Let's get your face washed, at least," he said, his eyes narrowing as they studied her. "That is, if you can walk."

"Of course, I can walk," Sybil said, drawing herself up straight only to list to one side. "I made it this far, didn't I? And my face is not dirty!"

With what sounded like an exasperated grunt, Robin's arm tightened around her, and before she knew what he was doing, he had picked her up and slung her over his shoulder. Sybil squealed as the already precarious ground spun beneath her, and she closed her eyes against an unwelcome vertigo, but in the blessed darkness that followed, she was distracted by the sudden onslaught of a scent—Robin's—and the feel of his hands upon her.

Abruptly taking an interest in her unique position, Sybil wiggled, and Robin put up a hand to steady her, only to remove it immediately. Sybil didn't know whether to be relieved or disappointed, but his touch upon her backside had gone a long way toward sobering her.

When he halted his steps, Sybil opened her eyes again to see that they were along the tree-lined brook, water dappled by the sun that peeked through the boughs overhead. She drew in a deep breath and smelled fresh leaves, new grass and Robin. Who could ask for more? she wondered giddily.

Yet Sybil soon felt a sense of want, a hunger, as Robin loosed his hold, sliding her down along his body to set her feet back upon the ground. She must have made some kind of noise, because he tensed, his grip upon her waist tightening, and his eyes narrowing.

"Don't," he whispered harshly.

"What?" Sybil asked, tipping her head back to search his handsome face.

"Don't...move." He grimaced and then drew a deep breath. "Don't make that sound, and most of all...don't look at me like that," he said.

"Like what?" Sybil asked, her gaze drawn to his lips. He was talking, after all, so it was only natural, though she could not so easily explain away her growing fascination with their shape. She jerked her attention back up to his eyes, as dark and clear as some sweet confection, and found herself equally enthralled.

Robin said nothing, but his expression became so intense that it nearly stole her breath. Her body suddenly grew tight and alive, her breasts full, her heart racing as she stared at him. Sybil felt a rush of heat, along with a heady sense of power as she realized that she held some sway over this man. As knight, lord and man, he was a formidable being, yet she affected him somehow, and the knowledge made her bold. Defying his warning, she moved, lifting her palms to his chest.

For a long moment, they simply stood there, Sybil trembling at the feel of his hard muscles beneath her fingers. She stared at her hands, amazed at her own temerity and the pleasure that flooded her at that simple touch. Even through his tunic, she felt his warmth, his strength, the very beat of his heart, which had picked up its pace. At that discovery, Sybil looked up into his face, but she had only a glimpse of his dark intent before he lowered his mouth to hers.

His arms closed around her, crushing her to him, and she slid her hands up his chest and around his neck, hanging on for dear life. His lips were even more wonderful than she remembered, firm yet soft, strong yet gentle, as they moved over hers. This time, when his tongue probed for entrance, she welcomed it. This time, when he pressed every inch of her against his body, she reveled in it, and this time, when he kissed her, she kissed him back.

And when she touched her tongue to his, his low growl of approval acted like a spark upon tinder. Sybil felt alight, inflamed, as she sought a deeper union. More than pleasure, more than the sensations her body gratefully accepted, she felt a connection to Robin himself, the very essence of him, as if he reached out for her soul.

His palms stroked her back as he angled his mouth, his kisses drawing away her breath and at the same time giving her life. Her fingers tangled in his thick hair, delighting in the texture, and time spun away. He laid her down in the soft grass that sloped down to the brook, amid the scents of early flowers and running water, and pressed kisses along her jaw and down the length of her throat. There he lingered against her throbbing pulse, and with a sudden, startled awareness, Sybil felt his hand upon her breast.

Her head fell back, and she sighed at the sensation. Her reaction must have been the correct one, for Robin shuddered. With a groan, he moved over her, his thigh parting her legs, his body hot and heavy upon hers as he took her mouth again with a new fierceness. Lifting one hand to her cheek, he angled her face, deepening the kiss. His fingers seemed to

search for her hair, straying to her wimple instead,
and then everything stopped.

With a great shudder, Robin lifted his head and
stared at her head covering as if it rebuked him, and
his expression, once so fraught with desire, hardened.
"This is wrong," he said.

"Nay," Sybil whispered, for nothing had ever
seemed more right. Twining her hands in his hair, she
pulled him down to her, imbuing only a small part of
the magnificent feelings roiling through her into the
press of her lips against his. The kiss was hot and
fierce and all too brief, for he pulled away again.

"'Tis wrong," he said, with a harsh finality. "You
are drunk."

"Nay," Sybil answered, for, in truth, she no longer
felt the befuddlement that came from too much ale,
but a far more potent entrancement.

Her denial was useless, however, for Robin rolled
from her and rose. "And what's worse, 'tis dangerous," he muttered, reaching down to pull her to her
feet. Although Sybil would have clung to him, he
released her immediately, as if the touch he had
craved now repulsed him.

"Let's go," he said, and without pausing to hear a
reply, he strode away, leaving Sybil to follow
numbly. Staring at his back, she could only wonder
at his swift change in mood. Had she done something
to drive him away? Had he found her lacking in some
way?

Reaching up, she fingered her wimple even as she
fought an urge to rip it from her head. Her cheeks
burned with shame at her own conduct, yet she felt a
far more powerful sensation of rebelliousness. She
had never taken her vows, and now, apparently, she

had discovered why. After what had happened, how could she even consider entering the cloister?

This afternoon, strange and marvelous and horrible as it had been, had acted upon her like a cock's crow to one who would sleep the dawn away, or as a call to arms that roused even the most cowardly to battle. No longer could she return to her slumbers or her complacency, as she had so often before, and her mind worked with a startling speed that drove away any lingering traces of ale.

Robin was nearly forgotten as Sybil considered her life, her world and her future with chilling deliberation. And all the way back to the nunnery, her resentment grew until she nearly cringed at the sight of its walls. And then, at last, she wondered if perhaps it wasn't long past time she left them for good.

Chapter Eight

Robin was so relieved to be back at the nunnery that he didn't even bother about Sybil's safety beyond seeing her into the building before fleeing to his own chamber. Yet even as he congratulated himself on his narrow escape from her clutches, he tossed and turned the night away, chasing half dreams and visions of a villain crawling into the novices' sleeping chamber and murdering them all.

Then he would wake up in a sweat, wishing he could be with her at all times, that she was lying there beside him, so that he could watch over her. And the feeling was so strong that he even conjured up plans to infiltrate the cloister, only to toss them aside as he vainly sought rest once more.

Tired and irritable come dawn, he sent out a messenger, rousing a youth from sleep to fetch some soldiers from Baddersly. Having learned that the man who might well have killed Elisa was free, Robin decided it might be wise to have extra guards. He couldn't be everywhere at once, and he didn't want to leave the nunnery unprotected while he looked for Tobias.

If the killing had been the result of a lovers' quarrel, the nuns were in no further danger, but Robin was not about to take chances. And he knew that while it was one thing for him to ride and walk about the countryside alone, it was quite another to take a novice with him. Even he might be overwhelmed by a band of ruffians, though he had to admit that the only threat to Sybil yesterday was from…himself.

The soldiers would do more than stave off any attack, Robin thought ruefully, they would serve as well-needed chaperones. Although for her own sake, he was determined to keep Sybil close, Robin had come to the conclusion that he could no longer be trusted with her. The lust that she effortlessly inspired had been bad enough when she was arguing with him constantly, her expression belligerent and her quips tart. But when she had lain back upon the spring grass like some kind of siren, all warm and welcoming, Robin had lost his wits entirely. And mayhap something else: his heart.

Robin refused to consider it.

He told himself that only desire drove him, for it certainly reigned supreme whenever he touched her. Yet, if that was all, why did he feel such an inexplicable longing not just for her body, but her entire being? It was as if the two of them created something wonderful betwixt them. Robin scowled. Naturally, that's the way it would seem, so that he would be tempted to take her to wife.

He was not going to marry her, curse or no curse. So what if Vala could no longer help him? He needed no magical aids to escape his fate. He was a de Burgh, and none could make him go against his own will, Robin thought righteously. He had found out what he needed to know about the last of the l'Estranges, so, as soon as he finished with the business of coroner, he would leave, never to see the novice again.

And if the thought of missing her taunts and kisses stung him somewhere deep inside, then that was bearable. He was strong enough to withstand the worst of physical blows; he would not break at the loss of company that irritated him more often than not. Aye, the sooner he was gone the better, Robin told himself.

However, solving the mystery of Elisa's murder was proving to be more difficult than he had ever imagined. Robin's brow furrowed at the number of suspects. Was it the thieving bailiff, the power-hungry nun or the laborer who might have been her lover? He fervently hoped that no others came forward, or he would be at his task until doomsday. Coroner, indeed! His brother Dunstan might well have informed him of the various offices that came with his holding.

Feeling cross and frustrated, Robin spent the day questioning the residents and trying to avoid Sybil's gaze. He took to leaning against the doorway, ostensibly to look out for spies like Maud, but also to keep as far away from his assistant as was possible within the confines of the novices' day room. Luckily, Sybil seemed as eager to forget her drunken lapse as he was, for she appeared to be deep in thought, distracted even, and said little to him beyond the necessary comments upon their task.

Unfortunately, they learned little from the other inhabitants of Our Lady of All Sorrows. Most of the servants were closemouthed, as if they feared being tossed from their home for speaking out. Or perhaps loyalty to the nuns kept them quiet, for male and female alike were fierce in defending their mistresses.

Were they protecting anyone in particular? Robin wondered, only to shake his head. Perhaps his strange findings about Vala, as well as the mysteries surrounding the murder, *were* making him see bugbears behind every bush, just as Sybil had suggested.

Robin was somewhat cheered when the men from Baddersly arrived, for here were representatives of the world with which he was familiar, far removed from the female enclave of the nunnery. The knights and outriders were welcome indeed, yet, troubled as he was, Robin might have wished for someone to share his trials, such as one of his brothers... But only Reynold and young Nicholas were unwed, and Reynold had made his position clear. Scowling at the memory, Robin set about finding housing for the new guards.

Although he had spent the evening drinking and dicing with the men from Baddersly, Robin hadn't really enjoyed himself, having suffered a sort of eerie discomfort, as if he were supposed to be somewhere else. When he realized that it was probably the curse working on him, he only threw himself more furiously into the gaming and ale. And now, the next morning, he had nothing to show for it, except even *more* discomfort.

Adding a throbbing head and another restless night to his list of complaints, Robin felt even less like his usual carefree self and more like his terminally temperamental brother Simon with each day, each hour perhaps. And when he mounted his destrier in preparation for the ride to Ryewater, he was surly and disgusted.

Sybil wasn't helping. "Are you sure the man at the alehouse said Tobias's relative lived in Ryewater?"

she asked, drawing his attention to her. Robin felt the familiar quickening of his blood, the race of his heart, the hot surge of longing that accompanied any awareness of her. Did she have to be so beautiful? he wondered as he studied the pale curve of her cheek. An ugly creature like Geoffrey's wife would have been far easier to resist.

"Well?" she prompted, a distinctly unlovely look upon her face as she glared at him.

"Yes, I'm positive," Robin said, urging his horse forward before she could start a lengthy argument. Now he was sorry he had agreed to take her with him. She was one of the reasons he had waited, for he was uncertain how long it would take to reach Ryewater and he had wanted a full day to make the journey. He also had insisted that another female come along to attend her, though Sybil looked as if she had no idea what to do with the young serving girl at her side.

Robin paused. It was rather refreshing to see a woman who knew how to fend for herself. Beyond his unique sisters-in-law, the noble ladies he met all seemed to be jaded, spoiled creatures, eager for a bedding, but petulant and demanding of luxuries and attention. Robin could not imagine Sybil ever acting that way, and perversely, he wanted to shower her with the indulgences that she had done without her entire life. She deserved better, he thought before catching himself.

With a frown, he rode ahead, staying as close to his men and as far away from Sybil as possible, but not too far away. Robin was still caught in the coil of that contradiction: while he didn't want to be near her, he didn't trust her safety to anyone else. 'Twas a predicament, but one that Robin tried to push out of his mind, concentrating instead upon the road to Ryewater and the man who had fled there.

He did rather well until they reached the outskirts of the small village. Then, Sybil, who had hung back during the long ride, appeared beside him, and Robin tugged at the suddenly tight neck of his tunic.

"Is your rash bothering you again?" she asked, with a sneer that little resembled the glowing admiration he had glimpsed yesterday.

"Yes," Robin snapped, disappointed in spite of himself at their return to adversarial mode. "Care to give it a good rubbing?" he challenged.

Despite Sybil's glare, her lips twitched, and Robin purred, "Scratch me and I'll scratch thee."

Her mouth quickly turned downward. "So you claim," she mumbled.

What? Robin blinked at her. Surely, she wasn't angry with him for stopping the madness by the brook? He hesitated as his mind jumped to a more unsavory conclusion. Maybe that lustful episode was all part of her insidious plan to marry him. Without pausing to consider that most of her behavior was more likely to send him screaming in the other direction, Robin scowled.

"Are your braies too tight, as well?" Sybil asked, lifting her brows slightly to mock him.

"*What?*" he nearly bellowed.

"You act as if something has you knotted up, what with your constant frowns and growls," she said, as if he were his brother Simon or some other glum character.

Robin glared at her, for he could not deny the accuracy of her accusation. "You seem inordinately

concerned with the fit of my clothing,'' he snapped
as he dismounted. ''Perhaps you've been looking a
bit too closely.''

In truth, he figured that his little novice had no idea
how often his braies were constricting him these days,
nor that she was the cause. And just like that, a wave
of desire washed over him so strongly that he actually
swayed on his feet, leaning against his destrier as he
dragged in a ragged breath. Wretched female! He
ought to show her just how well he filled his braies
and gain some relief.

But she was not drunk today. *More's the pity,*
Robin thought, remembering well when she had
yanked on his hair, pulling him down for a greedy
kiss, reluctant to loose him. With a low grunt, he
stepped away from his horse and strode toward the
first villager he could see.

''Stay there,'' he called over his shoulder to her.
''And *try* to behave.''

As he strode away, Robin heard a foul noise from
behind him that made him grin before he turned his
mind back to Tobias's uncle. In such a small community, it did not take long to gain news of the free-
man, and Robin quickly returned to the waiting train
with directions to the strip of land where the fellow
was working.

Past a copse of trees they found it, and Robin
tensed as he saw two men there. Dismounting once
more, he told the rest of the party to stay behind, but,
of course, one of them did not listen. Before he had
taken a few steps, Sybil was at his side, where, unfortunately for him, she seemed to belong.

''You forget that I am the only one who can identify Tobias,'' she said, that rebellious glint in her

eyes, and Robin just nodded, knowing that arguing would waste precious time. The two men ahead stopped to look up from their task, and Sybil grabbed Robin's arm. "That is him," she said.

Robin put a hand to the hilt of his sword, alert for any signs of flight, but both laborers simply watched them approach with wary expressions. When close enough to assure himself of their capture, Robin halted before them, Sybil safe behind him.

"You are Tobias?" Robin asked, and the taller of the two nodded his head fearfully. When he saw Sybil, unmistakable in her black novice's garb, he gasped, his expression crumbling. To Robin, his guilt was evident.

It was the older man, however, who stepped forward. "Who are you, sire, and what do you want?" he asked.

"I am Robin de Burgh, lord of Baddersly in my brother's stead, and as coroner there, I am concerned with the death of a nun at Our Lady of All Sorrows. I am here to speak to your nephew."

At his words, the older man appeared weary and beaten. He simply nodded and moved back, his shoulders slumped, leaving Robin to face Tobias, a young man of plain but steady countenance, tall and lean.

Apparently, the report of the bailiff's arrest, traveling as slowly as all news, had not reached Ryewater, for Tobias made no attempt to throw suspicion away from himself. Indeed, he made no defense at all, but simply stared at them with a stark expression that Robin found unsettling. The man, hardly more than a boy in Robin's assessment, did not look like a killer.

But appearances could be deceiving, Robin knew. Hardening his heart, he fixed the fellow with a direct gaze. "You worked at Our Lady of All Sorrows?" he asked.

Tobias nodded.

"And why did you suddenly leave?"

"My brother," he said, swallowing hard. "My brother talked me into running away. He knew about...about Elisa and me." He dragged in a ragged breath. "And he swore they'd hang me without waiting to hear my story."

"And what is your story?" Sybil asked, moving beside Robin, her lovely face grim.

"I didn't kill her!" Tobias cried. "Yes, I sinned with her, but I loved her. I would have married her, but she said that the bishop and all would never let her go, that they would hunt us down no matter where we went." He took a great gulp of air as if close to collapse, and Robin nearly reached out to aid him.

Of course, the nun had been right. She would rather be an adulterer than an apostate, breaker of all of her vows. The Church and State allied to return all those who strayed from the flock, and he had heard of those held in confinement against their will in lifelong punishment, a heavy fine to pay for a few moments of freedom. Robin shuddered.

"She never wanted to be a nun, but the old abbess insisted. They made her take her vows, so I didn't see how they could hold her to them. I was tired of sneaking and hiding, so when the fancy men came asking about her, I thought it was a sign," Tobias said, looking anguished.

Robin's eyes narrowed. "What fancy men?"

Tobias shook his head. "They came up to me when I was working in the orchard. I thought Elisa had written to them or told them about me, so they knew to come straight to me. They said they were relatives of hers, and I thought…'' He broke down, sobbing. ''I thought they'd come to help her, to get her out of the place somehow, with gold or influence.''

Then he lifted his head, revealing such despair that Robin nearly flinched. ''I didn't know they'd kill her. I swear I didn't!'' he cried. ''If I'd known they would kill her, I would have torn them from their fine horses then and there, though I be damned for it!''

''What makes you think these men did it? And why?'' Robin asked, though he felt a chilling sense of foreboding.

A fierceness crossed Tobias's face. ''When I met with her that night, she said she had no relations, that she couldn't remember anything before coming to the nunnery, except being hungry and cold. And the men, they never went to the nunnery, like they said. No one had asked for her, and there weren't any new guests in the tenant quarters, she said, or Sybil would have told her.''

Robin felt Sybil lurch beside him, and he reached out for her, only to drop his arm before making contact.

Tobias shook his head. ''I sensed something was wrong then. Why would these men ask all about her, then disappear? I tried to talk her into running away with me, but she wouldn't. I watched her climb the wall into the garden, never dreaming she was going to her death. I should never have let her go.''

''So you think these men followed you, knowing that you would meet her somewhere, then waylaid her when she returned to the nunnery?''

Tobias nodded, wretchedly.

"How many men were there? Can you describe them to me?" Robin asked.

"They were two, both average-looking, with dark hair. They looked like brothers, which made me believe them more," he said, shaking his head. "They wore fine clothes, and their mounts were big and black, not workhorses."

Robin nodded grimly, for Tobias's description matched the one the man at the alehouse in the village had given of the two strangers who had asked about the nunnery, the strangers who had talked to Maud. And Robin had a sudden, uncomfortable suspicion about their identities.

"Now I wish I'd never spoken to them, that I'd stayed with Elisa, that I had taken her with me, anywhere!" he said. "So what if the bishop would hunt us down like dogs? We would have had a bit of happiness first, and she'd be alive!" he said. And covering his face with his hands, he broke into wracking sobs once more, overcome by his grief.

"Where were these men from? Did they tell you?" Robin asked, a dark dread creeping over him to chill his heart.

Tobias lifted his face. "Wales," he said. Then he sank to the ground, his uncle coming forward to offer him comfort.

With one long, terrible view of the fellow's grief, Robin turned on his heel and strode away. He could hear Sybil hurrying behind him, but he didn't want to face her or his men, or even himself, not after the news he had just received. However, as usual, Sybil would not be deterred, reaching up to grasp his arm. Her touch pained him and Robin turned on her, ready to growl some curse, but instead of anger or contempt, he saw concern in her eyes.

"What is it?" she asked. It was the same tone she had used in those rare instances she called him by name. It always reached him, whether he will it or no, and he halted.

Blowing out a low breath, Robin glanced back at Tobias, then ahead to his men. "We can't talk here," he said. "I'll explain later."

He should have known better. Sybil's expression turned downright stubborn. "No. I want to know what is happening right now," she said. Darting a look around, she began pulling him toward a small copse of alders. Robin didn't know whether to laugh or rage at the thought of one slender novice moving his massive frame. In truth, he desperately needed a moment alone with his churning thoughts, but somehow, he couldn't bring himself to shake off Sybil's touch, which carried a warmth he could feel right down to his chilled heart.

Unfortunately, once they were within the leafy confines of the trees, she released him, jerking away abruptly to give him a prompting look. But what was he to say? The blackness that had lifted momentarily descended again with a painful lurch. Robin opened his mouth only to shut it again. Running a hand through his hair, he began to pace, caught himself and sat down on a large outcropping of rock. He felt dazed, each breath a struggle against the recriminations that filled him.

"Since you walked away from Tobias, I assume you believe his story," Sybil said. "Although I have to admit he sounds far more truthful than the bailiff, how can you be sure? Do you think those strangers were the same ones seen in the village?''

Robin nodded mutely.

Sybil made a low sound of distress. ''Then, perhaps neither the bailiff nor Tobias murdered Elisa,'' she mused aloud. ''Perhaps 'twas Maud. She could have hired those men to do the deed.''

Robin looked down at the toes of his boots. ''I think I know who killed Elisa, and it wasn't the bailiff or her lover or a jealous nun,'' he said, though the words came hard.

''Who, then?'' he heard Sybil ask.

''I don't know,'' Robin muttered.

''But you just said—'' Sybil began, her words trailing off as she made a noise of exasperation.

Robin lifted his head to face her. ''It's all my fault.''

''*What?* How?'' Sybil asked, waving her arm in a gesture of impatience.

''I went looking for Vala l'Estrange,'' Robin said, as if that explained everything. It had all seemed so innocent at first, sort of a lark, really, but now... He drew a deep breath. ''I asked about her and her child on the Marches because she had married a Welsh prince, and I think...I think someone else, alerted by my interest, came looking for her, too. And they got here first.''

''Are you saying that Vala was a Welsh princess?'' Sybil asked.

''She married a prince,'' Robin said. ''But she fled, why, I don't know. Perhaps she worried that her daughter would become a political pawn in the troubles between the English and the Welsh or even among the princes themselves. I don't know,'' he repeated, shaking his head. "But after I was there, after I learned where she had gone, someone else came looking for her, to kill her. And when they found out she was already dead, they murdered her daughter."

"What?" Sybil cried. "Vala, a daughter? Who are you talking about?"

"Elisa," Robin said, exhaling a harsh breath. "Vala brought her here for her own protection, and because of me, she is dead." If Sybil, Elisa's friend, came at him clawing and scratching, Robin would have welcomed it. He felt hollow, dead inside, for his part in a murder. It was one thing to slay warriors in the heat of battle, quite another to have caused someone to be killed by his own pointless blundering.

However, Sybil did not rage, though, she did argue with him, as usual. "I'm sorry, but I find all this impossible to believe. Vala as a Welsh princess? Elisa her daughter?" She shook her head, as if to imply that Robin was making up the whole incredible story.

He frowned. "The records at your nunnery show that Vala arrived with Elisa. Some here even thought she was her daughter, yet both women lived there in peace until I resurrected their names among those who had forgotten them! Whether Welsh or English, someone came here to eliminate the last of the line!" Robin's breath caught in his chest. "I might as well have killed her myself!" he muttered, looking away.

"Don't be absurd," Sybil said. "There is always trouble in Wales, and people were bound to remember this Vala sooner or later. She is a victim of her own choices, not your interference."

To Robin's surprise, he felt her hands upon him, gloveless and tender, as she took his face and turned it toward her. And that simple touch was enough to rouse him from his melancholy. He stared at her solemnly, noticing the way the sun filtered through the leaves, sprinkling her skin with light, like an angel. Yet there was solid, earthbound reason shining in those beautiful blue eyes and a fierceness in the way she offered him comfort that bespoke her humanity.

Indeed, she was all things to him because of the connection between them, that indecipherable something that made her *the One*. The sight of her sent a rush of feeling through Robin that he could not deny. And, as always, whenever emotions were running high between them, desire rose upon its heels, fast and furious.

Robin was in no mood to ignore it, and he reached for her, taking her mouth in a hot, reckless act of possession. She was his, by heaven, and he would mark her as his own. His arms closed around her, pulling her against him, drawing her onto his lap, but she still wasn't near enough. His hands roamed her back, moving down to the firm curves of her buttocks. He grasped them, squeezed and lifted and somehow she was straddling him, her gown riding upward, while his hardness strained against the juncture of her thighs.

"Yes," Robin muttered. Triumphant, he kissed her more deeply, as though nothing mattered but this woman, finally his. If only he could somehow crawl inside her, he would be whole, complete, *home at last.*

And Sybil did not demur. She met his mouth eagerly, her fingers delving into his hair, pulling him closer even as she pressed her breasts against his chest. With a groan, Robin reached up and tugged at her wimple, tossing it back from her head only to stare, his breath coming in great gasps, at the red-gold curls that spilled over his hand.

"Beautiful," he marveled. "Your hair is beautiful." He felt like laughing aloud with joy, for this was his lady, and she was fine and lovely. Bringing a fistful to his face, he drank in the scent of spring flowers and Sybil, then burying his hands in her locks, Robin drew her mouth back to his.

His need grew more urgent, and he gave in to it, desperate to take what he so desired before his wits had time to claim him. He wanted her now, had to be inside her or he would surely die of the lack. Gripping her behind, he rubbed against her body, groaning at the glorious pressure. *"Yes, oh, yes,"* he cried, breaking the kiss and throwing his head back in a burst of ecstasy.

Above them, Robin could see the tracery of leaves amid the blue sky, but it was as if they existed in their own haven, untouched by the world. For a moment, the sound of rustling in the trees distracted him, but then Sybil began whispering his name in a husky voice that enflamed him further.

Robin gritted his teeth, so close to the edge that he felt as though he might spill his seed into his braies like some untried lad. Unwilling to let that happen, he burrowed a hand beneath Sybil's skirts, between them, trying to free himself. He fumbled, his knuckles brushing against her moist heat, and she cried out his name in a hoarse shout that made him shudder with pleasure.

Then everything happened at once.

The rustling returned, so loud now that Robin could not ignore it, and with a start of horror, he could only assume they were being attacked. Cursing himself for dallying in the woods, away from the train, prey to any kind of ruffian and totally oblivious to danger, he reached for the hilt of his sword even as he rose to his feet, dumping Sybil from his lap onto the ground, where she fell in a heap.

Robin stepped in front of her, chest heaving, weapon drawn, only to stare as a massive buck crashed through the underbrush and veered away through the trees. Stupidly gaping after it, Robin was at a loss until he heard bells ringing. *Bells?* He turned, only to realize it was Sybil's laughter. She was seated on the ground, wearing a bemused expression, her gorgeous hair flowing over her shoulders and down her back in a sensual tangle.

Belatedly realizing that no one was assailing him, Robin became aware of another, far more insidious danger. He sucked in a harsh draught of air as he slowly regained his senses. And the reality of his situation turned the last of the lingering warmth inside him to a cold chill.

With a jolt of alarm, Robin realized that he had nearly deflowered Sybil, a novice, *the One*. And fast on the heels of his horror came anger. He glared at her, certain somehow that she had planned the whole thing to ensnare him. *Well, it wouldn't work.* He refused to marry her or anyone else. He wasn't handing over his freedom, his very self, for a few moments of pleasure, no matter how potent they might be. He might not be able to lift the curse, but he would be damned if he would succumb to it.

As he grimaced, still breathing hard, Robin watched Sybil's laughter fade and her amusement change to a look of stunned hurt that pained him, as well. Perhaps she didn't know, he thought. Perhaps she was as much a victim of this curse as he. Caught between conflicting emotions, Robin turned away and ran a hand through his hair in exasperation.

"Let's go," he said, stalking toward the edge of the trees and away from temptation. As he broke through the copse, he could see his guard waiting patiently and swore long and low. Chaperones, he had thought them! Now they would be sniggering amongst themselves as they speculated on just what he and the lovely young novice were doing alone.

Robin felt a new surge of anger and vowed that if word of this tryst reached anyone's ears at the nunnery, he would have their heads. *Every last one of them.*

Chapter Nine

They took refuge for the night at a Ryewater inn, Sybil and the young servant Robin had insisted accompany her tucked into a tiny chamber away from the main room that housed all the men. Having never seen an inn before, Sybil was unimpressed with the dirty, cramped quarters, but the odor and appearance meant little when she considered one small fact: it was the first night she could ever remember spending away from the nunnery.

Freedom had never smelled so sweet.

When they embarked on this journey, Sybil had thought of little except finding Tobias, but now, here in the darkness, awareness of her liberty thrummed through her blood like the beat of her heart. She could walk out of this place, and no one would stop her. It was such a heady notion that she felt dizzy from the force of it, as if her lungs could not take in enough air.

Of course, this was not the first time that her thoughts had turned toward escape. It seemed as if her mind had been wandering in that direction ever since Elisa's death, or was it Robin de Burgh's arrival?

Whatever the instigation, after long years of complacency, Sybil was forced to consider her position at Our Lady of All Sorrows. Perpetual student and novice, she had never been ready to take the next step of her vows and the commitment they required. Yet she had remained where she was, safe within the shelter of the walls, even as she yearned for a different sort of life outside.

Now she realized that fear had kept her here, fear of change, fear of the unknown, fear of her own independence. She felt ashamed of her own weakness, but determined that she could not continue on as before, serving the tenants while forever locked away from their world. These past few nights she had spent many sleepless hours considering her future and had come to one conclusion: she would never be a nun.

Perhaps it was Elisa's brief, unhappy existence that had decided her, or the recent trips outside the walls, or…Sybil flushed when she remembered what had made her feel most alive. But it was not the illicit pleasures to be had with a man that drew her, nor the false giddiness to be found in the ale barrel. It was the sweet delight of the sun on the fields at midday, the golden wash of evening gleaming off a brook and the heady knowledge that those simple pleasures were available at any time to those who lived outside.

Still, Sybil could not deny what had happened among the trees. When Robin had kissed her, she had seemed to lose all restraint, responding eagerly, allowing liberties that she had never dreamed about—and enjoying every one of them. When he'd pulled away, she had felt bereft, as if he made her whole and had left her with only a part of herself.

Sybil knew a sudden chill at the foolish notion. As ignorant as she was of the intimacies they had shared, she knew enough to be grateful that Robin had pulled away, thankful for the interruption that had separated them before it was too late. She could have been ruined! Sybil shuddered, for no matter how glorious she had felt in his arms, Robin de Burgh was a lord and she a novice. No pledges had he made to her, no words of love had he tendered. Indeed, he had glared at her with a fierceness that bespoke emotions far less tender.

That memory still stung, and Sybil swallowed hard against it. But she told herself that she neither wanted nor needed Robin de Burgh's good opinion. She had spent her lifetime obeying someone else's orders, following rules laid down by others, and she had no intention of binding herself to a new master, no matter how appealing he might be. She did not care to be any man's mistress, even Robin de Burgh's. Nor could she imagine catering to his erratic whims.

Let him go about his own business, for Sybil intended to go about her own, and it did not involve being chattel to anyone. As she listened to the night sounds of her strange refuge, the decision settled over her with a sense of rightness she could feel down to her bones, and Sybil knew what she must do.

Once she had seen justice done for Elisa, she intended to make her own plans, and she would not let her lack of money or resources stop her, as it had done so often before. This time, she would not wait for a chance that would never come, but would create her own opportunity. And it wasn't impossible, for in her position as mistress of the guest house, she knew worldly people with connections to the outside.

And lying there on her strange, narrow pallet, Sybil vowed to use those contacts to gain her freedom at last.

They left at dawn, Robin grimly eager to return to the nunnery, or rather, to return Sybil to the nunnery. He had spent the night alternately brooding over the deaths of Vala and Elisa and breaking out in a sweat at the memory of just how close he had come to burying himself inside the One, an act which would have sealed his fate for certain. He hoped that by putting Sybil back in her normal venue, he might stop wanting her so desperately.

Unfortunately, it didn't happen, for when they reached Our Lady of All Sorrows, Robin felt no relief. Even as he hurried away from Sybil on his mission to the abbess, his hunger for her remained. Unabated. Indeed, Robin gritted his teeth against the inevitable tightening in his groin. It seemed the only way to rid himself of his perpetual hardness was to think about Elisa's death or take himself in hand. But that thinking led inexorably to the memory of Sybil's touch, of how she had cupped his face in her hands and offered him comfort.

Robin frowned, but the recollection remained bright and vivid, conjuring a desire for more than just sex. How long had it been since he had received a woman's care? His mother had died bearing Nicholas, leaving their household nearly devoid of women, and his few liaisons had not been based on companionship. Robin shook his head in a kind of wonderment, as if Sybil had met a need previously unknown to him.

He growled a denial of the possibility that he might have lacked some tenderness in his life and sent a wary nun skittering away. With a certain fierceness, Robin told himself that he didn't need anything except the company of his brothers and their rough affection. Without it, he was alone, and no woman could take the place of the bond that had been forged by birth.

Yet, he couldn't dismiss the niggling notion that not just lust bound him to Sybil, but shared intellect, sensitivities, interests and yes, maybe even some heretofore unacknowledged craving for gentleness. Having never looked at a woman that way, Robin was nonplussed. He halted his steps, puzzled, before he decided he was going as soft as his brothers, which meant all his brooding was part and parcel of the curse.

The reminder of his original mission brought Robin's mind back to the murder for which he felt responsible, and he ducked his head, unsure exactly what to tell the abbess. The bailiff could be sent to the bishop's court because he had stolen from the church, but the coroner's jury would never meet unless Robin could discover the identity of the strangers he was all but certain had killed Elisa. Since he didn't even know if they were Welsh or English, Robin was not too optimistic about the chances of ever seeing justice. The knowledge gave him a sour feeling in his gut, but he wasn't going to give up.

Robin was drawn from his moody thoughts by the sound of his name, and he turned to find the nun

Catherine calling to him. She was in a small room with some heavy books open upon a table before her.

"Oh, my lord!" she said, raising a trembling hand to hail him once more. Having little patience for interruptions this day, Robin nevertheless stuck his head inside the doorway.

"The abbess said you were inquiring about Elisa's arrival," Catherine said. She had buried her head in one of the books, so she could not see his lack of enthusiasm, which was just as well, Robin thought. Taking a deep breath, he stepped inside and assumed a more gracious expression.

"Yes, I was," he answered, though the information was of little worth to him now.

"Well, here it is!" Catherine said, as if delighted to be of assistance. "She came to us in the autumn of 1265, as did another orphan found abandoned. Why, they were both no more than babies. So young!" she exclaimed, as though to herself.

Robin thought so, too. "Isn't that unusual?" he asked.

"Oh, yes. I didn't think we ever took in infants, but it seems that Vala, who also came to us at that time, arranged for them both to be accepted. I must admit that I am surprised, and even more so that they arrived within days of each other. But of course, that explains why Elisa and Sybil were so close!" she said, turning her head to give Robin an absent smile.

But Robin could make no reply. He felt as if someone had kicked him in the gut, nearly doubling him over. *Sybil?* He didn't even want to consider the ramifications of this bit of news, and yet he knew that he must. *Sybil and Elisa arrived at the same age, the same time and both because of Vala.* There was something here that roused his instincts to full attention, and it was all he could do not to bellow out loud.

Catherine's smile faded as she eyed him quizzically, and Robin ran a hand through his hair as he tried to regain his composure. "So Vala brought Elisa with her and Sybil as well?"

Catherine frowned and turned back to her records. "No, it seems that she arrived with Elisa, but that a day later Sybil came to us. "The child was found abandoned in the village and was placed in the nunnery school, according to Vala's instructions."

"Who brought her here, then?" Robin asked.

Catherine squinted at the text. "It just says a woman from the village, by the name of G-Gw—. Oh, dear, I'm not certain how to pronounce it. Gwerful, I believe."

A Welsh name, if ever he heard one, Robin thought, and she was a resident of the village? Suspicion made him growl as, for a moment, he forgot his company. Catherine's squeak of dismay brought him back to attention, however, and he forced out a smile. "Thank you," he said, leaving the nun to blush and titter at his exit.

Once in the corridor, Robin turned away from the abbess's room, retracing his footsteps to the guest house and beyond. Something wasn't right, he would swear to it, and he wasn't going to rest until he discovered just what had his senses screaming. He strode outside the building, planning to head for the village, then stopped, veering toward the stable where his destrier stood. The steed was faster than his feet and might be necessary, should his questions lead him somewhere else.

And with a pounding of hooves, Robin raced

through the gate, intent upon unraveling the mysterious antecedents of the dead woman, once and for all.

Once in the village, Robin returned to the alehouse where the owner had given him information before and found the old man just as voluble. Although he claimed not to know much of what went on at the nunnery, when Robin mentioned a village infant entering the school, the fellow scoffed.

"They don't take the likes of us there!" he said. "Why, all those students are from rich families who want to get rid of them. 'Tis just like the nunnery itself, you have to buy your way in."

Robin frowned. "I'm puzzled then, for I learned that the novice, Sybil, was an orphan taken there by a village woman," he said.

The old fellow screwed up his wrinkled face. "Sybil. Ah, yes, I know her, but she's not related to anybody here. I'll swear to that."

Robin frowned. Could this business grow any more complicated? "What of a woman named Gwerful?"

The man shook his head. "There's never been anyone living in this area by that name. I would have remembered the like of that."

"But 'twas a long time ago—" Robin began, only to be cut off by the old man's snort.

"Doesn't matter. I know everyone, and I've never heard of her," he said with certainty that was hard to deny. Baffled, Robin tossed him a coin and left. He had every intention of returning to the nunnery, for he was beginning to think he was seeing shadows where there were none. So Sybil had arrived right after Vala; it could be nothing more than a coincidence. And yet, as a de Burgh, Robin had learned to trust his instincts, and a gut feeling made him turn his destrier away from Our Lady of All Sorrows, back the way he had once come on his journey from Wales, back toward Baddersly.

There, in the village that spread below the castle walls, he discovered those who had heard of Gwerful, for she was a merchant's wife. Well known for her skill with a needle, she often dyed the cloth that her husband sold. Her home was a small cottage, where she and her husband also did business. After his long journeys of the day, Robin was weary by the time he entered the place, where he was greeted by a small woman with white hair, yet still slender and youthful looking.

"Are you Gwerful?" Robin asked, without preamble.

The woman nodded. "Are you here for some cloth, my lord?" she asked, taking his measure by the cut of his garments.

"Nay, but I would speak with you," Robin said. "I am Robin de Burgh, lord of Baddersly in my brother's stead." She nodded, apparently aware of his identity, but her manner turned more cautious than friendly.

"Many years ago you delivered a child into the care of the nuns of Our Lady of All Sorrows. Where did the infant come from?" Robin asked.

At the mention of Our Lady of All Sorrows, the woman's eyes grew wide. Clearly frightened now, she shook her head and glanced this way and that, as if looking for some way to escape from the tiny house.

"Fear not. I do not mean to harm you in any way," Robin said. He tried to appear more at ease, but every nerve in his body was taut, his instincts screaming that here, at last, he might actually find the answers he sought.

"I do not ask these question idly," he assured the woman. "As lord of Baddersly, I am serving as coroner for the area and am looking into a murder at Our Lady of All Sorrows. A young nun by the name of Elisa was killed recently."

Robin watched Gwerful's rapidly changing expression with interest. At the news of the death, she appeared horrified, leaning forward as if anxious to hear what he said, only to straighten once more, seemingly with relief, at the mention of the victim's name. "Did you know her?" Robin asked.

Gwerful shook her head.

"Then she was not the child you took to the nuns?" Robin asked, though Catherine had told him as much. "The infant you delivered there was Sybil?"

At first he thought she might deny it, but the woman slowly nodded.

"And how did you come about this child? Was she yours?" Robin asked, curiosity sharpening his tone.

Gwerful's mouth moved, but no sound came out. She cleared her throat, refusing to meet Robin's eyes. "I found her here in the village, abandoned."

"And why would you take her to Our Lady of All Sorrows? Why not to Baddersly?" Robin asked.

She licked her lips, as if to delay her reply. "'Twas well known that the lord at that time cared not for his people," she said, at last. "The nunnery had to because they are a religious house. They must take in the lost."

"Why would you think so? 'Twas no orphanage,"

Robin argued. The woman's obvious agitation was telling. All was not as it should be, and he did not need his well-honed de Burgh senses to tell him that.

"'Twas a school, and we thought—" Gwerful paused, obviously reluctant to continue, but Robin remained where he was, watching her expectantly. "That is, I thought that they would," she finally said, though it was evident she was still hiding something.

"And how did you and the child get from here to there?" Robin asked.

"We rode," Gwerful replied, as if confused by his question.

"You had a horse? If so wealthy as to own such an animal, then why did you not keep the child yourself?" Robin persisted.

"I could not! I promised Vala I—" Gwerful broke off, bringing a hand to her mouth, an expression of horror upon her features.

At last, the woman had slipped in her speech, and Robin's body tensed. Here was the link he had been looking for, but what did it mean? His heart pounding in his chest, his blood thrumming loudly in his ears, he no longer attempted to maintain the pretense of ignorance between them.

"Vala is dead," he said, seizing upon her blunder. "She died many years ago."

Obviously stricken, Gwerful let out an anguished sob and covered her face with her hands.

"You were her servant in Wales?" Robin prompted.

Gwerful nodded. "We had to flee. Vala feared for her life and that of her child. Her husband had been poisoned by someone in his own household, and she

wanted nothing more of the intrigues there. So she
ran, taking only the child and myself.''

As if a dam had been broken, the formerly reticent
woman released a torrent of words. ''She sought a
nunnery with a school, so they could both take refuge
there, but she still feared that her husband's family
would seek her out and find her daughter. So we
looked for another. When we reached this place, I
found a poor family with many children and an infant
daughter. I bought the girl from them, and we
switched the babies, giving the poor child Elisa's
name, just in case anyone would ever come looking
for her. At Robin's horrified look she stammered an
explanation. ''We thought to save the child from an
early death, to give her a better life.''

His nerves already straining, Robin felt his whole
body tense, as if preparing for a unavoidable blow.
''So Vala took this girl with her and left her daughter
with you?'' he asked, though he well surmised the
answer.

Gwerful nodded. ''I was to wait a few days, to
avoid suspicion, but I was so frightened! I was terri-
fied that something would happen to the princess
while in my care, and so I left the very next day. I
told the nuns I had found the baby in their village,
and Vala paid for her keep.''

Although Robin had known something was wrong
ever since his speech with Catherine and had felt an
unease that had only grown since confronting this
woman, her blithe confirmation of his suspicions sent
him reeling. It was as if the world had shifted under
his feet, so enormous were the ramifications of her
admission, and Robin could only stare at her in dazed
shock.

''And Vala renamed her own child Sybil, after the ancient oracles, a fitting one for a l'Estrange,'' he muttered, more to himself than to the woman standing in front of him.

All along, the novice who had driven him mad with her tart tongue and her stubborn behavior and her slender body had been Vala's daughter. For a moment, Robin fought against an urge to laugh at the vagaries of fate, at the irony of his destiny. He had come searching for a l'Estrange to lift the de Burgh curse only to discover that she was the one most likely to fulfill it. But swift on the heels of that insight came another, far more significant realization.

Sybil was in danger.

Robin drew in a harsh breath as the awareness struck him, rousing his protective instincts as nothing ever had before. Vala's daughter was alive, but might not remain so, for if he could ferret out the truth, perhaps others could, as well. Swinging toward Gwerful, he spoke with a new urgency.

''Come with me to Baddersly,'' he said. But he spoke more forcefully than he intended, and the woman stepped away from him, with a wary look.

Robin choked back an oath of frustration. Now that he knew Sybil was in danger, he cursed himself for leaving her. Why had he run off alone? He was hours away from the nunnery, even by the swiftest horse, and he had not the time or the patience to cajole this woman.

'''Twould be for your own safety,'' Robin explained, trying to dredge up the de Burgh charm that had been sorely lacking of late.

''I have a husband!'' she said.

"You may both come, as my guests," Robin said, but Gwerful only shook her head.

"Please, listen to me," he urged. "Someone murdered Elisa because they thought her Vala's daughter. And if I can follow her trail back to you, maybe they can, too." But Gwerful shook her head stubbornly, obviously more concerned with the present moment than what her future might hold.

"Let me speak with your husband, then," Robin said.

"He is a merchant. He is away," Gwerful answered, and Robin did not bother to test the truth of her statement. He knew he could forcibly abduct her, but the prospect of dragging an older woman away against her will was not a pleasant one. He could only hope that those who had murdered Elisa were long gone, satisfied that their job was done.

But Robin would not count upon that hope to protect Sybil. He would trust nothing and no one with that task except himself, and he felt the need to return to her pressing upon him like a weight that would steal his breath. With one last word of warning to Gwerful, Robin hurried outside to his destrier, but his eyes flew to the horizon, where the setting sun mocked his plans.

Swearing low and long, Robin knew he would have to spend the night at Baddersly...unless the moon would guide him on his way to the nunnery. Turning toward the castle, he urged his mount forward, stopping only long enough to summon soldiers to return with him, adding more to the guard that remained at Our Lady of All Sorrows.

As they headed off into the darkness, Robin counted himself lucky to have avoided Florian, the inquisitive bailiff, who would have pestered him with innumerable questions to which he had few answers. Although the murky history behind the murder at Our Lady of All Sorrows was not clear, that was about all he could claim to understand. Never before had Robin felt so at a loss, assailed by a host of emotions, all of them raw and new.

It was natural to want to protect Sybil, since he was responsible for her danger, yet no amount of rational reasoning could explain the frenzied way his blood pumped her name, feeding his frantic need to get back to her, to see for himself that she was all right. That she was *his*. To protect, not to possess, Robin told himself.

He was well aware that he had failed to do his duty in the past. Indeed, he frequently had vowed to avoid her, but circumstances had changed. She was his responsibility now, more than ever. His own petty selfishness had brought danger upon her head; now it was up to him to make certain she remained unharmed.

But even that decision, though simple enough, left Robin uneasy, for how could he protect her in a place where he could not roam freely? The holy grounds had not saved Elisa. And even if his guards surrounded the building, people would still have to come and go, servants and workers and messengers. How would he discern who might be intent upon evil? Walls could be scaled and even priests and nuns could be bribed and swayed.

He could restrict her to a room, but Robin knew Sybil well enough to suspect that she would not be caged. Indeed, she seemed already to be stifled by the walls that enclosed her; he could not imagine her agreeing to be further constrained. Of course, he

could go through the church, but a bishop might bury
her away at some other nunnery beyond Robin's
reach to fall prey to foul play. And what if such an
abbey held to sterner strictures? What if she were
forced to take her vows? Robin tried to beat back a
surge of panic so strong it nearly choked him.

He told himself that her status did not matter, only
her safety, but how was he to accomplish it? Her enemies were clever and determined. Perhaps they
thought their task completed, but if they somehow
suspected the truth, Robin knew that nothing would
stop them. The Welsh could be ruthless fighters, and
should some minions of the king come to claim her,
who was he to stop them?

'Twas a question that plagued him mightily all
along the road. Indeed, it wasn't until they had nearly
reached their destination that the answer came to him,
as sharp and stunning as the slash of a blade. Although he had no power over Sybil in her eyes or
anyone else's, there was one way in which he could
gain it, one way to protect her both day and night,
one way he could legally and morally spirit her away
from all threats. Unfortunately, that course was the
one which he had sworn to avoid: *marriage*.

To Robin's surprise, the prospect did not send him
flying into a rage or sicken his stomach, probably because it had nothing to do with the curse or commit-
ting himself to a lifetime of misery. Instead, the type
of union he was considering would be a temporary
arrangement, serving only to extend the full protection of the de Burgh name to an innocent novice.

There was simply no other way in which to insure
the safety of the woman whose life he had put into
jeopardy. Of course, Robin did not care for the so-

lution, but far stronger than his aversion to wedlock was the sense of honor and duty that had been instilled in him since birth. A de Burgh simply did not shirk his responsibilities.

That's what Dunstan had done. His eldest brother had married Marion to safeguard her. Of course, Dunstan and his wife were still wed, but Robin didn't dwell on that. His situation was different, and his wedding would be nothing like that of his brothers, for it would not be based upon love or even lust, but on circumstances that might easily be altered. Indeed, once the villains were discovered and routed, he and Sybil could sever their ties, claiming consanguinity or some other excuse to nullify their vows. 'Twould be easy enough, Robin thought.

Meanwhile, they could go to Baddersly, a stronghold defensible against all comers. Of course, Sybil would be safest at Campion, but somehow the idea of taking a false bride back to his father didn't seem like a good plan, and Robin shifted uneasily at the notion. His father, a notorious romantic, might not approve, and Robin did not care to test him. Indeed, the more he thought about it, the more Robin was convinced that no one need know of this marriage since it would be but an expediency.

Feeling better than he had in hours, perhaps even days, Robin approached the gate to Our Lady of All Sorrows, quite content with his course. Despite all, he knew a certain sizzling anticipation in his blood at the prospect of his meeting with his future bride, which he put down to the impending fulfillment of his obligations, *his protective obligations*.

Of course, it wasn't every day that a novice was given the chance to become Lady de Burgh, and

Robin couldn't help feeling a smug sort of satisfaction at the honor he was bestowing on Sybil, brief though it might be. He grinned at the prospect. For once, the One ought to be quite in charity with him.

Chapter Ten

Sybil was furious. It was bad enough that Robin had acted like a big, stupid oaf, barely speaking all the way back from Ryewater, but as soon as they had reached the nunnery, he had stalked off, even though they were supposed to be working together. And now she could not find him anywhere.

She suspected he was following the trail of the two men Tobias had mentioned without her, and the very thought roused her fury to a fevered pitch. Despite the abbess's decree, Robin was always running off on his own, making Sybil inclined to take action herself. In fact, she was tempted to confront Maud, who had been tied to the strangers by one of the brewers. But Sybil didn't quite trust her hazy memory of the ale-houses, nor did she want to send the nun fleeing, should the woman truly be guilty.

Although she had long suspected the powerful nun, the knowledge that she might be right gave Sybil a sudden chill, and she wrapped her arms around herself. She wondered if Maud, jealous beyond sanity, had simply come upon the strangers and hired them to commit the crime or whether she had sent for them with that specific purpose in mind, plotting her evil deed for months or even years.

Sybil shuddered, wondering if she ought to go straight to the abbess, without waiting for Robin. But what if Tobias were lying? And what about Robin's claims of political intrigues? Sybil shook her head, unable to believe that the friend she had known from childhood hid a secret past, let alone that the nun Vala had been her mother. Although both girls had been especially close to Vala, who had died when they were young, Sybil had never imagined such a connection. It made her feel strange and uneasy in a way she didn't understand.

Shying away from the sensation, Sybil blamed Robin. If he were here, she could question him, but he had disappeared, taking his wild theories with him. Along with her outrage at his defection came a familiar sting of hurt that he couldn't be bothered with her, despite all that had happened between them—or perhaps because of it.

In truth, Sybil had only intended to comfort him when he had turned moody, foolishly blaming himself for the murder. At least, that was her initial intention, but somehow her simple touch had incited a conflagration. It had been shameful and shocking, so why did it also have to be the most wonderful thing that had ever happened to her?

Sybil shut her eyes tight against the memory, not wanting to let herself be sucked into the maelstrom of emotions that threatened, unwilling to *feel* that much. She had spent years locked in her insular world, learning not to care that she didn't have a loving family, not to care when one of the nuns spoke sharply, not to care if someone left or died or...

With a small sound of dismay, Sybil lifted her fingers to her cheek, horrified at the tear that had escaped. She never cried, never wasted a moment on such a useless action. Forcing out a snort of disgust, she wiped the tear away with the back of her hand. Having always taken pride in her strength, how could she allow a few stolen kisses to disrupt her so completely? Obviously, her companion was not similarly affected, she thought dismally. Rather, he seemed to like it well enough at first, but then everything had changed.

When the deer came crashing through the trees, he had dumped Sybil on the ground, staring at her with a kind of horror that had stunned her. Was it because she had laughed at him? Or was he disgusted by her boldness? Heat washed Sybil's cheeks. Perhaps he thought her little better than some doxy!

What did she know of such things, or the whims of men? All the long way back to the nunnery Sybil had watched him avoid her and tug at the neck of his tunic and scowl into the distance. Finally, exasperated, she had told herself to be grateful for his black mood, for it had saved her virtue. Otherwise, she might now be ruined—or even with child. The thought, which ought to be horrifying, only seemed to cause more tears of loneliness and longing, until Sybil dashed them away.

What was wrong with her? She felt all jumbled inside, as if she regretted that more had not happened in the copse, instead of feeling ashamed of what had occurred. She ought to be planning her future, not wondering where Robin de Burgh had gone! But she kept seeing him stalking away without a word....

Sybil stiffened, struck with a terrible suspicion:

what if he had left the nunnery for good? Perhaps he
considered his business as coroner concluded, having
laid the murder at the feet of a pair of unknown
strangers. It would be just like him to meet with the
abbess without her knowledge! The idea that he was
gone, without even saying goodbye, sliced through
Sybil like a blade. And suddenly, she had to know if
it were true.

Heart thundering in her chest, Sybil hurried to the
guest house and, without even knocking, threw open
the door to his chamber. Her breath in her throat, her
hand to her mouth, she glanced wildly about the room
until her gaze came to rest on a leather pouch and
some clothing tossed across a chest, and she released
her pent air in a rush. Even a rich man like Robin de
Burgh would not have left such things behind, and
weak-kneed with relief, Sybil leaned against the
rough wall of the chamber.

Although the first rush of alarm had abated, a new
one rose to take its place, filling her with a different
sort of unease. *This was not good,* she acknowledged.
She should not care if this man came or went. Even
though he had not gone today, someday he would,
and soon. And she could not fall to pieces when he
did so.

Drawing herself up to full height, Sybil stood on
shaky limbs and told herself that it was the unexpected nature of his departure that had disturbed her.
After all they had been through together, she at least
deserved a farewell. Then she would be prepared,
would accept his goodbyes and move on with her life.

Yet even as she swore to do so, her body reacted
otherwise. Her feet took her restlessly around his

room, and she paused to touch each object that belonged to him, as if it were special somehow when she knew that it was not. Pausing before a discarded tunic, she ran a finger along the fine material, wondering why he always tugged at the neck opening. A memory of him offering to scratch her itch made her flush, and Sybil moved on.

But there was nothing left in the small chamber except the bed. Reaching it, Sybil stared, cheeks flaming, as she imagined Robin there, naked among the linens. She realized, with no little shock, that she would love to see his body, to feel it again, whether in pleasure or comfort or companionship. Reaching for his pillow, she drew it to her, inhaling the faint scent that lingered there. *His scent.*

"Sybil, you are going daft," she whispered, even as she clutched it tight. "You don't even like the man."

But she did. Despite her initial impression of him, Sybil found many things to admire about Robin. He was intelligent and sensitive and witty, as well as brave and strong. Without seeming intent, he drew from her the most powerful responses she had ever known, from rage to passion. And though she resented his ability to affect her so forcefully, Sybil had to admit that there was something to be said for that, uh, effect.

She sat down hard on the mattress as heat coursed through her, making her body feel all ripe and swollen. Who could ever have imagined these sensations? Was it any wonder that she was fascinated with he who produced them? Previously ignorant of men, Sybil could hardly blame herself for becoming preoccupied with the first one ever to stir her interest.

But even as she made excuses, Sybil knew that more
than curiosity made her cling to his pillow.

No matter. Whatever drew her to him, nothing
could come of it, and Sybil wrapped her arms around
herself as her heated flesh abruptly chilled. Seeking
warmth, she leaned back against Robin's bed. The
mattress was soft, the blankets tousled from his body,
and Sybil nestled there, feeling better, as though the
lingering traces of his presence reached out to her. It
was an absurd notion, but she was suddenly tired,
weary of wrestling with her problems and Elisa's
mysteries, as well as trying to keep to the usual demanding schedule of the nunnery.

Silently, she lay back against the sheets, eager to
close her eyes for just a moment. And then she slept.

Robin settled the new men in at the stables, then
went in search of Sybil, but a drowsy servant claimed
that all the women were abed, and he could hardly
barge into the novices' dorter. Still, the urge to see
her, to know for certain that she was well and safe,
consumed him until he told himself he was behaving
like a lunatic. No sane man would think of rousing
her when the nunnery kept early hours and she needed
her rest.

But he needed her. The thought flashed through
Robin's mind before he could catch it, and he just as
quickly denied it. He didn't need anyone except
maybe his brothers, and they were gone. His mood
soured, he marched to the guest house and his own
small chamber to gain some peace. Come morning
would be soon enough to propose, he thought, the
word jarring him as he opened his door. *Make ar-*

rangements, he decided, little liking the earlier choice of words.

Inside, the room was full night, except for a pale sliver of moonlight that fell through the single narrow window. Not bothering with a candle, Robin stripped in the darkness, tossing his clothing over a trunk and setting his boots on the floor. He lifted a blanket and put one knee on the mattress, but paused to eye the large mound of covers with some curiosity. As one who had put a few surprises in the beds of his siblings, Robin was wary, and tugging at one corner, he pulled away one layer only to stare in shocked silence at his discovery.

Sybil was in his bed.

She was lying on her side, one hand tucked beneath her chin, her lovely face so sweet in repose that it stole his breath. Her wimple was askew and great curls of hair escaped to fall over her cheek and throat, reminding Robin of their bright color and their sometimes fiery owner. He followed their path downward across the gentle curve of one breast, and swallowed hard. Robin knew what it felt like in his hand, and his entire body shuddered with the force of his desire. *She was in his bed, and she would soon be his wife…*

Only the swift, sharp reminder that their marriage was to serve solely as protection kept Robin from giving in to the fierce need that thundered in his blood. It was so overwhelming that he gasped for air, light-headed, and no wonder, for all the humors in his body had descended to one place, where they thrust forward eager and ready.

Groaning, Robin gritted his teeth. He had two choices. He could wake her or he could sleep with her. *Just sleep,* he ordered the nether regions that were clamoring for surcease. If he woke her, she would surely return to the dorter, where he could not be assured of her safety, while if she stayed here, he would have her near him, all night. Robin shuddered again as a new feeling, quite apart from his ardor, coursed through him, slow and sure and steady. *He had needed her, and here she was,* he thought, dizzily.

Frowning at that bit of whimsy, Robin turned his attention back to the bed and his own place in it. He could do this. He was not a slave to his body, as was the randy Stephen. He was a de Burgh, a warrior and his own master. Gingerly, he slipped between the sheets. But as he lay there, hard and throbbing, long into the night, Robin began to wonder if this marriage thing was such a great idea, after all.

Heat. Delicious, blessed heat. Sybil was surrounded by it. She couldn't remember ever being this warm. The nunnery was cold, the dorter more so, and she had spent a lifetime trying to cadge more blankets and heavier cloaks. But now, she felt just right, and something smelled so good. She snuggled deeper, but even her bed felt softer and more comfortable, and that discovery nagged at the edges of her mind, rousing her to wake.

With sudden awareness, Sybil's eyes flew open, and she blinked in horror at the pale light that signaled the coming of dawn. It was morning, and she was not in her usual place among the other novices. Where was she? She could recall looking for Robin and then… With a choked gasp, she realized that she had spent the night in his bed! Frantic, Sybil tried to turn, but something stopped her, and her breath caught as she realized she was not alone. Glancing downward, she saw a heavy arm flung across her body, just below her breasts, while farther down, she could feel an even heavier leg lying between her own.

Robin de Burgh was beside her, wrapped around her, his body giving off waves of heat like some great furnace, while his head was tucked above hers, his face buried in her hair. Sybil felt an odd sort of panic; she didn't know whether to laugh or cry, but a kind of gurgling noise that fell somewhere in between escaped her. Luckily, Robin's deep, even breathing didn't change, so he, at least, remained asleep.

How had she come to be here? Obviously, she had succumbed to her weariness, but when had Robin returned and why hadn't he noticed her? Sybil was relieved to note she was still fully clothed, though she must have kicked off her slippers sometime during the night. But what of her companion? Her heart, already thundering, picked up its pace as Sybil turned her head, afraid to look, but unable to do otherwise.

A quick glance confirmed her worst suspicions. *Robin was naked!* Sybil quickly closed her eyes tight against the revelation, but something, perhaps curiosity, urged her to open them again. After all, hadn't she wondered what he would look like lying here? And when would she ever have the chance to find out? Slowly, Sybil lifted her lashes and choked back another sound as a wide chest came back into view. It was broad and golden-colored and wholly alluring.

Shivering at the sight of one dark nipple, Sybil immediately trained her gaze upward over smooth skin to a huge, muscular shoulder. He seemed even bigger without his clothes. Bigger, and *so near*. Somehow, all the other times they had been pressed tightly together did not seem so intimate, for they both had been fully dressed.

Sybil stifled a moan of dismay as the memory of those times returned, bathing her with a new heat. Her body felt afire, her breasts full and sensitive, and she struggled against a sudden urge to turn in his arms, *to touch him.* Drawing in a deep breath, Sybil glanced farther down to find that the blanket hid the lower part of his body, but instead of being relieved, she was tempted to drag it away, to reveal all of his gorgeous form to her.

This is not good, Sybil realized, with no little dismay. However innocently it had occurred, she was a novice in bed with a naked man, and temptation was prompting her to even more mischief. Silently, she tried to ease away from her companion, but his fingers tightened around her waist, holding her fast, and Sybil gasped.

Mumbling something, Robin burrowed closer to her hair, making Sybil shiver. Then she felt him still, as if he, too, had roused to wakefulness, and she could only watch in horror as he raised up on one arm and looked down at her. Sybil tried to speak, but she could not. If she thought his body exquisite, his face truly stole her breath. His dark hair was tousled from sleep, his firm jaw shadowed and unshaven, and when he lifted thick lashes to reveal those eyes, the color of some syrup, slow and sweet and thick, she felt faint.

For Robin didn't appear shocked or even surprised by her presence. His expression held only sleepy desire and greeting, as if they were both right where they should be. Then, as she stared up at him breathlessly, a slow smile curved his lips that was bound to be her undoing. "Sybil," he murmured in husky voice, and she was lost.

He kissed her, and she met his mouth eagerly. He tossed away her wimple, and she was glad. He pushed aside the blankets and pressed his body, naked, to her own, and she welcomed it, her hands exploring the smooth surface of his skin, his muscular shoulders and the vast expanse of his back. When her fingers slid farther down, over taut curves, he groaned, thrusting heavily against her.

He stopped, muttered something, and Sybil wondered if he, of the two of them, had come to his senses, but instead he wrestled with her gown. She felt it being lifted, along with her shift, higher and higher, and she knew that she ought to protest, but she could only hold her breath until he pushed it over her head and off her arms and she wore nothing except her stockings. Her face flaming, Sybil knew she should be ashamed, but instead she felt beautiful and excited—and never more so than when Robin raked her with his gaze.

"Sybil," he whispered again, her name a celebration upon his lips, and she answered his smile with her own, as if their being together like this was the most natural thing in the world. He placed a hand upon her throat, and Sybil heard her own sigh of delight as his palm moved slowly down her chest, grazing her breast so lightly that she shivered. Then he squeezed, lifting it to meet his lips, and Sybil felt his mouth close over her nipple. When he pulled hard upon her, she cried out, moving restlessly, as if to meet some unknown destiny.

So lost was she in sensation that Sybil could not deny his touch, even as he moved over, fitting his

body against hers, enveloping her in his heat and
strength. But when she felt his hand upon her thighs,
spreading her legs, she made a squawk of protest. Her
objection was muffled in the firm press of his lips as
Robin kissed her again, so deeply that she could
barely breath, let alone speak, and whatever she was
going to say was lost in that delicious communion.

She could kiss this man forever, Sybil thought
dreamily, and never let him go. Yet when she felt the
thick hardness of him pressing intimately against her,
the alarm that she had ignored rushed through her
with renewed force. She broke the kiss to whisper
urgently against his throat. "No, Robin. We can't do
this," she murmured, echoing the words he had once
used against her. "'Tis wrong."

To her surprise, he did not rage at her, but only
stiffened, his already tense muscles becoming even
more taut as he seemed to strive for awareness. He
gasped for breath, his dark eyes unfocused as he lifted
his head, and Sybil felt a hot, new surge of desire at
his obvious excitement. She felt his body shuddering
beneath her palms and a mixture of power and awe
and yearning rushed through her that was nearly overwhelming, tempting her to put aside her hesitation
and give in to the wild wanting that drove them both.

Indeed, if he pressed her, Sybil knew that she could
not deny him, and so she waited, watching, for Robin
to make the choice. He was poised silent above her,
locked in a struggle with himself, and she wondered
if she had waited too long. Would there be no stopping him? Her pulse pounded frantically when at last
he met her gaze, his dark eyes bright with intent.

"If I vow that I shall not take your maidenhead,
will you let me... Will you trust me?" he asked, with

a kind of desperation that made Sybil's heart lodge in her throat. She could do naught except nod, wary but unable to argue, too lost to him to say nay.

Still looking into her eyes, he spread his own legs, closing hers together, even as he rose higher on his arms. Then Sybil felt his hardness touch the juncture of her thighs once more. She knew a moment's panic, but then the slow, slippery glide of that weight along the surface of the most intimate part of her body.

"Oh! But—" Sybil began only to lose her train of thought as Robin growled out his pleasure. The sound only stimulated her further, and she arched upward.

"Oh, yes," Robin growled. "Like this, my One," he said, grabbing her hips. And something in the way he spoke those words made Sybil hot and shivery. She felt the slow slide of the length of him again, creating a delicious pressure where he had once sought entrance.

"Squeeze your legs tighter," Robin urged, and when she complied, he growled again. "Ah, yes, *Sybil!*"

His obvious pleasure fed her own, and she reveled in this intimacy, not only the passion, but everything to do with Robin de Burgh. He surrounded her, his heat enveloping her, his scent filling her lungs, his skin smooth beneath her fingertips, his mouth lush and hot and potent against hers. They established a rhythm between them, simple yet complex, as they moved together, almost as one, and Sybil clutched at his shoulders when she felt a sharp burst of sensation.

"There! Right there!" she heard herself cry out, and Robin obliged her by positioning himself higher, his strong arms bulging as he held himself above her.

"Here?" he asked, in a deep growl of demand.

"Oh yes, oh yes, oh yes," Sybil whimpered as, conversely, she shook her head. She tossed from side to side and tried to open her legs, but Robin held her fast. He took mastery over her, and Sybil, who had never given over her will to anyone, succumbed to him helplessly. He groaned, quickening his pace, and that mysterious pressure seemed to grow and grow until Sybil felt as if she would come apart somehow.

And then she did, calling out her ecstasy even as Robin kissed her again, taking her cries into his mouth. She felt him thrust violently against her now-slack thighs, his body shuddering with the force of his movements and then heard his own harsh growl as he spent himself, his seed spilled between them.

Sybil took his weight, welcoming his heaviness, both astonished and enthralled by what had happened between them. His body was slick with sweat, and she wrapped her arms around him, reveling in his heat, in the wondrous joy that filled her, a sense of rightness so strong that she could only hug him to her more tightly. She never wanted to let him go, not now, not ever.

This is not good, her inner voice cautioned, but feeling warm and safe and *something* for the first time in her life, Sybil ignored the warning and gave herself over to Robin de Burgh.

Chapter Eleven

Her body replete, surrounded by warmth and comfort, Sybil was beginning to fall asleep once more when Robin rolled away, only to pull her close. Soon she felt him brushing the hair from her cheek and his lips, gentle upon the nape of her neck. Although his kiss was soft, Sybil sensed the underlying heat that could easily ignite the fire between them again.

This is not good, Sybil thought. Although her brain acknowledged the warning, the rest of her seemed to have other ideas entirely—strange, wondrous notions involving Robin de Burgh's body, and perhaps his heart, as well.

But just when they might have pursued their passions anew, there came a knock on the door that made Robin's big form stiffen and Sybil squeak in horror. Before she could dive under the blankets, he was gone from the bed, moving so swiftly and silently that she scarce had time to draw a breath. Sybil paused, staring at him in wonder, then began a frantic search for her clothing even as she heard Robin at the door, barring any intrusion.

"Yes, what is it?" he called.

"'Tis Abel, my lord. You bid me wake you at dawn."

"Yes, very good, boy. Return to the men, and tell them we ride away today," Robin answered.

Sybil was in the midst of shoving her arms into her sleeves when she heard the words that chilled to the bone. *Robin was leaving today? Now? After what had happened?* Sybil swallowed hard even as her own thoughts rushed to chasten her. *What did you expect, a profession of love? A proposal of marriage?* Although Sybil might swear she wanted nothing from this man or any other, still the news of his imminent departure, coming so swiftly upon the intimacies they had shared, struck her painfully.

And when have you known aught else? she asked herself. If she hurt now, she had only herself to blame for letting herself feel too much, too quickly, too foolishly. Although barely dressed, Sybil scrambled from the bed as Robin approached, wanting to get as far away from him as possible. He looked so big and tall and *naked* that she stared in dismay, and she couldn't help notice that a certain part of him had grown even larger. Wrapping her arms around herself, Sybil backed away, unable to look at him, for fear that her body might betray her once more.

All too soon, she realized that her worry was unfounded, for Robin made it quite obvious that he did not intend to return to the bed or her arms, the size of him notwithstanding. Indeed, he grabbed up his clothing, as if in a hurry to cover himself, and didn't even glance in her direction until he had donned it all, including his boots.

When he finally looked at her, his cheeks were flushed, whether with lingering heat or something else, Sybil could not say, but his demeanor was entirely different. His gaze darting away from hers, he ran a hand through his hair and cleared his throat, but said nothing. At that point, Sybil decided that if he tugged at the neck of his tunic, she would strangle him with the excess material.

Now what? Sybil's own awkwardness was vanishing as the silence lengthened between them, her distress transforming into anger. Was he going to say anything? She couldn't know the proper civilities for such circumstances, and besides, he was the one who had disappeared yesterday, only to reappear beside her this morning. He was the one who had seduced her. *He was the one leaving this day.*

Looking positively sheepish, Robin finally spoke. "I, uh, beg your pardon," he said, motioning toward the bed.

He begged her pardon? Even cloistered in the nunnery, Sybil recognized that his were not words of love or even simple wooing. *I beg your pardon* might work well if he had stepped upon her gown, not stripped it from her. *I beg your pardon* might suffice if he had bumped into her, not rubbed himself against her until he spilled his seed amongst the linens.

"*You beg my pardon?*" Sybil echoed, crossing her arms over her chest and glaring at the man who had so quickly lost his charms.

"Well, yes, I…I got carried away, finding you in my bed and all, but it doesn't matter now. I've got a plan."

"*It doesn't matter?*" Sybil repeated, her voice rising. She had been privy to some wild tales of life on the outside, but to hear such blunt speech from a knight and lord was appalling. Apparently, he cared

so little for her or her reputation that he would dismiss
what they had done outright as of no consequence
whatsoever?

The temper Sybil had tried so hard to tame roared
to life, and she was tempted to violence. Whether
Robin had unleashed all her passions, including her
rage, or whether she had just reached the limit of her
patience, Sybil knew only that she had to act, for
once, and she reached blindly for any object that
might conk some sense into the thick head of the man
before her. When her fingers closed around an empty
cup, she launched it at him with relish.

*"How dare you seduce me and say it doesn't mat-
ter?"* she shouted, even as he ducked and the wooden
vessel banged against the wall.

"Sybil! Calm down! What the…? That's not what
I meant!" Robin called out even as he dodged a
leather water flask she flung at his face.

"Then what exactly did you mean? And how is
that you climbed into that bed with me without a
word?" Sybil demanded, tossing a tunic at him. Running out of missiles, she was reduced to balling up
his clothing and throwing it, but the sight of the big
knight holding up his hands before him to ward off
her blows, was a balm to her tattered pride.

"And just where were you yesterday? How dare
you go off by yourself? Might I remind you that the
abbess told us to work together?" Sybil said, grabbing the pillow from the tousled bedding and smacking him across his massive chest. Of course, it was
too soft to do any damage, but she felt better for it—
until Robin snatched it from her hands and threw it
aside.

With a low oath, he grasped her wrists and crowded

her into the wall, leaning close, so that they were pressed against each other, both panting heavily. When Sybil saw him look down at her lips, she felt the heat flare between them—and promptly stomped on his foot.

"Ow!" he yelped, loosing her as he backed away with a growl. "Will you listen to me?" he asked, his voice a low hiss. "Or do you want to bring the whole nunnery down upon our heads?"

For one reckless moment, Sybil didn't care. What did it matter when she was leaving anyway? But the thought of being tossed out, rather than walking away, sobered her slightly. "All right. I'm listening," she said, crossing her arms in front of her.

Eyeing her warily, Robin ran a hand through his hair. "Very well, so I should have asked you to accompany me yesterday," he muttered, sinking onto a trunk with a scowl. "But at the time, I was so stunned and had no idea that my suspicions would prove so…" He lifted his head to fix her with his dark gaze in a rather unsettling manner. "Did you realize that you and Elisa came to the convent as infants, though no children that young have been accepted before or since?"

Sybil shrugged. She did not care to dwell upon the fact that her unknown parents had abandoned her. She had made a home here, taking what affection she could from the old abbess and a couple of favorite nuns, having long ago given up musing on her past.

"Thinking that was curious, I went to the village to pursue further information on your arrival here," Robin said.

Sybil felt her temper rise again. "You *what?* How dare you meddle in what is no business of yours?"

Robin's dark gaze held her own, unflinching. "Ah, but it turned out to be my business," he said, in a soft tone that chilled her. What had he discovered? Sybil wanted to cover her ears, unwilling to learn that the wealthy, beautiful parents she had imagined had not died suddenly far from home, that instead she had been born to a poor villein who, having no use for another girl child, had left her to die.

She must have given herself away, for Robin's eyes shone with sympathy. Sybil closed her own, dreading his next words, but when they came, she reared back in surprise. "You were not abandoned," he said softly, as if he could read her mind.

"What?" Shock, relief, and finally, pleasure flooded Sybil at the news that after all these years, someone, somehow, knew something of her parents. She felt faint, and, again, Robin seemed to know her mind, for he stood, reaching for her and easing her down upon the chest. Although normally she would have taken umbrage at his assistance, Sybil was glad of her seat when next he spoke.

"Vala was *your* mother," Robin said. "She had a servant buy a village child, one mired in poverty, to exchange places with you lest someone ever discover your whereabouts. That child was given a better life, but you are the real Elisa, though she renamed you Sybil, no doubt a testament to your l'Estrange heritage."

Sybil sucked in a deep breath, still dizzy and disoriented by Robin's claim. She had never quite believed his tale of Elisa and Vala, and now he would place her in it? "I'm a Welsh princess?" she asked, choking on a laugh. Was this some kind of joke he was playing on her? Surely, every orphan dreamed of one day reuniting with royal parents who would lavish them with love and riches.... Sybil brought her head up sharply. "I have a family?"

Robin must have seen the hope that, against all her good sense, rushed to fill the void inside her. "A family that might well be trying to kill you," he said.

Sybil felt another bubble of laughter escape, for she refused to consider the alternative reaction. Glancing about, she searched for some anchor in her careening world only to decide that she must be dreaming. Perhaps, all of it, from the moment she supposedly woke in Robin's bed, was one long nightmare. She was tempted to pinch herself—or maybe she should just pinch Robin, she thought, rather wildly.

It was too absurd, too horrible to contemplate the possibility that Vala had given birth to her, only to give her up, pretending she was nothing more than a stray child among many cared for by the nuns. Sybil couldn't accept such a truth. Nor could she face discovering at long last that she had relatives who not only didn't want her, but wanted her dead.

"Sybil," Robin said. His voice called her back from a bleak darkness, and she opened her eyes to find him kneeling before her. He took her hands in his, and she felt life flow through her again, warming her chilled heart and body. Was he the anchor she had been looking for, or the one that would drag her down? Sybil wasn't sure.

"This is serious," he said. "These men, whether Welsh or English, murdered Elisa because they thought she was you. I hope they will continue to think so, but I found out the truth, which means someone else might as well, and then it will be you who is in danger."

Sybil stared at him, unable to work up a fright over the bizarre possibility that some political assassin would discover her supposed identity. In fact, she could not conjure fear at all for the turmoil of other emotions. Resentment surged within her, toward Vala for not acknowledging her daughter and toward the nuns who had participated in the lie, knowing or not.

But most of all, Sybil resented Robin for disrupting her life, for giving her a parent only to take her away, for destroying her good memories of Vala and turning her entire existence upside down. Angry, she tugged her fingers from his and eyed him with scorn. Exactly what was she to do with this information he had thrust upon her?

Sybil was not left to wonder long, for Robin had an answer for that, just as he had for everything else. Rising to his feet, he drew a deep breath, as if he had more bad news to impart, and clasped his hands behind his back. He resembled a bishop scolding his flock, and Sybil had never seen anything more ludicrous than this errant knight assuming such a role.

"Since this is all my fault, it's my responsibility to see that no harm comes to you," he intoned, as though pronouncing a death sentence. "And after giving the matter much consideration, I have come upon a plan."

Sybil could only stare at him. Whatever the *plan,* it sounded both painful and abhorrent.

When Robin cleared his throat, Sybil narrowed her eyes, daring him to tug at his tunic. Luckily for him, he did not. He simply looked down at the floor and muttered, "We shall marry."

Sybil's mouth dropped open. *"What?"* she asked, unable to believe she had heard him aright.

"Marry." Robin spat out the word as if it were distasteful. He cleared his throat once more and nodded his head, seemingly to convince himself. "'Tis the only way to circumvent the villains who might target you next. 'Tis the best solution to our problems."

Sybil stared at him, stunned beyond speech. Of all the revelations of the last hour, this was surely the most shocking. Robin de Burgh was proposing to her—and not because of some measure of love for her, but to solve their *problems?* Sybil didn't know whether to laugh or break down and weep, so she simply gaped as he launched into his disclaimers.

"Of course, it won't be a true marriage," he said, and Sybil felt color wash into cheeks she knew had been lifeless.

"It will be for your protection. That way no one can touch you, legally or physically. We shall go to Baddersly, where I can see to your safety," he added.

It was all very logical—and so chilling that Sybil wrapped her arms around herself. Robin de Burgh wasn't pretending to feel anything for her at all, except responsibility. There was no mention of what had happened in the copse or in the nearby bed not long ago, no hint of the fire and passion that had blazed in him then. His expression was, in fact, rather grim, as he detailed what he called "the arrangement."

"You needn't worry. It won't be a true, binding contract," he said, totally oblivious to the subtle cruelty in his words. What other kind of marriage was there?

He answered her unspoken question with his own interpretation, as usual. "It will be a marriage in name only. You will have the protection of the de Burghs, and should any relatives or foes try to claim you, you will not be legally bound to any of them.''

''Except you,'' Sybil said, dully.

Robin cleared his throat. ''Well, that is simply a formality. Let me assure you that I do not expect any, uh, thing at all from you, but that you stay well-guarded until I can hunt down these killers.''

Sybil wondered if she had imagined the whole episode among the linens, dreamt the hot taste of his kisses, the hard, sleek muscles beneath her palms and the heavy weight of his naked body, both a bliss and a comfort. Obviously, he had not taken as much pleasure from their encounter as she had, else he wouldn't be standing here, refusing to look at her, while denying the slightest desire for her.

''And, of course, as soon as the threat is eliminated, we can dissolve the marriage by claiming consanguinity. People do it all the time,'' Robin added.

Sybil wondered how anyone would believe they were related, especially after Robin had hunted down the family members who were trying to kill her, and she felt another bubble of wild laughter rise in her throat, only to be suppressed. Thankfully, her initial shock and pain was turning into anger—at his wretched proposal, his toneless delivery and the qualifications he had tacked on—all to suit himself.

Sybil glanced up at him through narrowed eyes and saw that the cocky oaf was standing there looking rather proud of himself, as if she should be *grateful* for his ridiculous offer. She had discovered many facets to this man and changed her opinion of him several times, but now she had to revise her thoughts anew, for what she saw before her was a big, spoiled boy.

"Have you siblings?" she asked.

Robin looked flummoxed by her question, then answered readily. "Yes, six brothers."

"And all of them are older?" Sybil asked.

"No," Robin said, shaking his head with a puzzled look. "Two are younger. Why?"

"I would have thought you the youngest," Sybil said, with a snort of contempt. Then again, mayhap all men were this selfish, she thought, for what did she know of them?

Unlike most girls, growing up, Sybil had never dreamed of marriage, for she had no dowry, no way of coming to the attention of any eligible male. She was bound to the nunnery from birth, thanks to her mother, she thought, resentfully. Yet now that she intended to leave, such an alliance was not so impossible, and although she harbored no delusions of romance, she would expect affection at the very least. Else why should she surrender the independence she had yearned for for so long? This man tendered her nothing except the dubious offer of his "protection," and Sybil was not the least moved by it.

"Well, what do you think?" he asked, his handsome face still wearing that rather smug expression that carried with it expectations of gratitude. Hardening her heart to match his own coldness, Sybil stood.

"As to your proposal, my answer is no," she said, pushing past him toward the door. "I have other plans."

"Other plans? What *other plans?"* he demanded, grabbing her arm to pull her to him. At last, he was showing some emotion. Unfortunately, it was the wrong kind: anger and a bullying kind of interference.

"I don't believe that's any of your concern," Sybil said, staring pointedly at his fingers closed around her arm. Although heat rushed through her from even that small contact, she would not let him see it, and kept herself still, her expression closed.

Robin released her with an oath, as if he didn't trust himself. "It certainly is my concern! I'm trying to save your life, and you're acting like a senseless dolt! Do you have a death wish?"

Sybil glared at him in return. "No. I have a wish to live! I have spent my entire life behind these walls, and I don't intend to exchange one prison for another."

"Prison? What prison? Are you saying being married to me would be some kind of interment?" he growled, as if she had insulted him, and Sybil could have laughed at his outrage. The spoiled boy didn't get his way! Well, she had a lifetime of unfulfilled dreams, so she felt no sympathy for him. Her head held high, Sybil strode to the door.

"And just where do you intend to go? What are you going to do?" Robin demanded. For a moment, Sybil thought he might reach for her again, but he seemed to gain control of himself and ran a hand through his hair instead. "If you have some cockeyed notion of trying to travel to Wales, I'm telling you that you'll never make it. Even if the killers don't catch up with you right away, the country's at war!"

Sybil blinked. The thought had never crossed her mind, and she resented the insinuation that she was either so stupid or so desperate for relatives that she would rush off into a battle zone.

Her pause had conjured a hopeful expression on Robin's face, and Sybil could almost see his brain working from the outside in. "If it's family you want, I have plenty!" he said. "And some are even related to you! My brother Stephen married a l'Estrange, which was Vala's maiden name. And Brighid and her aunts are right here in England. In fact, that's how I…why I began looking for you. *Her*," Robin amended, suddenly looking uncomfortable.

"You could meet with them!" he added hurriedly. "The marriage would not be a prison, just a brief inconvenience, and then you could go wherever you like. They have their own manor house, and, well, I'm sure we could make arrangements for you to live anywhere you please."

There it was again, the dreaded "arrangements." The very word made Sybil want to scream, but Robin only eyed her confidently, as if well satisfied with his plan. And, in that instant, Sybil realized that she could not blame him for his passionless proposal. He was a man used to getting his way, to be sure, but he was doing what he thought was right. He could see no impediments to his logical, emotionless decision. And that's what hurt the worst.

"No," she said, and when he gaped at her answer, she almost felt sorry for him.

Robin watched her go, so dumbfounded he could not even find the strength to stop her from leaving. As the door closed behind her, he sank back down on the trunk, feeling stunned and drained, as if he had tussled with his brothers, only to be thrashed soundly, beaten both physically and mentally.

Loosing a long breath, Robin shook his head. As far back as he could remember, he had sworn never to marry, and now, when forced by circumstance to do just that, he was met with a refusal! And it wasn't as if he had asked just any female, mind you. He had asked *the One,* the only woman he had recognized immediately as his downfall. Perhaps he was mistaken about her, Robin mused, even as every nerve and muscle and bone in his body screamed in disagreement. *She was his.* How could she deny him?

Robin felt his face heat in anger and outrage. Not only was he astounded, but rather insulted, as well. All women want to be married. It was a known fact. And most would count themselves blessed beyond measure to wed a de Burgh. Wealth, power, safety, luxury and a certain, well, virility, came with the name. And this woman had even more reason than most to accept, for she didn't belong in a nunnery and he had offered her a chance to escape, only to have it tossed back in his face.

Robin growled low, seized by a primitive surge of possessiveness that made him want to throw her over his shoulder without a thought to her protests. And subduing her would be pleasurable indeed, he mused, only to shift uncomfortably. He turned his head to stare at the bed and sucked in a harsh breath. The blankets were still tousled, one pillow still sunk with the impression of her, and Robin's body hardened painfully.

Sighing, he put an elbow on his knee and sank his forehead in his palm. What had he been thinking? But he knew the answer: he hadn't been thinking at all. He had woken up slowly to find her in his arms, her scent stirring him, her body soft against his own, and he had done what any man would do. He had forgotten all cautions, all his own vows, and knew only one thing: the need to touch her, kiss her, *be inside her.*

Robin shuddered, feeling the desperate urge all over again. But of course, he had only complicated things. He had realized that later when, at last, his good sense returned. And he had tried to ignore it, which probably hadn't been the wisest course, considering how upset Sybil had been about the whole thing. He had tried to assure her that he wouldn't impose upon her again with this marriage, but that hadn't seemed to placate her either. Although not as persuasive as Stephen, Robin had long been known for his glib tongue, yet nothing he said had worked.

She had refused him.

Groaning, Robin felt oddly bereft as he considered the situation. And as he sat there, head in his hand, he became aware that, perversely, he now most desired that which he had disdained before. In fact, instead of putting him off, Sybil's refusal only made him more determined to wed her, not because of any nonsense about her being the One, of course, or even any half-buried hopes of getting naked next to her again. Really, he had no choice in the matter. He was bound to protect her.

She had lived many years inside these walls, her spirit yearning for more, and must have reached her limit of patience. And the thought of what she might do next scared him spitless. In her current reckless, headstrong state, Sybil just might take off for Wales, marching into the midst of war in an effort to search for a family that might very well be trying to kill her. And obligated as he was, Robin would have to chase after her, a dangerous and onerous task.

He scowled at the thought. Then he cursed his own

wagging tongue for bringing up the aunts. What if she went to live with them? Now that he knew Sybil, the last thing he wanted to do was introduce her to those two, let alone let her live in their lunatic household. Why, even Stephen's wife had seemed all too happy to leave it. And what about all that soothsaying nonsense? Robin shuddered. Stephen might accept his wife's oddities with equanimity, but Robin liked Sybil the way she was. He didn't want her turned into some kind of witch!

Of course, then maybe she could lift the curse… Robin shook his head, blowing out an exasperated breath. Even to his own mind, he sounded as mad as the two aunts. He was suddenly uncomfortable. There was really no need for Sybil to ever find out exactly why he had begun searching for her mother. Better that she stay away from the aunts, who would undoubtedly prattle on about it, making Sybil think him a fool or worse.

Then she would never marry him.

Robin straightened at the sharp sense of panic that sliced through him. He didn't try to analyze this newfound desire to wed beyond a de Burgh's devotion to duty, honor, and the protection of the weak. Weak? Pah! Sybil could hardly be classified as such, and yet, she was as vulnerable as any woman to men bent upon murder. Rising to his feet, Robin vowed grimly that no harm would come to her, not now, not ever. Unfortunately, Sybil didn't believe the seriousness of the threat to her life.

It was up to him to convince her.

Chapter Twelve

Sybil wasn't really surprised that Robin came looking for her. He could be a formidable fellow when he chose, and she suspected that he would not be deterred so easily from his "plan." Apparently, he felt responsible for her, and he was a man who took such things seriously. Although Sybil decried his actions in this instance, she knew she would not have him be any other way. And, despite her distress, she felt a sizzle of anticipation run through her at his arrival.

Steeling herself against that telling response, Sybil continued talking with one of the servants, but the appearance of the big knight sent the girl skittering off. Sybil was not so easily intimidated. Turning her back upon the man even as he called out to her, Sybil spoke over her shoulder.

"I have nothing further to say to you, unless you want to discuss something about Elisa's murder in your…supposed role as coroner," she said, while she grabbed the clean linens the girl had left behind and began making up the bed.

"Sybil, you are not taking this threat to your life seriously. Whatever you think of me, whatever your feelings about my, uh, proposal, you must consider the danger to yourself!'' Robin replied.

Sybil kept at her task, snapping the sheets crisply. ''You'll pardon me, if I fail to take your word about it,'' she said.

''Sybil.'' Sybil shivered at the sound of her name on his lips, and something in his tone made her stop and turn around.

He was eyeing her soberly, his cheeks flushed. ''De Burghs do not lie,'' he said softly. ''You have my word as a de Burgh, as a knight, and a man of honor, that what I say is the truth.''

As if she had no will of her own, Sybil felt her heart begin pumping frantically and her body heat, just at the sight of him, so serious, so intent, so wretchedly handsome. She drew in a shaking breath.

''But there is another who can verify what I say. In fact, that's where I was yesterday. I was looking for Gwerful, the woman who brought you to the nunnery. She lives only a few hours ride away, in the next village. Will you come? Will you hear what she has to say?''

In the end, Sybil agreed. She told herself it was curiosity that drove her to examine this reputed heritage of hers and not the dubious attractions of Robin de Burgh at his most persuasive. Of course, the promise of a day spent away from the nunnery held its rewards, too.

Robin was in better spirits after her acceptance, making an effort to charm her, and though well aware of his tactics, Sybil enjoyed herself. The ride was very different than the one from Ryewater when he had ignored her so rudely. This time he stayed by her side, entertaining her with a merry wit, and Sybil had to admit that she liked the attention. Although she knew he was only trying to get his way, she felt a small measure of triumph that he put himself out, a bit of balm to her sorely battered pride.

As if to lure her to wed him with the promise of relatives to embrace her, Robin began to talk about his family, and Sybil quickly found herself entranced. His father, the Earl of Campion, was a wise and strict, but loving parent, bound to his seven sons by respect and affection. However, when Robin spoke of the earl's recent marriage, Sybil sensed a subtle undertone of disapproval. Although Robin seemed to like the woman named Joy well enough, he appeared to have reservations about the union.

Sybil wondered about that, but kept silent as he recounted stories about each sibling with varying degrees of admiration. And when he told tales of growing up in this rambunctious household, Sybil felt a sweet envy, along with a dangerous softening toward the man who put things in his brothers' beds, cut their hair with a sword and generally played tricks upon the whole family.

Sybil could envision the young man Robin had been, the jokester she glimpsed on more than one occasion and would like to see more often. There had been little laughter in her life, and now she found herself yearning for it, for the carefree character Robin resembled when not serving in his burdensome role of coroner. Obviously, that had made him more somber, and Sybil sensed some other, underlying tension, as well.

Although it didn't sound as though he was estranged from the relatives he spoke of so glowingly, Sybil guessed there was something he wasn't telling her. And despite an unruly urge to probe further, to understand everything about this man, she told herself that Robin de Burgh was not her concern. So, when he changed the subject, she did not press him.

Still, the day passed comfortably, with the kind of easiness between them that came rarely. For once, there was no arguing or awkwardness or wildly heightened passions, beyond the subtle awareness of heat that always grew between them. Sybil liked to think that she had come to her senses at last, but perhaps she enjoyed her freedom so well, savoring each new bit of countryside, that she would waste no energy in tumultuous exchanges. More likely, they managed so well was because Robin was on his best behavior, lest she turn back toward the nunnery, and Sybil delighted in keeping him dangling beside her, while the men that hung behind prevented him from getting too close.

It was only when they reached their destination that Sybil began to grow uneasy. Although she still wanted to dismiss Robin's story as an elaborate hoax, she could not ignore his sincerity. Whatever the truth, he certainly believed what he claimed, and suddenly Sybil wasn't sure if she wanted to hear someone corroborate his tale. That would make it *real,* and then she would have to give serious consideration to a past wholly different from the one she had grown to accept.

It was only natural to be anxious, Sybil told herself, yet she began to feel such a strong sense of foreboding that she was reluctant even to dismount. But she would show no weakness to her companion, and so she followed him into the small cottage, even though apprehension dogged her.

"Gwerful?" Robin called aloud, but there was no answer, and Sybil wrinkled her nose. She caught the hint of an unpleasant odor in the air, something that seemed familiar and yet distasteful. Suddenly, the dread that had been growing fairly choked her, and she made a low sound of dismay. But Robin was already wary, putting her behind him as he slowly moved around the heavy table scattered with bolts of cloth, until he stopped abruptly.

Peeking around his arm, Sybil saw what had halted him, and she drew in a harsh breath. A women lay sprawled upon the tiles, as dead as Elisa, only her wound appeared to be from a knife or sword plunged into her body. Whether this was Gwerful or not, Sybil did not know, but the woman would speak no more, to anyone. Turning her head away, Sybil pressed her face into Robin's upper arm. Although she did not think of herself as squeamish, this was the second murder victim she had come across in only a few days, and she did not care for the sight.

And there was something comforting about leaning against Robin's strength. His arm was hard with muscle, yet his sleeve was soft, and the scent of him, now so sweetly familiar, filled her head. Sybil made a small, incoherent noise, and the arm lifted, closing around her to pull her against his mail-clad chest.

She half expected him to taunt her, for she had lashed out at him over Elisa's body, but he only held her tight, his big body a solid wall of protection against all the ills of the world. Even as Sybil realized the foolishness of such musings, for a long moment she remained tucked next to him, struck by a desire that had nothing to do with kisses. It was a deep, soul-stirring sort of yearning, as if this closeness might fill the emptiness inside her that she had never even acknowledged.

Sybil sucked in a ragged breath and felt Robin squeeze her arm in reassurance. "Better get behind me, lest the villains be lingering here," he said, and she moved reluctantly from her place, following him as he drew his sword and went through the rest of the small cottage. But whoever had done the deed was gone, and when they returned to the body, the ramifications of the killing struck Sybil forcefully.

"Is this…the woman you wanted me to see?" she asked.

"Aye. 'Tis Gwerful. Someone is on our trail," Robin said. He turned his head and muttered a low oath. "I should never have brought you here." Blowing out a long breath, he swung toward her and took her hands, pulling her near. His face hard with intent, he spoke with a new urgency. "You must marry me," he said.

Sybil fully intended to refuse. Despite his attentions this day, nothing had changed between them. He still proposed to her only out of duty, and she still preferred freedom to his cold "arrangement." Although for the first time since finding Elisa dead, Sybil felt real fear that she, too, might be marked for murder, she did not see the necessity of marrying the man who would protect her.

But when she looked up into his handsome face, his expression, both fiercely determined and rather desperate, seemed to seize up her speech, preventing her answer. He towered over her, big and handsome and close, this man she had known only a few days, yet who had affected her more than anyone in her lonely life. His eyes, the color of dark honey, pleaded with her, the scent of him filled her lungs and the heat of him enfolded her.

And somehow, instead of denying him, Sybil said, "Yes."

Leaving one of his men at the cottage, Robin made sure the rest surrounded Sybil and himself as they headed toward nearby Baddersly. The sooner he got her inside the stronghold, the better he would feel. Unaccustomed to the fear that had him in a fierce grip, Robin did not care for it, but he knew some measure of relief that at least she had accepted him.

Finally, she had seen the danger and the necessity, and Robin was grateful for that. She had agreed to marry him for protection, which was just what he wanted. So why did he feel a certain dissatisfaction? Maybe it was because he'd practically had to force her. After all, a man liked to think he wasn't totally repulsive to women, especially to the One he suspected was destined for him.

Unfortunately, Sybil never really acted as though she liked him at all, except when she was kissing him, but he couldn't think of that. That was not part of the arrangement. Robin gritted his teeth as he shifted in his saddle, desire raging through him with sudden intensity. With a frown, he tried to ignore it, concentrating instead on the more pressing question of just how to hunt down the killers.

He had barely helped Sybil dismount when Florian came rushing out of the great hall to greet them. The steward of Baddersly was competent, if a bit mannered. He drove Simon to distraction with his meddling, but Robin had always gotten along well with him, at least until now. When he thought of introducing Sybil into the household, however, Robin wasn't so sure.

"There you are, my lord! We have been worried about you," the steward said, and Robin suppressed a smile. Surely, no one had ever expressed such a sentiment to him before, and though he didn't mind, he could just imagine how grating Simon would have found it.

"Coroner, indeed! Why you should have to dirty your hands investigating some murder that is plainly the province of the Church, I do not know! Probably because those fat bishops are too lazy to send someone to do it themselves," Florian said, with visible disgust. "But, come, have you eaten? And who is that with you? Have we guests, my lord?" he asked, turning toward Sybil, and Robin's grin faded as he hastened to forestall the questions he could see coming.

"Florian, this is my betrothed," he said quickly. The words sounded strange to his ears after all the years spent avoiding them, and yet he felt right speaking them. "Will you please summon the priest? We've decided not to wait any longer to be married."

Robin eyed his steward expectantly, but, for once, Florian had no easy reply; he appeared positively flummoxed. "Your *betrothed?*" he echoed finally, his jaw sagging. Then, staring at Sybil, he gasped aloud. "You're marrying a *nun?*"

"She's not a nun. She was a novice. But she's going to be my wife. *If* you would please fetch the priest," Robin said, his voice rough with impatience. He wanted everything all legal and public, so that no questions could be raised later, and the sooner they were wed the better. He didn't want to give the notoriously recalcitrant Sybil time to change her mind.

And, in truth, now that the moment was upon him, Robin was seized by fierce urgency.

He wanted to marry her. *Now.*

Florian gave him a startled look, but did not rush to do his bidding. Instead, he turned toward Sybil again. "I'm afraid someone has not properly introduced us," he said, with a reproving frown toward Robin.

"You may call her *Lady de Burgh,*" Robin cut in, seeing no reason to mention Sybil's identity any more than necessary, even here. And since Florian showed no signs of moving, Robin took her elbow and hurried her through the wide doors, leaving the steward to gape after them.

Once they were inside the familiar hall, Robin felt a small measure of relief. He sent his train back to the gate, to bar it against all strangers, and gave another man a message to take to the nunnery, all the while keeping Sybil close at his side. Although she didn't look particularly pleased by his behavior, Robin didn't think he could let her go now even should she scream a refusal and start throwing things at him again.

She was going to be his. *At last.*

The knowledge seared through his body like wildfire, and no matter how hard he tried to contain the conflagration with his usual platitudes, it continued unchecked. It didn't matter now why they were going to marry or how much he had initially disliked the idea, Sybil would be bound to him, and he felt a primitive sense of victory that overwhelmed all reasoning.

Robin leaned close to her, delighting in that small pleasure. "You might want to remove your wimple," he suggested, though he itched to do it himself.

"Oh! Yes, of course," she said, carefully loosing the fabric. As she pulled it away, her hair spilled out, rich and fiery, a mass of curls that hit Robin like a kick to the groin. All he wanted to do was sink his hands into those locks and hold on for dear life. He must have made a sound because Sybil glanced his way, only to gaze, wide-eyed at the look on his face. No doubt, the raw hunger there was enough to scare any woman, let alone a novice, but she didn't turn from it. Indeed, her blue eyes took on the dazed aspect of desire until the air between them crackled with it and all they needed was one single spark to ignite them both.

Without breaking the connection between them, Robin was just about to bellow for the priest when the man appeared, looking as bewildered as Florian had. "This is quite sudden, isn't it?" the fellow asked.

While Florian nodded, Robin shook his head. "No. 'Tis a betrothal of long standing."

"Ah, uh, yes," Florian echoed. "We've been expecting these nuptials for some time."

"It was arranged between our families years ago," Robin added, ignoring the startled faces of both Florian and his intended.

"I see. Very well, then," the priest said. Clearing his throat loudly, he announced his intention to join them together in holy matrimony, then turned to Robin. "Will you have this woman as your wedded wife?"

Although he had insisted on the rush, the sound of the question he had so long disdained made Robin tug at the neck of his suddenly tight tunic. Around them, he could sense the hall falling into silence as he stared at the priest, but he couldn't seem to respond. His tongue had cleaved to the roof of his mouth. Only a slight noise from beside him stirred him at last, and he turned his head to look at Sybil, who was eyeing him with no little annoyance. Her expression definitely was not that of a woman working her wiles or even of a besotted bride, and he knew that if he didn't speak soon, he would lose her for good.

"Yes, sir," he said, the words ringing out, loud and clear, in a tone that none could dispute. And he smiled at her, a grin of reassurance, of complicity, and, perhaps, of something else.

"Will you find it at your best to love her and hold to her and to no other to your lives' end?" the priest asked.

"Yes, sir," Robin answered, without a thought to any other outcome. Forgotten were his plans to annul this marriage as soon as the killers were found. Indeed, as he looked into his bride's blue eyes, he could see no future except a long and fruitful one, full of passion and delight.

"Then take her by your hand and say after me," coached the priest, "I, Robin de Burgh, take thee, Sybil, in the manner of the holy church, to be my wedded wife, forsaking all others, in sickness and in health, in riches and in poverty, in well and in woe, 'til death us depart, and thereto I plight you my troth."

Robin repeated the words with a certainty born of heart and body, and for once, his mind did not dispute them. At last, Sybil was his, and he was too exultant to consider what lay ahead, especially when this moment felt more like a victory than his downfall. All he wanted to do was to throw her over his shoulder and carry her up to the great chamber.

But before he could even consider such a mad action, the residents of Baddersly swarmed about them both, tendering their wishes, and Florian was shouting orders to the kitchens that would begin a feast of celebration. And in his ecstatic mood, Robin joined in as cups were raised in goodwill and trestle tables were hastily assembled.

Even Sybil seemed to throw off some of her prickliness and delight in the fine food and convivial atmosphere. In his few moments of lucidity, Robin wondered if she, too, had forgotten that theirs was an arrangement, not a true marriage. As for himself, he was ready to toss aside the plan entirely and enjoy the spoils of it, for his blood ran hot, his body hard with wanting her. She was his at last, and he wanted to make it true in all ways. Only his ingrained de Burgh honor kept him from plying her with wine to improve his chances.

Instead, he relied solely on the charm that had stood him in good stead over the years, along with the heat that always blossomed between them, whether either willed it or no. And as the afternoon wore into evening and Badderlsy's villeins arrived, games and dancing ensued and the hot press of his desire was tempered by his joy in teaching Sybil these small pleasures.

It wasn't until evening when Robin's thoughts began once more to turn insistently to his wedding night that he realized the truth with a sudden heart-stopping jolt. No matter what happened or didn't happen between them, he and Sybil would be expected to share the great chamber. The mere thought sent blood rushing to his nether regions with renewed force, and he gripped the arms of his chair in a white-knuckled grasp.

Robin was afraid to look at her. Had she an inkling of their situation? Would she go with him willingly or deny him? His heart lurched in a sort of panic. How could he protect her, if she were not with him? He would demand it, he decided. They must share a room, if only to maintain the pretense of this marriage, for he hated to think what kind of talk separate chambers would engender, especially from the notoriously gossipy steward. They must stay together this night and every night, he thought, his blood thrumming and his body throbbing as his glance strayed to the stairs and the great chamber beyond.

What they did there was up to Sybil.

Sybil felt drunk, though she had consumed little enough of the potent wine. The euphoria came from life itself, from a world wholly unlike the stifling walls of the nunnery, from the warmth of the people of Baddersly, from the fantastic feast, from the elegant surroundings and the freedom to play games and dance. And, most of all, from Robin de Burgh.

Her husband.

Although some small portion of her brain kept warning Sybil that theirs was not a true marriage, she found it difficult to remember exactly what Robin had proposed when he made her laugh with some witty observation or when she held his hand as they danced along with the rest of the revelers or when he fed her small dainties from his trencher.

The number and variety of dishes spread before them had staggered her, and more had arrived, making the impromptu meal last until the time she would have partaken of supper at the nunnery. Although she swore she could not take another bite, Robin kept tempting her with morsels, such as a sugared almond or a date, delicacies that Sybil had never tasted. His latest offering was some sort of small cake drenched in honey. He gracefully tore off a corner and reached out to give it to her, and, laughing, Sybil could not refuse.

But this treat was a bit more difficult to manage than a nut or a fruit, and Sybil had to lick errant drops of honey from her lips. When she did so, Robin paused, his fingers poised before her, his liquid gaze hot and focused, and she felt an answering warmth deep inside. Slowly, deliberately, he touched his fingertip to her mouth, catching a bit of honey. Her heart hammering, Sybil accepted the drop, sucking it from his skin. Then, flushed and rather embarrassed, she nipped at his finger, trying to recapture the earlier playful mood.

But it was gone, replaced by something far more intense and dangerous. Emitting some kind of choked sound, Robin pushed back his chair with a loud scrape against the tiles. "'Tis time to retire," he said, his voice hoarse. Around her, Sybil could hear the laughter and ribald shouts of the people who lingered in the hall, but they were only a shadow on the edge of her awareness. Every thought, every glance, every fiber of her being was directed at one thing and one thing only: Robin de Burgh.

He held out his hand to her, and she took it, shivering as his larger fingers enclosed her own, at the rough brush of his palm against her, at the heat that radiated from the tips of her nails through the rest of her body, making her feel weak in the knees. She wondered wildly if she could even walk as she stepped forward, never taking her eyes from his. Dark and delicious as the honey itself, they held a promise of forbidden delights beyond the hours of food, drink and dancing.

And yet Sybil could summon no will to refuse him. Like a dreamer, she went with him as he led her to a curving stair, up the steps and into a luxurious chamber, soft with firelight and exotic carpets and tapestries. But she was no passive wraith passing through on her way to waking. Indeed, her nerves sizzled with expectancy, her very being alive as never before. And when he shut and barred the door, the room faded from thought and there was nothing except the man who took her in his arms.

He was fierce, pushing her against the door, crowding his hard form against her own, but Sybil found an answering ferocity within herself that rose up to meet him. She lifted her arms around his neck and buried her fingers in his thick dark hair, pulling his head down to hers. And when their lips met, it was as if the earth shook.

He plundered her mouth, and she entwined her tongue with his, seeking out every part of him, every secret, every nuance. He rocked on his feet, as if he, too, were dizzy, and Sybil felt herself being lifted up, carried across the room and tossed upon the wide bed. She had but a moment to catch her breath, and then he pounced on top of her, a low, eager growl coming from him. Kicking away his boots, he pulled off her slippers with rough impatience, and in between long, wet kisses, he tugged at her clothing.

In turn, Sybil pushed at his tunic, making a low

sound of pleasure herself when her hands found his bare chest, so wide and smooth and beautiful. With a grunt, Robin rose to his knees, pulled the garment over his head and tossed it away, but she followed him, pressing kisses against the massive wall of golden skin. The action, delightful as it was to Sybil, seemed to inflame him beyond endurance, and as if possessed, he threw her back down upon the bed, stripping her garments from her and struggling out of his braies and stockings with several muttered oaths.

Sybil lay back, laughing at his haste, until he came down upon her, bare flesh to bare flesh, and then she could only gasp in pure rapture. It was only when he once again rose to his knees, spreading her legs before him, that she knew a moment's doubt. His man-part was huge and hard and the look on his face was fierce and intense, his intent all too clear. With a cry, Sybil struggled and sprang from the bed, though her limbs shook beneath her.

"This is madness," she cried, stalking away, only to turn around and stare at Robin, helplessly, her own desire warring with what little good sense she still possessed.

He had fallen onto his back, his enthusiasm visibly flagging at her words. "What?" he croaked out.

"Have you forgotten your own *arrangement* so quickly?" Sybil demanded, still breathing hard. Just the sight of him, so big and muscular and naked was enough to make her will waver. "'Tis no true wedding night between us, but a false one that you swore never to consummate."

"Huh?" Robin looked at her with such a bewildered expression that Sybil was tempted to laugh. Even now, after all that he had put her through, her heart softened with just one glance at him. *This was not good.*

"Oh, I don't know why I let you do this to me! You didn't even want to marry me! You don't even want me!" Sybil said, throwing up her hands in exasperation.

As if to defy her words, a certain part of Robin's body grew to enormous proportions again. He sent her a glance that was part glare, part plea. "Sybil! By faith, I've never wanted anyone or anything more in my life," he ground out, as if each breath were painful. "I try not to touch you, for both our sakes, but I can't help myself."

He threw an arm over his face, and Sybil's body, unruly and reckless as it was, took a step toward the bed. Her mind found it hard to concentrate when the rest of her yearned for him so fiercely that it seemed she would die if she did not return to his arms, to his strength, to his passion, to give him what they both wanted.

"What of your promises to leave me a maiden?" Sybil whispered, in a desperate last stand. "There can be no child, for I won't have one born of a temporary union."

For a long moment, Robin was silent, then finally, his voice came, a muffled groan from beneath his arm. "There are other ways," he said.

"What?" Sybil prodded him.

"There are other ways of pleasuring that would leave you with your maidenhead," he muttered.

"So you are an expert on these matters, are you?" Sybil asked, annoyed somehow by his wealth of experience. Suddenly, she wondered just how many women had fallen sway to the wiles of Robin de Burgh.

"No, but my brother Stephen is, or was, before his marriage. And, he, uh, often talked of such things with us." Robin lifted his arm to look at her, his cheeks flushed as if in embarrassment, and Sybil's sudden pique faded.

"And…just what are these other ways?" she asked, a bit breathlessly.

"Come, Sybil, and let me show you," Robin urged, a grin breaking across his beautiful face. And without another thought to the rightness or wrongness of it all, Sybil moved forward, toward the massive bed and the man who seemed to have stolen her will. He just might have stolen her heart, as well, but Sybil refused to consider that now, when his great body gleamed golden in the firelight, when his muscled arms reached out for her, and she was his wife, at least in name.

So she went to him, every inch of her tingling with anticipation, and she was not to be disappointed. Again, Robin laid claim to her mouth and her body. His big hands roamed over her, stroking her skin, tangling in her hair, and his lips often followed. Although Sybil felt him shuddering beneath her palms and could hear the harsh cadence of his breath, he moved slowly, deliberately, selflessly, as he roused her passions once more.

When he suckled her breasts, she cried out, lifting her hips in helpless abandon, but he did not move over her this time. Instead, his hand slid up her thigh, in between her legs, caressing her there until Sybil was writhing, tossing her head from side to side in frantic ardor.

"Yes, please! Right there, Robin!"

"Where? *Here?*" he asked, hoarsely.

"Oh *yes*. Oh, please! Robin, do something!"

"You told me not to," came the growl of amusement at her breast. But when she kicked at him with one foot, he nipped at her with his teeth and thrust one large finger inside her. Gasping, Sybil had but a moment to be startled by the invasion before her body closed around him in great, hot spasms, and she nearly wept with the force of her pleasure.

"Shh. Shh." She heard Robin's low voice, rather strained, as he held her close, and she buried her face into his shoulder. It was only when the last ripples of passion died away that Sybil realized he was unchanged. She reared back to look down his form.

"But what of...you?" she asked, staring at that part of him that remained huge and hard.

Robin smiled, albeit painfully. "I was hoping that you might...touch me," he whispered, his voice definitely strained.

"Oh," Sybil said, swallowing hard. Her heart, having slowed a bit, now was picking up its pace as her body seemed to take an enormous amount of interest in Robin's.

"How?" she whispered, reaching out to put a tentative finger to the tip of him.

Lying on his side, Robin muttered a harsh oath as his body jerked in response. *"Anyway you want,"* he said.

"What do you call it?" Sybil asked, curious.

Robin made a garbled sound. "I don't have a name for it!"

"But I don't even know what it's called!" Sybil protested. "We don't learn such things in the nunnery, and even though I have contact with the widow ladies who—"

"A tarse. Just call it a tarse," Robin muttered through gritted teeth. And Sybil smiled. She realized suddenly that she had quite a bit of power over this man, *and she liked it*. With certain, slow movements, she ran a palm up the inside of his thigh, thick with muscle, and heard the harsh groan escape his throat. Then she let her fingers roam farther up, cupping and stroking, and finally taking the oddly named body part in her hand. She felt strong and female and excited as she closed her fingers around it.

"Tighter," Robin said on a groan. "Harder!" Muttering something unintelligible, he covered her hand with his own and showed her just what he wanted, until they were both panting and slick with sweat and then as Sybil watched, wide-eyed, he exploded into her fingers, hot and wet, and she felt her own body shudder in reply.

"Robin!" Sybil cried out his name as she threw her arms around him. He pulled her close, and enclosed by his massive strength, she felt safe and warm and wonderful, enveloped in a pleasure more poignant even than that she had just experienced. For this feeling went beyond her physical response, deep down into her soul, and even as Sybil surrendered to it, she suspected it wouldn't be as temporary as her marriage vows.

This was love, and whatever the future held, it was forever.

Chapter Thirteen

It took Robin a few long, dazed moments to come awake. The sun was slipping through the shutters, the fire had long since sputtered out, and he was still abed. Even more unusual was the warmth that filled him, not a weather-induced heat, but something that worked from the inside out. He realized as he drew a deep breath, that he felt better than he had in years, blissful somehow. Reaching up to stretch, he discovered the reason for his contentment when his hand brushed against skin. And not just any skin: *Sybil's*.

Robin stared down at her, expecting to feel horror at his own lapse, for taking her to bed again when he had sworn not to touch her. But he couldn't conjure up any trace of regret. Indeed, as he lay studying her sweet face, his throat constricted with some unknown emotion, and then, as his gaze drifted lower, he felt another, far more urgent tightening down below.

She had freckles. Robin had discovered that last night, and now he wanted to investigate every one of them. He wanted her again, in every way possible, and most especially he wanted to be inside her. With a groan of need, he lifted a hand toward her only to pause at the sound of knocking against the door. Robin grunted in annoyance. Undoubtedly, it was that meddlesome Florian. "What is it?" Robin called, even as he felt Sybil stir beside him.

"Good morn, my lord. I have a bit of food and drink for you to break your fast. And perhaps a bath for my lady?" the steward answered.

A bath. Robin blanched. He supposed that there should be blood on the linens, and for one wild moment, he wondered whether he ought to prick himself. But then what would be said when the marriage was dissolved? Robin frowned. He didn't care to think about that right now, not when Sybil was beside him, all warm and soft and tousled.

He glanced her way, only to find himself staring at the fiery hair that tumbled about her creamy shoulders, replete with delightful freckles, and the way the blanket dipped when she moved, revealing the dark, tempting cleft between her breasts. An incoherent noise escaped his throat as his body hardened even more, and he wanted nothing so much as to bury his face in those curves.

"My lord!" Florian's voice had never been more unwelcome, and Robin was beginning to realize just why Simon found him so irritating.

"Go away!" he shouted.

"Robin!" The breathy sound made him drag his attention up to Sybil's face, where he focused on her lips. The sight brought back a memory of that mouth pressed against his chest, and he groaned, unable to concentrate on what she was saying. Something to Florian about giving her a few moments? Few moments? Fie! He would banish the steward and every other resident of Baddersly for the rest of the day, maybe even the week. Or a year. In an effort to sway her to his way of thinking, Robin reached for her once more, but she moved away with a laugh.

Rolling onto his back, he laid an arm across his face and groaned again. She wasn't going to be prickly this morning was she? Somehow, Robin didn't think he could stand it if she went back to throwing things at him. But instead of squawking, Sybil gave him a slow, sultry smile and slipped out of bed, dragging the sheet with her. When she wrapped it around herself, Robin got a glimpse of a bare backside that made him gulp.

He had thought she disliked him, but now he wasn't so sure. And, obviously, he was in deep trouble if she didn't. There was a new confidence about her today, a subtle feminine power. She had always seemed assured, but slightly vulnerable to the stifling world of the nunnery. Now, she seemed to have found her place at last. God help him if it was at his side!

And, yet, with the lingering taste of her on his lips, and the memory of her curled beside him all through the night emblazoned on his mind, Robin found it difficult to remember just why he hadn't wanted to marry her in the first place.

"I'll have to send to the nunnery for my things, unless you want me to wear the same gown day after day," she said, as she walked toward the door. Gown? Robin didn't want her wearing anything at all. Ever. His gaze followed her around the room, hoping for some slip in her makeshift garment, only to narrow when she began to unbar the door.

"Wha—? What are you doing?" he asked. But it was too late. In bustled Florian with a large platter, which he set down on a chest beside the hearth. As

Robin watched, frowning, he put out bread, cheese, small, hard apples and a bit of that honeyed cake that Robin recognized from the night before. Just the thought of it made him growl in frustration, but no one seemed to hear him.

"Florian, is it?" Sybil asked in a gracious tone she never used when speaking to *him.* And even the steward looked entranced as he nodded. "I wonder if you might be able to find me a robe. I'm afraid my things haven't arrived here yet."

"Certainly, my Lady de Burgh!" he said. The name rang in the air loudly, yet Robin wasn't jarred by it so much as by Sybil's pleasant manner. Why couldn't she be that sweet to him? "And a bath, as well?" the steward suggested.

"Oh, that would be *wonderful,*" Sybil replied, and Robin scowled. He wasn't so sure he liked this new confidence of hers. In fact, he was certain he didn't want her plying anyone else with her freshly honed wiles. And when she slipped out the door, presumably to use the garderobe, Robin nearly called out to stop her. *Simply for safety reasons, of course.* Even though they were at Baddersly, Robin intended to keep his eye on her every moment. He got to his feet, but frowned, for no matter how congenial she seemed this morning, he couldn't imagine Sybil allowing him to follow her into the garderobe.

"Some delicacies to tempt you, my lord? You must keep up your strength," Florian said, with a sly look that made Robin want to cringe. "I brought them myself, for I didn't think you wanted everyone gaping at the newly marrieds."

No, you wanted to gape at us yourself, Robin thought churlishly. He pulled on his clothes, just in case he had to go after Sybil. *For her own protection, of course.*

"Such a lovely lady, my lord! Though I must admit the suddenness of the nuptials caught me by surprise," the steward commented, as he fueled the fire.

Uh-oh, here's where the interrogation begins, Robin thought, and he wasn't about to share the truth of his union with the most notorious gossip in the area, perhaps in the entire land. But when Robin glared at the steward, Florian didn't even blink. Apparently, he had too much experience with the de Burghs to be easily cowed.

"Of course, I am proud of the little feast we threw together yesterday, but I look forward to a much more elaborate one," Florian said, smoothly. "I admit to being a bit put out when Simon insisted on getting married at Ansquith, but here, at last, is our turn to shine, to show the de Burghs just how well Baddersly can welcome them all. Although we haven't quite the size or resources of Campion, I think we can manage a wedding celebration the likes of which few have seen."

Robin blanched. Yesterday was bad enough, but now Florian wanted to hold another observance, a bigger one, that his entire family would attend? "I'm afraid that's not possible," Robin replied in a harsh tone.

Florian put his hands on his hips. "You cannot mean you are taking her back to Campion? Why, you have been here hardly at all! Do not say you are removing from Baddersly permanently!"

"No! Not yet, at any rate," Robin muttered. He lifted his head. "And we are not traveling anywhere. We are staying right here."

Florian practically rubbed his hands together in glee. "Then, when can we hold the—"

Robin cut him off with a wave of his hand. "There will be no other celebration."

"What?"

"Not now. Not ever. And I don't want to hear any more about it," Robin added, as Sybil entered the room.

Shooting him a look of disgust, Florian headed toward the door, only to let fly one parting arrow. "By the way, your brother sent word he would like to talk with you. Apparently, he's wondering just where you are and why you haven't paid him a visit."

Robin swore under his breath, for he knew that word would soon reach Simon of his hasty wedding, and then he would have some explaining to do. Florian smiled wickedly. "I'll bring the bath," he added, nodding graciously at Sybil and leaving Robin to glare after him.

"Come sit down and eat," Sybil said, taking one of the two heavy chairs that sat near the hearth. "I vow I shall be as fat as a pig ere I leave here."

Robin scowled. He didn't like this talk of leaving. He sat down hard and took a hunk of bread, just for something to do, but he had no idea what to say.

"What's the matter?" Sybil asked, giving him an innocent look.

Everything, he thought. He had been dragged from his bed, where he had been very happily ensconced, and now this talk of Simon and *leaving.* He didn't like it.

"Aren't you hungry?" she asked, her expression a little too guileless to be believable. Oh, he was hungry all right, and he ought to show his bride just how voracious was his appetite. But thoughts of Simon and *leaving* brought his mind uncomfortably back to the danger that faced them.

"You aren't going anywhere," he muttered. For some unknown reason, he felt like starting a fight, maybe to distract himself from all his worries. Or maybe because when passions ran high between them, Sybil usually ended up flat on her back. But, for once, she didn't dispute him, and Robin immediately wondered if she had concocted some plan to depart the moment he turned around.

Robin shook his head at his own fancies. She looked content enough, and she was safe at Baddersly, he told himself. Then why did he want to lock her in the great chamber, preferably with him? He ran a hand through his hair. The best thing he could do would be to leave her here while he tried to find the killers, but every nerve in his body screamed a protest at that notion.

And even though she wasn't arguing, how could he be certain the notoriously rebellious Sybil would stay put? He could place guards at the door, but Robin didn't trust anyone else to watch over her as would, even should he advise them of the dangers. The mere thought sent the now-familiar rush of protectiveness through him so swiftly, it was dizzying. In an instant, he knew he could not leave.

He could send one of Baddersly's knights on the trail of the strangers, but it was a delicate situation, and none of those simple fighting men were versed in subtlety or cunning. Nor could he think of a one to whom he would commit his wife's future. With a frown, he realized that there was no one here able to take on this task for him.

"So what do we do now?" Sybil asked.

Robin glanced up sharply, blood rushing to various parts of his body in swift response. He knew what he wanted to do, but he suspected that going back to bed wasn't what his bride had in mind. He frowned. "You stay here," he said, gruffly. "I'm going to have to find the murderers, or get someone to help me do it."

"One of your knights?" Sybil asked.

Robin shook his head. "No. There are none I'd trust with the task. 'Tis work for one of my brothers," he admitted. Robin's first thought was of Geoffrey, the most clever and learned of the de Burghs. But Geoff was far away and occupied with his family, *as they all were*. Robin stifled that bit of resentment and put his mind to his siblings. But there was no getting around it. The only one close by was Simon, a good man in a fight, but not exactly the most easygoing. And he was already miffed at his younger sibling.

Robin stifled a groan. "There's no help for it. I'm going to have to go to Simon," he said.

Sybil looked as if she meant to ask him more, but just then the door swung open and the servants entered with water for her bath. Robin watched them empty the buckets into the wooden tub Florian had dragged near the hearth and wondered if drool was running down his chin. His body had long since seized up at the thought of Sybil, naked, in the bath. And when the servants left, he sat there for a long moment, staring at the tub, strangled nearly to incoherence by lust.

"Well, then, you had better be off after your brother, hadn't you?" Sybil said, giving him a questioning look that he suspected wasn't quite as innocent as it appeared. But Robin had no time to dally here, and he knew it. The sooner he found the killers, the sooner this sort of unholy temptation would no longer be a part of his life. The knowledge, instead of cheering him, made him growl out a rough farewell through gritted teeth as he marched from the room, Sybil's soft laughter ringing in his ears.

Calling hoarsely for a guard, Robin made sure that no one would enter the chamber except himself, not even the servants in his absence, then shouted again for a messenger. He thought about heading down to the hall, but felt a reluctance that made him turn to the more private solar instead. Soon a young man arrived, swift and eager, and Robin carefully sorted out the message he was to take to Ansquith.

After the messenger left, Robin called for the knights of Baddersly and explained to them that two strangers were doing murder in the area. Without going into too many details, he told them of the threat to his wife and entertained suggestions to further protect the castle. He felt marginally better after reinforcements were sent to the walls and gate, but after they left, Robin found himself pacing the small room restlessly.

His mind wandered, all too quickly, from defenses to Sybil, and he felt a sudden, urgent need to see her, to assure himself of her safety, simply to *be* with her. There was really nothing further to do until he heard from Simon, he told himself as he took a few steps toward the door. Even though he knew the trail of the murderers was growing colder the longer he waited, he could not bring himself to leave Sybil here alone. Indeed, he was just convincing himself that he should return to the great chamber, where, surely, she had finished with her bath, when a roar erupted from the doorway.

"What the devil do you think you're doing?"

Simon's bellow was unmistakable, and Robin flinched as he glanced over to see his brother filling the entry. Slamming the door behind him, Simon faced him with the kind of expression that was known to make grown men quail in battle, but Robin had seen it all before. Nevertheless, he steeled himself.

"I barely had returned home when I heard that you have returned to Baddersly without a word to me. Not that I care, but Bethia seems to like you for some inane reason," Simon growled. "Before she could even plan a visit, I heard that you were lodged at a nunnery, investigating a murder that by all rights should be the province of the bishop! This is all hearsay, mind you, for you couldn't be bothered to contact me or keep me informed of anything."

Although the most warrior-like and quick-tempered of the de Burghs had mellowed somewhat since his own marriage, right now he looked pretty fierce, and Robin was well aware of his temper as he raged on. "Then, this very morning, I have to hear from a villager about my *own brother's wedding!*"

Things being what they were lately, Robin wasn't really in the mood for a brawl with his elder, so he hastened to explain before it went too far. "Now, Simon, it's not a real marriage," he said, holding up a hand to stave off his brother's wrath.

"Not a real—?" Simon sputtered, then swore under his breath. "What do you mean? *Is she ugly?*"

"No, of course not. She's the most beautiful—" Robin began, only to have Simon cut him off.

"Then she's some kind of shrew, like Geoff's wife?" his brother asked.

"No! She might get a bit testy at times," Robin said, remembering how he had been forced to duck the missiles launched at his head. "But she's—"

"Stupid?"

"No!"

"Spoiled?"

"Certainly, not!" Robin sputtered. Sybil had never been granted a thing in her life, and now he found himself wanting to shower her with luxuries. But before he could say as much, Simon was blurting out another question.

"Bound to someone else?" he asked.

"No!"

Simon frowned, as if in thought, then gave Robin a queer look. "So she's cold in bed. Is that it?" he asked.

"Now, wait just a moment—" Robin said, surging forward.

"Obviously not," Simon said, sidestepping him easily. "What then? Does she make you unhappy? Ill?" he asked, fixing Robin with a sharp gaze.

"No! I feel wonderful!" Robin protested.

"Well, then, what's the problem?" Simon demanded, crossing his arms over his chest as though exasperated.

Robin felt just as aggravated by his brother's interrogation, unwelcome and intrusive. "There is no problem because this isn't a real marriage. I just gave her my name to protect her from harm. It's a temporary thing, and when the threat has passed, we'll, uh, annul it," Robin said, though he found himself frowning. No matter how logical that inevitable end might be, he just didn't care to think about it.

Simon threw himself down upon a settle and propped his feet up on a nearby chest, eying Robin curiously. "Now let me get this straight," he said. "You feel *wonderful?*"

Robin nodded, rather reluctantly.

"Better than you have in your whole life?"

"Well, I don't know about that," Robin muttered. But when Simon studied him sharply, he flushed. "Well, some of the time, maybe." Like this morning, waking up next to Sybil. *When he wasn't thinking about the whole marriage thing.* "Yes," he replied, with a scowl.

Simon's dark brows lifted in a gesture that reminded Robin of his more caustic brother Stephen. "And you want to get rid of her?" Simon asked, as if he weren't hearing correctly.

"Well, not exactly," Robin said, disliking both Simon's attitude and the direction of the conversation. It was more complicated than that. Simon, who always saw things in black and white, obviously couldn't grasp the intricacies of the situation. Robin opened his mouth to explain more carefully, but Simon barked out a laugh.

"You love her!" he accused in a gruff tone of triumph.

"*What?*" Robin shouted. "I do not!"

Simon didn't flinch. In fact, his lips curved into a wicked smile, as if Robin's denial simply had confirmed his opinion. "You love her, don't you?" he repeated.

Robin blew out a breath and sank down onto his

seat, reaching up to run a hand through his hair. "Well, if I do, it's not of my own free will," he said.

"What the devil does that mean?" Simon demanded, in a thunderous growl.

"It's all part of the curse!" Robin said.

"*Curse?* What curse?" Simon asked, crossing his arms in front of him again, as though talking to a recalcitrant child.

Normally, Robin would bristle at the posture, but he felt a little reluctant to bring up his little theory to Simon, who never believed anything he couldn't see for himself. However, his brother was glaring at him in a way that told him he was going to have to come up with something. It might as well be the truth.

"I've decided there's some kind of spell over the family because everyone's getting married when we were perfectly happy as bachelors," Robin muttered.

Simon appeared thunderstruck. "You're telling me you were perfectly happy a month ago?" he said.

"Well, not exactly. Everyone's all scattered about because of these women," Robin complained.

Simon raised his brows.

Robin felt his face flush. What did Simon know? He was a deluded as the rest of them! "Pardon me, if I don't want to be led around by the nose like all of my older brothers!"

Simon looked as though he was going to explode, and Robin braced himself for a fight.

"You're saying Bethia leads me around by my nose?" Simon demanded. For a moment, Robin thought he was going to lunge across the room, but he only shook his head, as if Robin wasn't worth the effort. "If we dote on our wives it's because we want to. We haven't given up anything, not our so-called

freedom or manhood, but have gained everything,''
Simon muttered, waxing poetic in a way Robin had
never seen in him before. Then, as if embarrassed by
his words, he glared at Robin.

"But if you're too stupid to understand that, you
must at least see that nothing in the world remains
stagnant. You don't have to have Geoff's brains to
realize that! Children grow up. They leave their
homes and make new families. Otherwise, there
would be no future generations! You'll see, when
your wife is increasing—''

"No, I won't!'' Robin said, surging to his feet.
"I'm not consummating this marriage because it isn't
a true one.''

Simon stared at him with a blank look of incom-
prehension. "You have this woman you say is beautiful and holds her own against a de Burgh, meets you
on your own terms, who is intelligent, exciting, interesting, and you want to get rid of her and go back
to being alone? Worse yet, you want to return to your
childhood, to the life of a boy?''

Robin frowned down at his feet. "I didn't mean it
that way,'' he muttered. He had never thought of
Simon as particularly clever, but his normally dull-
witted brother was twisting everything around.

"It's time to grow up, Robin,'' Simon said harshly.
When Robin lifted his head to glare at his brother,
Simon held up a hand as if to ward off a fight. "I'm
just telling you to think about what you have before
you throw it away.''

Robin turned aside. He didn't want to think about
the future or the dissolution of his marriage, but neither was he about to surrender after all these years to
the very thing that had disrupted his formerly idyllic

existence. He heard Simon grunt in annoyance, then take a deep breath.

"In the meantime, why don't you tell me why your wife is in danger?" Simon said.

Relieved at the change of subject, Robin explained as best he could, and Simon's face hardened at the news of the two murders. However, he didn't seem to be as eager for a fight as he used to be. Indeed, when Robin asked him to go after the trail of the killers, Simon looked a little pained.

"Now, let me get this straight, I'm supposed to do your work for you while you're cozily locked up here with your bride?" he asked.

Robin flushed again. "I just don't trust anyone to guard her!" he sputtered.

"Well, the obvious course would be to send her home. None would dare seek her out at Campion," Simon said. He paused to give Robin a sharp look. "But, somehow I don't think Father would approve of this sham marriage of yours."

Robin shifted uncomfortably. He didn't care to consider his father's reaction, and besides, he had no intention of letting Sybil go that far away. "I can't waste such time! We need to act now, while the trail of the killers is still reasonably fresh."

Simon grunted. "Well, I can see why you don't want to leave her here. Baddersly's too big. There are too many people here to protect her properly," he said. He paused, as if reaching a decision. "She can stay at Ansquith, while you and I both go after the murderers."

Robin knew Simon preferred his wife's smaller holding to the larger castle of Baddersly, but he wasn't so sure. In truth, he wasn't so sure about leaving Sybil *anywhere*.

"Ansquith is safe," Simon said, with a growl, ready to defend any slur against his home.

"Of course," Robin said. He looked down at his feet. "It's just that I don't like going away, especially when she has no one else."

"I understand," Simon said gruffly. "But it must be done lest you look over your shoulders for the rest of your lives."

Robin nodded, his throat suddenly tight. Once they found the two strangers, there would be no ever after, at least not with Sybil.

"She can stay with Bethia," Simon said. "That way she'll be protected, and she won't bolt."

Robin lifted his head. What made Simon think his wife was going to *bolt*? He glared at his brother, but Simon simply shrugged. "Women are like that," he said.

Robin frowned. "And how can you be sure she'll be safe?"

Simon had the audacity to laugh. "Are you joking?" he asked. "She'll be with Bethia."

Chapter Fourteen

Sybil leaned against the side of the tub, reveling in the hot bath perfumed with scented soap. Such luxuries, as well as the privacy in which to indulge them, had been few and far between at the nunnery. And although Sybil knew she should not put an excessive value on such worldly things, she couldn't help enjoying herself. She felt like singing, and she hummed a tune that someone had played last night for the dancing. Surely it was not a sin to be destined for a life outside Our Lady of All Sorrows, for that was the conclusion Sybil had reached: that here, at last, she had found her place.

This was where she belonged.

The past stretched out behind her like a cold, dim and narrow tunnel, while it seemed as though her new life, with all its brightness and color and warmth, had begun the moment she wed Robin de Burgh. Oh, she knew that theirs wasn't a true marriage, and she decried the reasons for it, but Sybil could not deny how well she liked being Lady de Burgh. The castle, the food and the appointments were enough to satisfy anyone, and she drank them all in like an awestruck

child. Yet it was the people and the glorious freedom
to be had that most enthralled her.

And, of course, Robin.

Her lips curving into a smile, Sybil lifted up one
leg and studied it, moved by a new awareness of her
body and herself. She half hoped to hear him at the
door, interrupting her bath, and she imagined, with
delicious abandon, the two of them wet and naked.
Shivering in both delight and embarrassment, she let
her leg fall with a splash and sank down to her chin.

But she had seen the passion shining in Robin's
eyes this morning. Indeed, he had made his disgrun-
tlement at Florian's entrance quite obvious, and that
knowledge gave Sybil a secret thrill. She felt
strangely powerful, for she knew that no matter how
he might dispute it, she had the ability to affect Robin
de Burgh, knight, lord and formidable man.

With fresh insight, Sybil judged that his feelings
for her went beyond duty and protection, but just how
far, she hesitated to speculate. Robin certainly looked
hungry for her all the time, and she took what comfort
she could from that knowledge. But her experience
with men was so limited that she could not claim he
felt any bond between them except a physical one.

Her own emotions were far too easy to gauge.
Somehow, over the past few days, she had gone from
despising Robin for his strength and his power over
her to surrendering herself to it. Although she didn't
plan to give up her first taste of independence, it
seemed to her as if they could coexist: her love for
him and her own sense of herself. Indeed, she was far
more free here than she had been at the nunnery. And,
in some way, this passion gave her a new strength
that she didn't understand.

At the back of her mind, the truth of her situation nagged at her, warning her that despite her current euphoria, this marriage was not real and her devotion to her erstwhile husband was *not good*. But she ignored it, for how could something that felt so right be so wrong? At one time, she had condemned Elisa for these very emotions, but now she wondered why Elisa had not trusted to her heart, reached out and seized her opportunity for happiness. Sybil frowned. Luckily, their circumstances were not the same, and for now, she was content to live the lie.

Tomorrow would come soon enough.

Meanwhile, she would breath and stretch her wings and discover the great, wide world. And she would be herself. Sybil smiled, struck again by the odd notion that finally, she was where she was supposed to be, doing what she was meant to do, even though she knew it was absurd. She gave a little laugh at the thought, for even in her wildest dreams, she was not destined to be Lady de Burgh.

Sybil finally left the bath when it had cooled and she was fairly certain Robin would not return to frolic in it. Marveling at the elegant clothing Florian had sent along with the hot water, she dressed carefully and brushed out her long hair, leaving it to hang free down her back, a refreshing sensation. Then, aided by the novelty of a small mirror, she peeked at the person she had become and drew in a sharp breath. She really looked like Lady de Burgh, she thought, even as she told herself not to grow accustomed to her title.

With nothing else to do, Sybil prowled the great chamber, gazed out all the windows at the vastness of Baddersly and was just beginning to grow restless when she heard Robin's voice at the door. She whirled, eager to see him, only to sit down abruptly. Although a novice at this business between men and women, Sybil knew better than to show Robin just how she felt, especially when he did not seem to return her affection. The man was far too smug already.

So she waited, carefully cultivating a casual air as he entered, lifting her head in greeting only when she saw another man as well. Sybil's eyes widened as she studied the fellow, a taller, darker, more gaunt and grim version of Robin. This must be his brother, Sybil realized at once, but she suppressed a shiver nonetheless, glad that this man had not answered the cry at the nunnery.

"Sybil, this is my brother Simon."

"Lady," Simon said, bowing his head slightly in deference.

Sybil opened her mouth to deny that she was a lady, only to smile instead as she realized she was. Lady de Burgh. *For now anyway.*

Simon studied her with narrowed eyes as if he were judging her worthiness, and Sybil rose to her feet, meeting his scrutiny with her own, for she refused to bow to any man, no matter how intimidating he might be. Dimly, she wondered if all the de Burghs were so intense and how one managed to hold one's own against several of them. But Simon's harsh face broke into a smile when she returned his gaze, and he slapped his brother hard on the back.

"Congratulations are in order, I understand," he said, as if pleased, while Robin looked as if he would like to protest his brother's choice of words. Before he could do so, Simon spoke again. "But, there is no time for that now. You are in danger, my lady, and I think you would be safer at my holding, Ansquith. So we shall repair there immediately.''

Was Robin ridding himself of her so quickly? The thought struck Sybil painfully, her own expression of welcome faltering even as Simon stepped forward.

''Robin, as well,'' he added, leaning close, before his brother elbowed him out of the way, and suddenly, Sybil had two de Burghs dancing attendance on her, each vying for her attention. It was almost more than she could bear. Sybil smiled. *Almost, but not quite.*

Ansquith was smaller than Baddersly, neat and tidy and rather cozy, Sybil thought as Simon led her through the great hall of the fortified manor house. The owner was resting and would have to meet with them later, Simon said, surprising Sybil, for she thought surely he was lord. She could not imagine the grim knight serving under anyone, but Robin explained that Simon had married the daughter of Sir Burnell, who had been ill for some time and was only now recovering.

Sybil had barely digested that information when they reached the solar and were greeted by Lady de Burgh herself. And she looked far more suited to the role than Sybil. Tall and beautiful, with a blond braid hanging down her back, she held herself with regal authority. Indeed, Sybil would have thought her cool and unapproachable, but for the hand that rested on the swelling at her belly. The slender woman was obviously pregnant, and Sybil drew in a sharp breath of surprise and pleasure.

After giving Sybil a scrutiny much like that her husband had conducted, Bethia de Burgh welcomed her warmly. She listened soberly as the men explained the threat to Sybil and their plan to search for the two strangers suspected of the killings. And before Sybil had even begun to think of settling in at another new residence, they spoke of leaving. At once.

Sybil fought against an errant twinge of disappointment that Robin would be going away so soon, but whatever she was feeling must have been echoed twofold by the other de Burghs, for Simon suddenly drew his wife into a hasty embrace and kissed her full upon the mouth. Stunned, Sybil turned to Robin, hoping that he did not expect the same sort of farewell, for she was certainly not ready to display her feelings so publicly.

To her relief, Robin only took her hands and looked at her, but his gaze was so intent that Sybil's heart thundered and her breath caught. Her new confidence seemed to flee in the hot intensity of his gaze, as did any reluctance on her part to engage in telling goodbyes. If he had thrown her on the floor, she probably would have let him, despite their audience.

But it soon became all too apparent that kisses were not what was on Robin's mind. "Don't leave this room. If you have to use the garderobe, take Bethia with you. Don't go anywhere without a guard," he said. Sybil's initial excitement at his focused attention was dampened by the fact that he spoke of protection and nothing more. As usual.

"I'll be careful," she said, more sharply than she intended. Then her momentary pique vanished as she realized that Robin could be hurt as well in his pursuit of the killers. Although she suspected he was well able to handle any challenge, she felt a tingle of unease. She would have nothing happen to this man she loved, whether he cared for her or not. "You, too," she added.

Robin shrugged away her concern. He opened his mouth, as if to say more, but closed it again when he glanced toward his brother. His gaze returned to her, his eyes dark and intense with some unspoken message, then he squeezed her hands and strode to the door, where his brother was waiting. Simon called for a guard, and the heavy oak swung shut with a loud thud, closing the men out and the women inside. Sybil felt a new pang, an ache that came with this brief parting, which she recognized all too well as an unpleasant harbinger of what was to come.

Absently, she heard Bethia step forward to bar the door, but her mind remained on Robin, and she moved to the narrow window, looking out to the bailey and beyond. The seriousness of the threat to them both struck her more forcefully than at any time since she had looked upon Gwerful's body, and she worried for his safe return. And then what? she asked herself, as she wondered about her future. The euphoria of her wedding had carried her through the night and most of the day, but now, with Robin's departure, it seemed to flee, leaving her feeling bleak and alone once more.

"How long have you known him?" The question jolted Sybil from her reverie, and she turned to see Bethia de Burgh studying her.

"Only a short while," Sybil said, though even she found the answer difficult to believe. It seemed more like a lifetime that she had known Robin, with a lifetime and more stretching out ahead of them, as well. She shook her head.

"That's long enough," Bethia said, with a wry

smile. Her hand drifted again to her belly, and Sybil
felt a twinge of envy for the real Lady de Burgh, her
union a true one, her husband's devotion apparent to
all.

"I'm sorry to be thrust upon you unannounced,"
Sybil said, suddenly uncomfortable.

"Nonsense! I am eager for a guest, especially a
sister-in-law," Bethia answered.

Sybil flushed, embarrassed by the lie. Although
Simon had explained the threat to her life, no one had
mentioned that it was the reason behind her hasty
nuptials. Perhaps Robin had kept silent in order to
protect her, but Sybil could not accept this woman's
hospitality under false pretenses. "It's not a real marriage," she said, even though the words were difficult
to voice. She swallowed hard.

To Sybil's surprise, Bethia evinced no shock at her
bald admission, but tossed back her long braid and
laughed. "For a de Burgh, there is no other kind,"
she said.

Sybil glanced away, struggling with the thickness
in her throat. "Perhaps most of the time, but in this
case, Robin married me to keep me safe."

Again, Bethia did not react as expected but chuckled aloud, and Sybil eyed her sharply. Was the
woman taunting her? "Pardon me," the beautiful
blonde said as she swallowed another laugh. "I am
sure Robin told you that was why he took you to wife.
Perhaps he even believes it himself. Although clever
as a rule, in some areas, the de Burghs are remarkably
slow-witted," she said.

At Sybil's bemused expression, Bethia smiled. "He
might be able to fool himself and you in the bargain,
but he can't fool me or his brother," she said. "I've

seen Robin look at you, and 'tis not the look of a man who is simply doing his duty.''

Sybil gaped at the other woman with a mixture of chagrin and pleasure to hear her own suspicions spoken aloud. The hope that Robin felt something for her returned, with new fervor. After last night, she had been certain of it, but doubts still assailed her, especially since she didn't know how much of his interest in her depended upon their…intimacy.

''What do I, a former novice, know of men's…'' Sybil paused, intending to say *lusts,* but reluctant to speak so boldly, ''…behavior?'' she amended.

Again, Bethia laughed, a wonderful, husky sound that set Sybil at ease even discussing this delicate topic. ''If you are trying to understand the behavior of men, you might as well hope to fly to the moon! But 'tis obvious that Robin not only wants you, but loves you, as well,'' she said.

Sybil's heart pounded in response, and she felt shaky at the sudden leap in her pulse. Sinking down upon a settle, she drew in a ragged breath, eager to believe Bethia, but still wary. ''How can you tell?'' she asked.

''Well, I suppose the way he parted with you, as though wholly unwilling, gave me a clue,'' Bethia said, with a chuckle. ''He's got that possessive air about him that fairly shouts you are his and woe betide anyone who thinks otherwise—even you!''

''What?'' Sybil asked, not a little puzzled. She frowned as she mulled over Bethia's words, at once both eager and reluctant to believe them. ''If 'tis as you say, then why doesn't he speak of it?'' she asked. There had been plenty of opportunities for Robin to confide his innermost feelings, especially last night in bed.

Bethia made a sound suspiciously like a snort as she took a seat beside Sybil. With the air of one who has knowledge beyond her years, the other woman leaned forward and smiled. "Let me tell you a little bit about the de Burghs."

Sibyl listened, rapt, as Bethia spoke of the Earl of Campion and his seven sons, a predominantly male household with few feminine influences. "Oh, the older boys remember Campion's second wife, but not the younger ones," Bethia said. "Robin was still a little boy when she died, so he and Reynold and Nicholas grew up without a mother. For all of their good looks and charm, they are unused to dealing with women, and often need a cudgel to the head—or the heart—in order to admit to a weakness for anyone."

Bethia shook her head. "I've spoken with the other wives and it's always the same thing: getting them to say the words is like pulling teeth!"

"So you had that problem with Simon? How did you get him to come around?" Sybil asked.

Bethia loosed another deep-throated laugh. "Well, I had several problems with Simon, the main one being his tendency to try to direct everyone and everything in his path, which continues to this day." She leaned back with a smug smile. "But I've learned how to manage him. And as for you getting Robin to come around, you'll just have to use her head—and your body."

At Sybil's shocked expression, Bethia laughed. "They say that anything is fair in love or war, and sometimes I don't think the de Burghs know the difference," she said.

Encouraged by this extraordinary woman, Sybil felt her confidence resurge. Her future, once seemingly set in stone, now twisted and veered in different directions, and she could not say whither it would take her. But she could not go back, nor would she care to do so. This new life was too interesting, too exciting to forgo, whatever the consequences.

"And speaking of war," Bethia said. "Have you done any fighting before?"

"Just with Robin," Sybil answered wryly.

"Well, then, the first thing we must do is to teach you to protect yourself because as much as he might want to stay close, *and I do mean close,* to you day and night," Bethia said with a grin, "there may be instances, such as today, when your personal guard just can't be with you. Or there may come a time when you're both threatened. Although the de Burghs think of themselves as invincible, I know for a fact that they aren't," she added, with a knowing expression.

Sybil smiled at that announcement before the ramifications of Bethia's speech struck her. "But aren't we safe here?" she asked.

"As safe as can be made possible," Bethia answered. "But castles and manor fortresses are made to defend against attack by a host of warriors, not one or two men determined to gain entry. Even if Simon barred the gate against all comers, I would still maintain a cautious vigilance. And, should nothing ill occur, then you have done no worse than to learn a valuable skill that might come in handy some day. What say you, sister?" she asked.

Swallowing hard against the emotions that title invoked, Sybil simply nodded her head, though she had no idea how a pregnant woman was going to teach her how to fight. However, whatever doubts she had soon vanished as Bethia walked over to a heavy chest, opened the lid and tossed her a couple of nasty-looking knives. Then, as if that weren't enough, she pulled out a long, deadly sword with an expression of pure delight.

"Let's start with this, my weapon of choice," she said, smiling eagerly at Sybil.

Robin didn't like being away from her. After all, she was his responsibility, and he was never one to shirk his duties. Well, maybe he had tried to escape some of them as a boy, but not now, and especially not where Sybil was concerned. He frowned as he remembered their parting. He had wanted to say…things, but with his brother and Bethia there, it had been impossible. And, anyway, his tongue seemed to tie itself in knots when he looked into the face of his One.

It was all part of the curse, no doubt, but in truth, Robin wasn't much concerned with that anymore. He had too many other things to consider, like wondering what Sybil's new assurance meant and whether she was smiling at any of the guards at Ansquith. And why she couldn't have said something when he left, like *I'll miss you.*

Aye, that was likely, Robin thought, with a grimace. She had seemed only too happy to be rid of him. She hadn't even bothered to argue about the move to Ansquith, though Florian had. The steward had been quite put out at the thought that not one, but two, de Burghs, had abandoned his far bigger, luxurious castle for the smaller manor house. He had grumbled and complained, even appealing to Sybil, who laughed and told him they would be back. But would they? Robin didn't like to think that far ahead.

At Ansquith, he had tried to appear confident and controlled, for Sybil's sake, but, in truth, the idea of parting from her, which had never seemed like a good one, had torn at his insides. And Simon was no help. His elder seemed to derive special delight from his younger sibling's current misfortunes, and Robin found himself regretting every prank and jest he had ever played at his brother's expense.

Far from being sympathetic to his feelings as they left Ansquith, Simon had shown him to a sleeping chamber, only to promise to set aside another for his bride "since yours isn't a true marriage." Robin had glared at him, but Simon had only guffawed in a bizarre juxtaposition of their former roles. Robin was the one who had always laughed at Simon, the brother too literal to take a joke. Now, his elder seemed privy to a secret world that not only excluded Robin, but made him a source of amusement, as well.

Deep in these unpleasant thoughts, Robin was only vaguely aware of a harsh curse from nearby, and he jerked upright to face a scowling Simon. "I should never have brought you along!" his brother muttered.

"Wha-what?" Robin asked. "Did you say something?"

Simon swore again. "Yes! I've really been enjoying a long conversation with myself! Fie, I suppose it's hopeless," he muttered.

"What are you talking about?" Robin demanded, his attention finally caught.

Simon grunted. "Remember how I was when you came to Ansquith last autumn, after Bethia and I had

had a fight? I was moping around like the vanquished and even let that fool Stephen get me drunk!'' Simon said, with a shudder.

"Yes,'' Robin answered slowly. He wasn't quite sure what that had to do with their current pursuit of two killers, but obviously, his normally taciturn brother felt a need to babble these days.

"Well, you are acting as I did,'' Simon said, shaking his head. "And there's only one cure for it.''

"I am not moping!'' Robin answered. "I'm, uh, thinking. And, anyway, Sybil and I didn't have a fight.''

Simon laughed, humorlessly. "Maybe not, but you certainly haven't settled things with her.''

Robin said nothing. He had no interest in discussing his bride with his brother again, but something, maybe curiosity or maybe his own dissatisfaction with how things were, finally prompted him to speak. "So what's this cure?'' he asked.

Simon roared. "I would say marriage, but since you've already done that, you're going to have to make it a true union, one based on love, not expediency.''

Robin grimaced, and Simon chuckled again, but both men grew quiet as they approached the cottage where Gwerful had been killed. Robin nodded at the guard he had posted, and they dismounted. The cottage was much as he had left it, the body having been taken away for burial by neighbors, for her husband was still away.

"How do you know the merchant didn't kill her, in a mad fit?'' Simon asked, grimly. "It happens sometimes.''

"Too much of a coincidence,'' Robin answered.

"They lived peacefully enough until I appeared, asking questions."

"You can't blame yourself," Simon said in a gruff tone.

"I can, and I will," Robin answered. Simon didn't know the half of it.

Simon grunted, then knelt to inspect the floor where the woman had lain. Robin looked around the rest of the small building once more, but found nothing.

"Not much of a struggle," Simon said.

"Anyone could have walked in, and she would have welcomed them as potential buyers," Robin noted.

"But men bent on stealth might very well not want to come in the front," Simon said. He looked at Robin, and, as one, they headed toward the rear, where a small door led to a patch of garden, planted with beans and such. There were no animals, but this was not the home of a villein, and meat could be taken in trade. Robin surveyed the area, while Simon knelt again, presumably looking for telltale signs of hooves in the grass.

"Here," he called. He had reached the end of the garden, where blackberry bushes rose before a tract of woods, and Robin hurried toward him.

"They are careless," Simon said. Nearly as good at tracking as the eldest de Burgh, Dunstan, Simon followed the trail through the trees, across a furlong of plowed land and back to the road.

"Now, what?" Robin asked, harshly.

"We follow the road and watch carefully for any diversions," Simon said, heading back toward the waiting destriers.

"Mayhap they returned to the nunnery," Robin said with an uneasy look in that direction, for the road led to Our Lady of All Sorrows and beyond.

"We shall see," Simon said, and with a curt nod, Robin mounted his horse and urged it toward the road.

It was slow going, and Robin was forced to curb his growing agitation. Never the most patient of men, he bristled at the pace, while the thought of Sybil made him doubly anxious.

"They probably set off straight for the nunnery once they found out Sybil was the real princess," Robin muttered as Simon studied both sides of the route with infinite care. "They may have hurt one of the other nuns or be there, even now—"

Simon cut him off with a rude oath. "I should have brought Bethia along, instead of you!" he said. "You're thinking too much with parts other than your brain."

"I am not!" Robin replied, indignant. He hadn't once thought of *that* since leaving Sybil. He was too worried about her.

Simon swore again. "I'm talking about your *heart,* you idiot!"

Robin would have denied it, but Simon had stopped by a thicket and raised his hand in a signal to halt. As Robin watched, his brother dismounted and studied the ground. "This way," he finally said, getting back into his saddle.

"But how do we know these hoofprints belong to the men we are seeking?" Robin asked, though he knew they had no other course except to follow.

"We don't," Simon said. "But I'm thinking that they saw your party coming yesterday and hied themselves off the roadway, perhaps just to avoid any other travelers. Then, they just might have recognized you as the coroner and saw that a novice rode with you."

Robin sucked in a deep breath, his gaze flying to Simon's as fear seized him in a harsh grip.

"Perhaps, perhaps not," Simon said.

But Robin was not placated. He knew what his brother was thinking as surely as if Simon had spoken aloud. The killers just might have followed them back to the village and on from there to Baddersly.

And then to Ansquith.

Chapter Fifteen

Sybil couldn't recall when she had enjoyed a day more, for she was thoroughly taken with Bethia de Burgh. A woman who did not hide her strengths, Bethia had made her own way in the world, despite hardships and vulnerabilities. Having grown up without a family, with no choice of her home, Sybil felt a kinship to this woman who had spent many years in drudgery to relatives who had tried to break her spirit, to no avail.

Bethia was an example, in more ways than one, Sybil thought, nursing her aching muscles. Accustomed to hard work at the nunnery, nevertheless, Sybil was unused to throwing a knife or wielding a sword. And although the other woman claimed her weapons were lighter than most, Sybil could feel the effects of hefting them in long practice. Still, she welcomed the signs that she was mastering a skill that gave her new power and confidence.

She felt *good*. She had claimed friendships over the years, especially with Elisa, but that quiet young woman had been very different from this outspoken lady who seemed so much like Sybil herself. Again, she knew that sense of being home at last. And although she told herself not to become attached to Bethia or the trappings of a noble life, Sybil realized that no matter what became of this marriage of hers, she was looking at a better future. She was making new friends and gaining new experiences. She was *in the world,* and it was right.

Sinking down upon a chest with a groan, Sybil begged for a rest, though Bethia didn't even appear winded. With a laugh, the lady took a seat upon a settle, dropping her sword beside her with a natural grace. Sybil brushed the curls out of her face and drew in a deep breath as she surveyed their work. The once-elegant solar now looked decidedly odd, its few pieces of furniture pushed against the walls to make room for swordplay, while a straw pallet stood upright, riddled with the marks of knife points.

"It looks a bit different than when I came in," Sybil observed, and the two women dissolved into giggles like girls until a knock at the door interrupted their laughter.

"Yes?" Bethia asked.

"'Tis Gerbold, my lady," answered a voice on the other side of the door.

"Come in, then," Bethia called, and a big knight strode inside, bowing courteously.

"My lady, two priests are here, asking to see the novice from Our Lady of All Sorrows. They are investigating a murder," he said.

Out of long habit, Sybil felt a chill, and even though she told herself that no one, not even the bishop, could touch her now, she glanced nervously at Bethia. A lifetime of bowing to the whims of the hierarchy made her wary of the vast and rarely disputed influence of the Church. But one look at Bethia's calm and steady countenance roused her own faltering courage, and she lifted her chin and squared her shoulders. She was no novice now. She was Lady de Burgh.

"Very well," Bethia said. "Escort them in."

The two priests walked in and bowed low to the women, introducing themselves in low tones as Paulinus and Randal. They wore dark cloaks and appeared bent by their labors, though their faces were unlined.

Bethia acknowledged their greeting with a grand nod. "As lady of Ansquith, I welcome you," she said. "I understand that you wish to speak to my kinswoman, Lady de Burgh, formerly of Our Lady of All Sorrows," she noted, nodding toward Sybil.

At her words, the priests exchanged a startled look, then gaped at Sybil. "Why, uh, congratulations, my lady," Paulinus said, and both bowed again. Sybil felt the breath she had unknowingly been holding release in a low rush.

"We give you good greeting, Lady of Ansquith," the other priest said. "But we must talk privately with your kinswoman. 'Tis Church business of the utmost importance."

"Of a private nature," Randal added.

Bethia's face hardened. "I'm afraid that isn't possible. Gerbold——" she began, only to be cut off by a sudden flurry of activity. The formerly bent and unobtrusive priests straightened, and one of them put a knife to the throat of the knight before he could begin to respond to Bethia's summons.

"I'm afraid I must insist," Randal said, with a

snarl. His hood fell back, revealing a decidedly unholy expression.

"You are no priests, nor are you investigating any murderers, for you are the two who did the deeds," Bethia said, rising to her feet in outrage.

"Stay where you are, lady," the fellow called Paulinus warned. "You aren't the one we want!"

"But 'tis me you're getting. It's one thing to attack a defenseless nun in the dark, quite another to challenge two armed women in their own keep," she said, lifting the discarded sword that lay by her side.

The two killers took one look at Bethia, beautiful, richly gowned and visibly pregnant, and they burst into harsh laughter. Even Sybil, who had seen Bethia wield a weapon, felt a sudden fear, especially for the woman's unborn child. This was her fight, not Bethia's, and she could not live with herself should the lady or her baby be injured. Her fingers closed around a knife that still lay in her lap.

"No!" Sybil shouted, leaping to her feet, blade in hand. She was not sure whether she intended to throw herself or the weapon at the man called Paulinus, but before she could do anything more, Bethia struck. Sybil's cry had distracted both killers, and in the moment their attention was fixed upon her, Bethia lunged.

Sybil, as stunned as the two men, watched in horror as Paulinus doubled over the sword protruding from his stomach. Randal, who had his knife to Gerbold's throat, jerked forward with a shout, only to be struck by both Bethia and the knight, who took advantage of the man's loosened hold.

Sybil could only stare, wide-eyed, as Bethia put her sword to the now-prone villain's throat. "Who sent you?'' she demanded, but the man shuddered and died before he could respond. Overcome by the grisly sight, Sybil sank to her knees and covered her face, her courage faltering as she was wracked by tremors and a longing for the solid strength of her husband.

Perhaps life in the wide world wasn't so wonderful, after all.

The moment they reached Ansquith, Robin knew there was trouble, for even at the gate the guards were in an uproar, waving them through with grim faces. Seized by a fear far stronger than any he had felt these last few days, he did not stop to find out what was happening, but raced onward. He galloped into the bailey, bellowing his rage, Simon at his heels, stricken by a breath-robbing terror that he was too late, that his One was dead.

It was only when Simon pointed out Bethia waving from an upper window that Robin paused long enough to hear her shouts that all was well. He shoved his sword back into its sheath, sweating and shuddering with the force of his relief. It took him a full moment to gasp for air, and when he did so, he glanced over to see Simon, white-faced and tense as well.

Neither brother spoke as they made their way into the hall and up to the solar, where Bethia met them with the tale of what had happened. Robin listened as best he could, but he had eyes only for Sybil, who sat by the window, clutching a cup in strained fingers. He rushed to her side, knelt before her and put aside the hot wine to take her hands in his. They were cold, and he chafed them between his own.

"Are you all right?" he asked, his voice hoarse, his throat thick with emotion.

She nodded, but her expression was bleak, a shadow of her usual confidence, and Robin felt as though his heart were being wrenched from his chest. Better that she toss things at his head than look so lost and alone. She turned to him, finally, and lifted her chin. "I didn't faint," she said, and Robin swallowed against the feelings that swamped him.

She was strong-hearted by nature, but her sheltered life had left her vulnerable, a fact that she didn't care to reveal to anyone. Yet that endeared her further to Robin, especially since she had the power to make him feel weak himself. Seeing her now, like this, he didn't wait for permission, but swept her up in his arms and rose to his feet.

Ignoring her feeble objection, Robin turned to see that they were alone in the solar, but he didn't pause. Carrying her to the chamber that had been set aside for him, he slammed the door behind him with all the fierceness that filled him. Protectiveness, possessiveness, worry, relief, and yes, love, surged through him until he could think of nothing except Sybil. She was the very air he breathed, the very blood that pounded through him, setting him afire.

"I'm not hurt, Robin," she protested, as he laid her down upon the wide bed. "I don't need to lie down."

"Don't you?" he asked, even as he rose over her. "Well, I do."

Cupping her face, he held her still for his mouth and kissed her with all the strength of the feelings in his heart. She gave him no resistance, but answered his ardor with her own, and soon they were rolling across the wide expanse in a tangle of bedding and clothing. Garments were shed in a flurry of haste and with a rip of fabric, but Robin didn't care and Sybil didn't complain. She seemed as possessed as he was, as determined to forget the last hour of cold fear in the blaze of passion. And when, at last, they were both naked, Robin held her tightly, unable to get close enough, unable to stem his frantic need.

He wanted to be inside her. He wanted to shout that he loved her and claim her as his own. But the bargain they had made, the last lingering suspicions of the curse, and his own tumultuous thoughts kept him silent. He would not take that last step in the heat of the moment, stealing from her forever her maidenhood without her will.

Telling himself that this time was for her, Robin leashed his own raging desires and began to stroke and caress her. He touched her everywhere, grazing her smooth skin with his fingers, his lips, his body. He suckled at her breasts and moved lower, laving her belly, dipping his tongue into that indentation and spreading her legs with shaking hands.

He kissed her there, and she made that low noise in her throat, part shock and part delight, which only excited him more, and carefully, he used his fingers, his mouth, his tongue, all of him, to bring her pleasure. Her musical cry was his reward, and he pulled her close, ignoring her whispered concern about his own body, still hard and aching. And he coaxed her to sleep.

But his own thoughts were not so peaceful, churning with a mixture of frustration and rage at what had happened here in his absence, along with other feelings, deeper, stronger, that threatened to upturn his very existence. Robin knew he should be relieved at the day's outcome. No one was hurt; the murderers were killed. And yet, he felt weighted down by some dread that kept making him reach for Sybil. Gradually, he was nearly overcome by the urge to wake her and take her as his own. *Now. Finally.* To forget all else but the bliss he would find in her body. *Now. Forever.*

Finally, he rose from the bed, amazed to see that his hands were shaking. With one last glance at his wife, he forced himself to walk away from temptation and close the door quietly behind him. As usual, when uneasy, he gravitated toward his family, but Simon was not in the hall nor could Robin find him anywhere. Finally, he returned to the solar, where he paced impatiently until his brother appeared, looking slightly disheveled. "What happened to you?" Robin asked.

Simon glared at him until Robin realized the significance of the disappearance of both the lord and lady of the manor. He laughed, then colored, for he didn't care to contemplate Simon's recent activities in any detail. Glancing away, he cleared his throat to mutter an apology, but Simon was already striking back.

"So the murderers are dead. The threat has passed. Now, it remains only for you to dissolve your marriage," Simon said. "When will that be?"

Here at last was the demon Robin wasn't prepared to face as yet, the cause of his dread and source of his discomfort, and he didn't care to hear it brought to life by his brother. He swung round, a denial on his lips, only to see Simon wearing a rather smug expression. He tugged at the neck of his suddenly tight tunic even as he wondered, suspiciously, if his brother was enjoying this.

"I'm not certain. I will have to discuss the matter with my lady, of course," Robin said.

"Of course," said Simon snidely. "But you might want to get the process going. You know how slow these ecclesiastical courts are." He smiled as if in sympathy, but Robin got the impression that he was being baited.

"Now, what reason exactly were you going to be using?" Simon continued in a blithe tone. "I don't think Father would approve if you both claimed that she was coerced into marriage."

Robin shook his head numbly. He didn't want to think about this at all, let alone talk about it.

"What about claiming a prior marriage? Most of those are false, of course, but if you hand out enough coin, you can free yourself from any old tie," Simon said.

Robin bristled, disliking not only the subject, but the tenor of his brother's conversation. He had heard of randy old men who disposed of their first wives that way in order to wed someone younger and more comely, but he didn't like it. Nor would he ever declare himself bound to anyone except Sybil. *Ever.*

"You wouldn't even have to claim the prior contract yourself. I know how much you oppose marriage! All you would have to do is hire someone to claim he married Sybil before you did. That fellow could live with her as man and wife, and then you'd be rid of her, for good," Simon said.

Robin felt his blood boil at the thought. *No one, no man, living or dead, was going to take Sybil from him!* And, if Simon uttered one more word about it, he was going to thrash him. He didn't care if Simon was older or tougher, he had reached his limit, and he swung round to face his brother, his hands balled into fists.

Simon paused as though mulling over the situation, then grinned wickedly. "I have it! There's another reason for annulment that you've never mentioned and one that would suit you perfectly!"

"What?" Robin said, stupidly. Relieved that Simon was changing his tack, he relaxed from his fighter's stance.

"It requires nothing on your part really, and is even quite truthful, considering your situation," Simon said, in a breezy fashion that should have warned Robin of what was coming. "All your lady would have to do is tell the court that you are impotent."

"What?" Robin roared. With a bellow, he lunged for his brother, who dodged away, guffawing loudly. He turned and sucked in a deep draught of air as he considered thrashing or being thrashed. He might feel better for it, but he knew that no amount of pummeling would change the facts. The truth was that he wasn't ready to end the marriage as yet, and Simon knew it.

But Robin wasn't about to concede victory to the big lout. Straightening slowly, he glared at his brother. "We have no proof that these two worked alone. More could come," he said. And it was true. He would not let Sybil go until he was certain that no one posed a threat to her. *For her own protection, of course.* "In fact, I was going to ask you if you have a trustworthy man to send to Wales to find out whatever can be learned about the two killers."

Simon fixed him with a look that told Robin he

well guessed his motives. He heaved a scornful sigh. "Yes, I have a man who can undertake such a mission," he said, at last. "But if you want to keep your wife, you had better tell her so instead of wrapping this marriage of yours in excuses."

Something about Robin was different.

Sybil couldn't put her finger on it, but he seemed nervous somehow. Although she found it hard to believe that the most arrogant man she had ever met was unsure, there was no denying that he wasn't quite himself. For one thing, he had taken her to bed, then insisted she rest without seeing to his own needs, an act that spoke of a selflessness Sybil hadn't expected of him.

And she had done so, the excitement of the past few days, along with some spiced wine and Robin's diligent attentions, allowing her to sleep throughout the evening and night, as well. But when she woke in the morning, eager to take her turn at pleasing him, Robin was gone and the linens cold. She wondered if he had even slept there, an odd circumstance considering that since their marriage he had been all too eager to dally with her.

Then, there was his manner when she met him in the great hall, guarded but overly pleasant. Sybil began to wish he would start arguing with her again, just to prove he was the man she had come to know. When he led her to table in a solicitous fashion, she eyed him with new suspicion. Just what was he up to? Robin's attempts to charm usually meant he wanted something from her. But what?

Sybil found it hard to eat when his gaze lingered on her, only to dart away, all during the midmorning meal. So occupied was she with her speculations that she only listened with half an ear as the men spoke of sending someone to Wales. Robin made it quite clear that he did not think the threat against her had passed with the death of the killers. And his vague allusions to a continuing danger would have worried her, if she weren't so busy wondering just what *he* was planning.

Perhaps he wanted to dissolve the marriage at once, Sybil decided, her heart sinking. Obviously, he hadn't intended to be obligated to her for an indefinite period of time. And she could hardly blame him, yet she bristled at the way he was going about it. Why didn't he just state his intention outright, instead of treating her so gently? Did he think she would break at his departure? Well, she wouldn't, Sybil assured herself, *at least not in his presence.*

After the interminable meal, he drew her away to a corner of the hall, annoying Sybil further. Why couldn't they conduct their conversation in the privacy of their chamber? she wondered. When she saw the eyes of both host and hostess follow them with interest, Sybil was about ready to pick up something and throw it at the man.

He cleared his throat, avoiding her gaze, and Sybil crossed her arms in front of her, tapping her toe impatiently. Whatever he was about, she would have done with it, rather than continue this stalling.

"Sybil, I, uh…"

She stared at him. Hard.

"I'm sorry I wasn't here yesterday when you were in danger," he said. His face darkened, and he seemed himself, at last. "I'm sorry that you were put at risk, but now, I think, you finally see the danger you are in," he added, avoiding her gaze, once more.

Danger she *had* been in, Sybil silently amended. Somehow, she didn't think that an army was out searching for her. If she were a queen, perhaps, but not one of the many so-called princesses in the tiny country of Wales. She might know little about politics, but she suspected that much at least. She tapped her foot, waiting.

"I'm very grateful for Bethia's help, but since it might be a while until we find out more about who's behind this threat to you, I think we ought to return to Baddersly," Robin said.

Sybil lifted her brows. "And?"

"And we must continue to be wary, and, uh, of course, we will still need to maintain the, uh, marriage," Robin said, tugging at the neck of his tunic. "Just for your protection, of course," he added.

Relief flooded Sybil, though she didn't show it. He might be up to something, but at least it wasn't ridding himself of her. Yet. And the knowledge gave her new boldness even as she remembered Bethia's advice. "Has your rash returned?" she asked. Stepping forward, she pulled at the top of his tunic, trying to get a better look at his throat, but he batted her hand away.

"No, I'm fine, really."

Although Sybil had hoped to interest him with her attentions, their closeness was affecting her, as well. Robin's heat washed over her, his scent filled her lungs, and when his fingers closed over hers, her heart pounded out a frantic rhythm of joy that she would stay with him a while longer.

"Why don't we repair to our chamber, so I can have a closer look?" Sybil asked.

Robin's dark liquid eyes widened, and she heard him catch his breath. "When we get home," he said, squeezing her hand, his gaze filled with promise. "When we get home."

Sybil smiled, her confidence returning at this evidence of her power. "Perhaps there is some salve I can...rub on you," she whispered.

Robin cleared his throat. "I'm, uh, sure that can be arranged," he said.

"Good," Sybil said, stepping back at last and smiling up at him. They were together. Robin was himself again, and all was well. For now.

All was well, Robin thought smugly. Despite all his brother's warnings and his own worry that he wouldn't be able to talk Sybil into returning to Baddersly with him, everything had turned out just fine. In fact, now he wondered why he had let Simon bother him, and he felt like laughing when he thought of the difficult night he had spent away from temptation, certain Sybil was going to toss missiles at his head, should he insist upon continuing their relationship. *Just for her own protection, of course.*

He had parted from his brother with an arrogant grin, the future too far away to concern him. And he had undertaken the journey home without fear of attack, for even if the two killers had been carrying out another's orders, it would take some time, if ever, for news of their deaths to reach the Marches. Meanwhile, he was looking forward to the promise of Sybil's hands on him just as soon as they could reach the great chamber.

Surely, his life couldn't possibly improve.

He even managed to ignore Florian's effusive greeting when they dismounted in the bailey at Baddersly. The steward was babbling on, happy at their return, and whispering eagerly about some "surprise" that awaited them in the great hall. Another celebration, no doubt, Robin decided, his good mood allowing him to bear what would likely delay his tryst with his wife a little longer.

But he could afford to be generous with his time, for he had many long days and nights ahead of him not only to dally in bed with Sybil, but to make her his, at last and forever. Such thoughts had him walking a bit stiffly as he led her through the tall doors only to stop in surprise at the sight of two women.

"Just look who's here!" Florian said, throwing his arms up with a flourish.

"Robin, dear!"

Robin heard it, but he didn't believe it. That voice, along with an odd sort of jingling, sent a tingle up his spine, and he blinked in shock as his eyes adjusted to the dimness of the interior, allowing him to recognize the Mistresses l'Estrange in all their glory. A low noise came from his throat, halfway between a grunt and a groan, as horror rooted him to the spot.

"Oh, he's so surprised to see us, just as you said, my dear steward," Cafell said, clapping her hands in apparent glee. She moved forward, and Robin reeled.

"He probably wonders what we're doing here," Armes said, tersely. "Cafell had a premonition," she explained.

"Actually, dear, it was a dream," the shorter sister amended.

"A dream then," Armes said.

"A dream about Vala," Cafell said, leaning close. "I'm afraid it was rather vague. Dreams can be so ethereal, you know. Not as clear as looking into the water," she added in a whisper.

Robin could only gape at them, his tongue cleaved to the roof of his mouth.

"But I was able to discern, at the very least, that she was trying to tell me something about her daughter, and I thought it might prove of value to you. He's on a quest, you know," she said, turning to Sybil. Robin made a strangled sound, his arms flailing blindly to prevent any further speech on this subject.

"Here, sit down, young man, you don't look well," Armes said, pushing him into a chair with an inordinate amount of strength for an old woman.

"A quest?" Sybil asked.

"No, I—" Robin began.

"Now, don't be modest, my lord," Florian said. Always eager for gossip, he gave the old ladies an encouraging smile. "Do tell us all!"

"No!" Robin surged to his feet, seized by a premonition of his own that he had better stop this before it went any further.

"Nonsense," Armes said. "What are you doing?" she asked, as Robin grabbed Sybil's arm to lead her away.

"We have to go," he said, first steering Sybil in the direction of the stairs, then back toward the main doors. Back to the safety of Ansquith.

But Sybil dug in her heels. "Robin de Burgh! What is the matter with you? Let go of me!" she said, giving him a suspicious look.

"Oh, dear! Perhaps it's the curse working on him!" Cafell suggested.

"A curse!" Florian's eyes practically popped from his head in excitement. "What curse?"

"No curse! There is no curse!" Robin said, but his protests fell on deaf ears.

"Why, that's not what you told us," Cafell said, looking at him askance.

"Indeed, you seemed most desperate to avoid the fate of your brothers," Armes added.

"I was drunk," Robin muttered. But no one was listening to him, and he sank into his seat, doomed. Even if he cloistered Sybil in the great chamber, there was no way to prevent the aunts from talking. He might as well try to stop the sunlight. And in Florian, they had found a perfect audience. Soon the entire castle would be abuzz with the story of the accursed curse. He felt like sinking his head into his hands and moaning like a wretch.

"It has to do with marriage," Cafell confided. "Poor, dear Robin is convinced that someone has laid a spell upon the de Burghs since so many of them have wed of late. I must admit I was skeptical at first, but—"

"He wanted us to remove it," Armes cut in, dryly.

Robin could feel eyes on him. No doubt, Florian was barely containing his merriment. And as for Sybil's reaction, he didn't even want to consider it.

"But, of course, we couldn't. Brighid wouldn't like it, and that sort of thing really isn't our specialty," Cafell admitted. "However, he suggested that we recommend a colleague who could do the job for him."

Robin groaned. It all sounded so much worse when recounted by these two.

Armes huffed. "Naturally, it's not something just anyone can do."

"So we suggested some relatives," Cafell said.

"Vala in particular," Armes noted.

"Though we weren't exactly sure what had happened to her," Cafell mused. "We knew only that she married a Welsh prince."

"So he went in search of her," Armes said.

Cafell must have turned to him. "My dear boy, I wish you had let us know what happened. We were quite in a dither as to your future, you know," she said, apparently oblivious to the fact that he was sunk over his knees, head in hand.

"Cafell was concerned," Armes said.

"So I looked—" Cafell began, only to trail off with a nervous laugh. "Rather, I had the dream, you see, and Vala's daughter seemed destined to play some part in it. Your future, I mean."

At that point, Cafell seemed to pause to take a breath, while everyone else began to talk at once, especially Florian. But then Robin heard it, the voice he had been dreading, its steely tone silencing the others.

"Are you saying that Robin set off to find Vala in order to lift a curse he thinks compels his family to marry?" Sybil asked.

"Well, yes. I do believe he feared that he might be next," Cafell confided.

"But, he already is—" Florian began, only to shut his mouth, apparently struck by a rare attack of tact.

"I can imagine how repulsive that thought would be to him," Sybil said, and Robin groaned at the sound of her voice, cool, calm and lethal.

"Yes, the poor boy seemed to clutch at his neck every time he mentioned it, just as if a noose round it was imminent," Cafell said.

Robin groaned again.

"I can just imagine. Indeed, I've seen him do it myself. And here, I thought it was a rash, a rash that needed *tending*," Sybil said.

Flinching, Robin lifted his head at last, the memory of the promised rub returning to taunt him.

"I'm sorry, dear," Cafell said, eyeing Sybil with some curiosity. "I'm afraid we were never introduced."

Sybil smiled graciously, but her expression didn't fool Robin, who moaned in anguish as she spoke to her eager audience.

"I'm Robin's wife."

Chapter Sixteen

Sybil couldn't believe it. She didn't know which was worse, that a grown man could believe in things like marriage curses, or that by his own bumbling, he had ended up in the very predicament he wanted to avoid at all costs. "What an oaf! What an idiot! What a lout!" Sybil chanted aloud, as she packed her few belongings.

In her absence, they had arrived from the nunnery, but now they could just go right back, as could she, Sybil decided, only to pause, swallowing hard against the lump in her throat that seemed to encompass her chest as well, a great, fat lump of hurt where her heart had lodged. No, she wouldn't slink back to the nunnery, tail between her legs; she would go somewhere else, anywhere else. Bethia would take her in, or perhaps the Mistresses l'Estrange, who were bound to her by blood, not some fake alliance.

"Sybil. Let me in."

She glanced up, unsurprised to hear the great, oafish lout himself at the door of the great chamber, demanding entrance. "Go away!" she shouted.

"Sybil, open this door or I'll rend it asunder.

What's more, I'll wrench each piece of rock from the walls and destroy the whole wretched castle, if I have to!'' Robin bellowed.

Heaving a loud and hearty sigh, Sybil threw down her burdens and strode to the worn wood, which she unbarred. Then, without a glance in the direction of her temporary husband, she returned to her task.

''I'm leaving, so you can dissolve this distasteful union,'' Sybil said, over her shoulder. ''Indeed, I'm shocked that you even went through with it, considering your *rash*. Your guilt must have weighed heavily upon you.''

''Of course, I felt guilty, but it wasn't that. I felt—'' Robin began.

''I know. *Responsible*,'' Sybil said bitterly. Had she really imagined that anything else drove this marriage? Duty, protection, *lust* maybe, but certainly not affection. Bethia had been mistaken, and Sybil had joined in, imputing her own motives to a man who possessed no tender emotions.

''Yes, but—'' Robin began.

But Sybil cut him off. ''It really doesn't matter,'' she assured him. She had her pride, and she wanted no pity from Robin de Burgh. Nor did she care to hear any long, involved explanations of his brilliant reasoning. The man was an idiot!

''But it's not as they say,'' Robin protested, and to Sybil's surprise, he had the audacity to reach out to grip her arms.

''Let me go,'' she demanded in a low, even tone, but he only turned her around to face him. Although she considered implementing some of the disabling tricks that Bethia had taught her, Sybil decided against fighting him, for he just might win, and then where would she be? Flat on her back, as usual, she thought, flushing hotly. Instead, she stood still and tried not to look at him. However, he was so close, it was unavoidable, so she focused on a spot on his tunic and tried to convince herself to hate him even though his touch roused her body and heart to a painful yearning.

"I was drunk when I came up with that stupid notion," he said.

That pathetic excuse made Sybil lift her head to glare at him. "And you managed to ride all the way to Wales in this stupor?" she asked.

"No, but—"

Angry again, she tried to shrug off his hold. "Let me go!" she shouted.

"Look, throw something at me. Strike me, if you will, but I can't let you go. I can't," he repeated, his voice hoarse, his dark eyes stark with something raw and desperate.

His tone halted her struggles, and Sybil searched his gaze, hardly daring to hope. "Why?" she asked.

"Because," Robin answered. Turning his head, he drew in a great, ragged breath. "Because it's not safe. I have to protect you."

With a violent lurch, Sybil pushed him away, disappointment swamping her. He didn't care for her, but he wasn't going to let her leave, either, she realized with sickening clarity. "Protect me then, but stay out of my bed!" she cried.

"I can't," Robin whispered in a strangled voice, as though tortured.

But Sybil had no sympathy for him. "You claim that honor is so important to you. Then, act honorably! Because if you don't, I'll hie myself to the cloister, where you'll never be able to touch me!''

Her empty threat must have convinced him because he looked sorely pained. Indeed, his expression reminded her of a spoiled boy being refused his treat, a mixture of frustration, anger and denial. "All right," he muttered. "But I'll stay here in this room with you. *For your protection.* Besides, we need to keep up appearances. No one can know this isn't a real marriage.''

Sybil laughed, a bitter, unhappy sound. "And how do you expect to do that while the hall buzzes with the news that the Mistresses l'Estrange brought?''

"I don't care what those two say. I don't care what anyone says. You're my wife," Robin insisted, through gritted teeth. And his manner was so convincing that Sybil might have believed it herself, if she didn't know just exactly what Robin de Burgh thought of marriage.

Robin sat in the corner of the hall, sunk in gloom, wondering what he had ever done to deserve his fate. Unfortunately, the answer came to him readily enough, and he rued the day he had come up with the notion of a curse on the de Burghs. After all, what kind of being, wizard or witch or whatever, would have the power to work such magic? And why, if they held a grudge against the de Burghs, would they force weddings on the family? Now that Robin thought about it at great length, such a spell didn't seem like much of a punishment. And to what end? A bunch of new de Burghs!

Robin shook his head. He supposed the whole idea was pretty stupid. At least, that's the conclusion he had reached after plenty of contemplation. And he'd certainly had time for contemplation as one week of marriage turned into another and another, while his wife continued to avoid him.

Oh, she seemed to be enjoying herself well enough, Robin thought as he watched her move around the hall with a heart-stopping grace, spreading warmth to everyone from the aunts to Florian down to the meanest of servants. *Everyone except him.* He didn't care much for that. Jealousy flared within him, hot and urgent, whenever she even smiled at someone else, and telling himself that it was just the curse didn't work anymore. *Nothing worked.*

Each night he tossed and turned on a pallet by the door of his own chamber, ostensibly guarding it, when he wanted nothing more than to crawl into his rightful bed beside Sybil. He burned, not only with the desire to touch her, but with the need to simply hold her, her slender body tucked against him in some kind of silent communion. He *needed* her and not just glimpses at a distance, but with him, body and soul.

He was miserable, more miserable than when any of his brothers had married and left home, more miserable than when his father had taken a new wife, disrupting the last of their bachelorhood, more miserable even than after the death of the mother he didn't really remember. Robin leaned back against the wall with a sigh. He hadn't thought of *that* in years, and he tried and failed to capture much more than the faint whiff of flowers, of warmth, of love.

What he did recall was clinging to his older brothers. Too young at the time to discern his own need, perhaps he had clung a little too tightly. Nicholas had been a newborn, Reynold a toddler and already lost in his own world, so Robin had turned to his elders. He had jumped into a rough-and-tumble society that held little tenderness, softness, or nurturing. And for long years since, he had disdained such things as unnecessary. Only now, with the need for Sybil pulsing through him like the flow of his own blood, could he finally admit that perhaps something had been missing.

He had a wonderful family, and he was grateful for it beyond measure, but at last he acknowledged, if only to himself, that he had missed his mother and the presence of a woman in his life. He realized that the loss had changed him, that none of the pranks and jests and carefree behavior he had adopted had ever quite filled a certain emptiness at the very core of him.

But Sybil could.

Robin knew it, with a certainty that he could claim for little else, and he lifted his head, searching the hall for her until his gaze lighted upon her, arrested. She was sitting on one of the long benches next to a young serving woman, holding a small child on her lap. And at the sight of her, leaning close, her face wreathed in smiles, Robin was seized by a hunger so great that it stole his breath.

His chest hurt as he watched her whisper and coo to the babe, and at that moment he wanted nothing more than to see her round with his child, to create his own family. For once in his life, he didn't equate the word with his siblings, but with sons and daughters yet unborn. Dragging in a deep, ragged draught of air, Robin realized the truth. He didn't want to return to his childhood, where the last, vague memories of his mother lay. And even if he could go live with all his brothers in some kind of bachelor reunion, he wouldn't. He would rather make a life with Sybil.

Simon was right. People grow and want different things, and until it hits you, you don't realize the strength of that desire. Robin decided that he owed his brothers an apology, for he could see now that part of his unhappiness sprang from jealousy at what his brothers had. When he saw Geoffrey and Dunstan with their children, he had felt rejected, set aside, as well as envious that they had found something they valued more than life at Campion. No matter how he had disdained them, he had coveted their joys, though he didn't know it and certainly didn't know how to gain them for himself.

But now he did.

He would make a good father, Robin thought, choking back emotion. He would play with his children and laugh with them, a more approachable sire than the omnipotent Campion, but, he hoped, wise as well. Only, right now he didn't feel so wise. He felt incredibly stupid.

With a groan, Robin scrubbed his hand over his face as he remembered Reynold's reaction to his pet theory of the curse. And Simon's. No wonder they had thought him mad. What had possessed him to come up with such a scheme? When he thought of the death of Elisa and the danger to Sybil, he felt even worse.

"What's the matter, dear?" A soft voice at his elbow was accompanied by a gentle jingle, and Robin glanced up to see Cafell, concern wrinkling her forehead.

Robin shook his head. "'Tis the whole business of the curse. How could I have been such a fool? How could you have encouraged me?'' he asked, with a groan.

She reached out to pat his arm, the tiny bells on her sleeve ringing softly. ''Now, now. If you had not gone in search of your destiny, how would you have found it?'' she asked.

Robin paused, dumbfounded. He usually didn't waste his time considering such questions, for philosophy was Geoffrey's forte, but now he wondered. If not for his foolish quest, what, indeed, would have taken him to My Lady of All Sorrows? Or even to the village nearby? How would he have ever met a young novice hidden away in the nunnery? Panic seized him at the thought that he might never have found Sybil, never have looked upon her or touched her or held her close.

''See? You must do what you must do,'' Cafell said. ''And sometimes a man's route takes many twists and turns.'' Robin listened in awe until he realized she was basically a soothsayer, and he didn't even want to know his future. He could envision it well enough without any magical intervention. At some point, the threat to Sybil would pass, and he would lose her. And he would spend the rest of his life wallowing in his loss.

Not a pleasant fate.

''But 'tis up to you, dear, which path to tread,'' Cafell said. ''You must make your own future,'' she added, gently, with a nod toward Sybil.

Robin hesitated, too bleak to rouse himself, and the old woman leaned close. ''You love her, don't you?'' she asked.

And, suddenly, Robin felt as though he had been struck upon the head, as he had been often enough during a rousing practice of arms or a brawl with his brothers. Whether it was caused by Cafell or his own awakening, Robin's ears rang with the force of the blow. *Of course, he loved her.* And it was no trick of a curse or anything else. *He loved his wife.* And all he could think was: what the devil was he doing? Why was he trying to avoid the very thing that would save him?

He looked across at the hall at Sybil, and he knew what he must do.

Sybil watched the baby on her lap blow bubbles, and she felt a wonder and delight that she had rarely known. She had had few chances to hold babies at the nunnery, and she was discovering just as much about this one as the little fellow was learning about her. The mother sat by, enjoying the last of the mid-morning meal, and giving the child dollops of honey.

"Oh, isn't he a love?" A soft voice, accompanied by a tinkling made Sybil turn to see one of the l'Estranges leaning close, and she nodded happily. "But his hands are all sticky," Cafell exclaimed. "Armes, fetch a bowl of water, won't you?"

"I'll get it, Mistress," the child's mother said, but Cafell shooed her away.

"Freshen yourself up. We'll take care of the little one."

And, indeed, before Sybil could barely draw a breath, Armes had placed a basin in front of her, but it wasn't one of those usually used for washing before eating. "What an odd bowl," Sybil said, pausing to study the wide vessel. It appeared to be made of some kind of beaten metal and was far larger than they needed, but what did these ladies know of babies? Probably no more than Sybil herself.

She moved the child closer and tried to dip his hands in, but as soon as he touched the water, he set up a merry splashing and laughing. Sybil could only join in, as droplets flew about. Then she reached out to push the bowl away only to catch sight of her reflection there. She paused, staring, at the picture of herself and the child—and someone else. Who was that behind them? Robin? Sybil swung her head round indignantly, but he wasn't there. In fact, no one stood near her.

Blinking, Sybil looked back into the basin, where the eerie, unreal reflection floated on the now-still liquid, Robin clearly recognizable to her eyes. She watched in fascination as the figures began to move, Robin leaning close to lift the baby, and she realized that it wasn't the blond child on her lap that he held, but a dark-haired boy, the very image of himself. Sybil knew the child's identity immediately, as well as a sharp sense of yearning for him—and for his father.

A small sound escaped her lips when, as if bearing out her most secret desires, the three images embraced as a family. And then, it all faded away, until she was staring at nothing except clear water filling the beaten bowl. Gasping, half in startlement and half in loss, Sybil swung round again, but Robin still was not there. The baby's mother bent near, taking her child with a smile, and Sybil felt an ache of emptiness even as she gave him up.

"Did you see something, dear?" The voice, near and unexpected, startled her, and Sybil whirled in surprise to see Cafell at her elbow. Confused and shaken, she shook her head in answer to the strange query.

"No?" Cafell asked, as if she didn't believe Sybil's denial. "Well, that is too bad, really. Your mother was so talented! And with that l'Estrange blood running in your veins, I was so sure you would catch a glimpse of the future. Your future," she added.

Sybil gaped at the little old lady who smiled at her just as though she were discussing the weather and not something wholly bizarre. She had heard whispers since the arrival of the sisters, rumors of healing and special powers associated with their name, but Sybil hadn't taken any note of such nonsense.

"Of course, some don't want to see, especially if they are not inclined toward their fate," Armes noted as she retrieved the strange bowl from its place on the table.

"Still, I find it always helpful to gain some understanding of one's destiny, perhaps just to nudge it a little," Cafell said, with a wink.

Sybil could only gape after them as they wandered away, chatting blithely of things she had never before considered possible. How could anyone look into the future? Still unable to accept her own murky past as a Welsh princess, she was hardly ready to call herself a soothsayer, as well. But there was no denying she had seen *something*. Had the l'Estranges put it there? She shook her head, for the two little old ladies didn't seem capable of such a feat. Indeed, Cafell was uncommonly forgetful.

Perhaps the bowl itself held the key, Sybil mused. Although she had been brought up to believe in nothing except the doctrine of the Church, the servants and villagers believed in enchanted objects and lucky talismans. And, of course, relics of the saints were well prized by all. Sybil frowned, ready to dismiss the entire episode as a figment of her imagination, or, more likely, her own most hidden longing, one she hadn't even admitted to herself. For that is exactly what she had seen: she and Robin and their child together, a totally impossible vision when her marriage was only a sham, soon to be annulled by a man who despised the union.

And yet, despite knowing all that, Sybil felt a stirring of hope for the first time since she had learned of Robin's so-called quest. Automatically, her head turned toward where he spent most of his time, slumped in the corner like a spoiled child deprived of his will. But he wasn't wearing his usual sulky expression. Instead, he was staring at her with such intensity that it nearly took her breath away. And against all her best sense, she trembled, her heart began pumping and she burned with the familiar need for him, stronger and deeper than ever before.

As she had at the vision trapped in the water, Sybil could do nothing but stare at her husband as he rose to his feet and began moving toward her. She tried to gather her resources, but suddenly, she found it difficult to remember just why she was so angry with him. As he walked across the tiles, she didn't see a spoiled boy, but a grown man who knew what he wanted. And he wanted her. Sybil saw it as surely as she saw him. But how? And how much?

As he neared her, Sybil stood as well, and the entire hall, with its vast elegance and the people lingering after the meal faded as if all were unreal, and only Robin, approaching her with sure intent, was the true reflection. Sybil didn't know exactly why she left her seat, perhaps with a thought to avoiding him, but it was not her way to run and hide, and so she faced him, as if facing her very future.

Certainly, it was too late to avoid him, for he was before her, tall and handsome and beloved, in a way no other man could ever hope to be, affecting her as no one ever had before or ever would again. He halted, so close that she could reach out and touch him, and the look in his dark liquid eyes made her forget all else. She had the unruly sensation that should he sweep her off her feet and take her to bed, she would do naught to stop him.

Sybil had no idea what she was expecting, perhaps that very action, but certainly not the words he spoke. "I've been a fool," he said.

The baldness of the statement jarred her, but what had she been hoping for, an avowal of love? "Yes," she said, in answer to her own silly fancies, as well as his pronouncement.

"And in being such a fool, I caused Elisa's death and put you in danger," Robin said.

Despite her own disappointment, Sybil rose to his defense. "You did not cause Elisa's death. There are far too many circumstances involved for you to claim such omnipotence," she replied. Then she drew a deep breath. "As for me, if you had never asked about me, where would I be? Withering away at the nunnery, day by day, hour by hour, without the impetus to change my life. You gave that to me. And I will always be grateful," she said, and she realized it was the truth.

He reached for her, and Sybil knew she was lost, but before he could claim her, without one word of the affection she craved, a noise erupted at the tall doors to the hall. She turned her head to see Simon enter with another man.

"Robin!" he called. "I was headed to Baddersly and met this messenger on the road. He has a summons for you," he added, his face grim.

A summons? Sybil glanced up to Robin in question, but he shook his head and turned away. "Let us repair to the solar then, to see this missive," he said. Before Sybil could protest, he, his brother and the stranger were heading to the steps for a conference. And for a woman who claimed no presentiment of the future, she felt an ominous sensation of dread.

Chapter Seventeen

Robin blinked down at the parchment in his hand, the words swimming before his eyes, then stared up at his brother. "'Tis a summons to the ecclesiastical court, demanding an annulment of my marriage," he said in a hoarse croak.

"What?" Simon bellowed.

Robin glanced over the rest of the page even as he continued speaking. "They are claiming Sybil had a prior contract to marry, a binding betrothal arranged at birth, to a prince of Wales." His blood thundering at the very idea, Robin went on, his voice rising. "They claim that it has precedence over the *clandestine union* alleged by one Robin de Burgh, *who did forcefully and without consent or permission of the abbess, steal the novice known as Sybil from Our Lady of All Sorrows nunnery.*"

Robin broke off to deny that charge most vehemently. "'Twas no clandestine union, but one held in public and with the participation of a priest. And how dare they say that I stole her from the nunnery?" he demanded.

Simon grabbed the missive from his hand and

looked it over, only to snort in outrage. "'Tis a slew of lies. But to what purpose?"

"To take her away from me, of course!" Robin said. The words ripped through him like the point of a blade, but the pain that accompanied them was far more agonizing than any visible wound.

"The Marcher lords can't be behind it, then," Simon said. "Not one of them would dare challenge the de Burghs."

"Aye. 'Tis the Welsh. Her relatives," Robin muttered through the growing thickness in his throat. Panic beat at his ribs, robbing him of breath, and he sucked in a deep draught only to blow it out as Simon smacked him hard on the back.

"Obviously, they don't know who they're dealing with," his brother said. Robin realized the blow was Simon's idea of comfort, but he took no cheer from it until he looked into his brother's face, grim but determined. His eyes held an evil glint as he spoke once more, his voice rife with the promise of retribution.

"It's time to call for reinforcements."

By the time Robin and Simon had conferred at length and sent out their own messengers, it was late afternoon and Sybil was no longer in the hall. Seized by a growing desperation to seek her out, to prove to himself that she remained his, now and forever, Robin strode through Baddersly until, at last he found her in the great chamber, surrounded by sewing. And when he saw one of his own tunics among her mending, he swallowed hard. Some of the stark emotion must have shown on his face, for she looked up with an expression of concern.

"What is it?" she said.

Robin barred the door, and then moved forward, toward where she knelt upon the tiles. "They have made their move," he said. "And 'tis a cowardly one."

"Who? My...enemies?" Sybil asked.

"Aye," Robin said with a nod. "'Tis your relatives, for none among the English would challenge a de Burgh openly. Intrigues are not uncommon at court and among the great landowners, certainly the Marcher lords whom I originally suspected, but none of them would do this." He tossed the hated missive into her lap.

"What is it?"

"'Tis a call to court, not the king's court, but an ecclesiastical court. In their efforts to wrest you away, they are now claiming our marriage invalid."

Sybil paled, and Robin flinched, wishing there was some way he could spare her all this. "How?" she asked.

"They say that you were already contracted to marry, an arrangement made at your birth with another of the great lines of Wales," Robin muttered, though the words were hard to voice. His own feelings surged again, hot and powerful, at the thought of his wife with another.

Sybil made a dismissive sound that would have drawn a smile from him, had the situation not been so serious. "How absurd! They can't get away with this, can they?" she said.

Falling to his knees before her, Robin took her by the shoulders, savoring the first touch of her that he had known in long, endless days. "I won't give you up," he said, with grim determination. "Not now, not ever."

Sybil eyed him somberly. "But what of your plans for annulling the marriage?"

"There will be no annulment," Robin said, and he meant it.

His wife appeared unconvinced, for she studied him with open speculation. "And what about the curse?" she asked.

Robin shook his head. "A foolish notion, born of jealousy for a life I did not have. But I won't deny it played its part, for it brought me to you," he said.

"And if—"

Afraid of what she was going to say, Robin didn't let her finish. "No one will ever take you away from me," he repeated, tightening his grip. *"No one. Ever."* He had never been more serious in his life. Couldn't she see it? Couldn't she forgive his past foolishness?

Her blue gaze met his, direct and challenging. "Why?" she demanded.

"Because you are *mine,*" Robin said, in a harsh voice. And, looking into her eyes, he knew that finally he would prove it. He would mark her as his own, *now and always,* and he bent his head to seal the promise.

The moment his lips met hers, Robin felt the heat pulse between them and the excitement dance in his veins, along with a new poignancy, a rich, deeper current that sprang from his love. This woman was the One destined for him, and though he had married her in haste, with a host of excuses, he intended to keep his vows always. Drawing in a shaky breath, Robin kissed her long and deep, putting everything he felt into the merging of their lips, hoping that she could tell what was in his heart.

When she broke away, he nearly cried out, struck by a new kind of fear. It wasn't the heart-stopping terror he had known when Sybil was endangered, but a kind of soul-wrenching wariness that, after all this time, he would lose her, not because of his own mistakes, but because of her feelings—or lack thereof. It seemed he had been struggling with his emotions since their first meeting, but what of Sybil? What if she didn't share his ardor? In the last few weeks, she certainly had kept her distance. She hadn't seemed to miss their dallying—or even his company.

Robin stared down at her, holding his breath, preparing himself for the worst, though he was not quite sure how he would manage to survive should she spurn him. But she only smiled up at him, her fingers drifting up to caress his cheek and dip into his hair.

"And what of your vaunted honor, Robin de Burgh?" she asked. For a moment, he blinked, unsure of her meaning, until he realized she referred to his promise not to touch her. Then, he let out his breath in a snort. He had no intention of keeping that particular vow any longer.

"Honor has nothing to do with this," he muttered, seizing her again in a fierce grasp, and he heard her laugh against his mouth, a sound of delight that filled his heart with joy. He lifted her in his arms even as he kissed her, carrying her to the bed with sure intent. And there, in the gathering twilight, he stripped her of her clothing, while she eagerly tugged at his own.

And when they were finally blissfully naked, he came over her, reveling in the sight of her fiery curls spread across his pillow, the touch of her body against his own, and the heady scent that spoke of her growing desire. In their times together, Robin had come to know her body, and so he wooed her maiden's flesh with his hands and his mouth, with the press of his thigh, the stroke of his tongue and the scrape of his teeth. And when she cried out in pleasure, he kept pushing her to new heights, until he heard her again and again, and she finally lay prone against the linens, gasping for breath.

Only then did he mount her, spreading her legs and finding the slick center of her ready for him. At the very first touch, he jerked, already overcome with need, his long wait over. And when he thrust himself deep, he was hardly aware of the words that sprang to his lips.

"I love you!" he shouted, as he spilled himself inside the hot, welcoming haven of her body.

Robin muttered her name like a prayer as he slumped over her, panting and shuddering in the final throes of passion. And when, eventually, he was able to move, he drew her into his embrace and looked into her face, just so there could be no misunderstanding between them this time, and said it again.

"I love you," he whispered. "You are my wife, not just for now, but forever, *my One,* my Lady de Burgh."

The weeks until court passed far too swiftly. At last, Robin had Sybil in his life and his bed, but the shadow of the summons hung over everything he did. His passion was filled with a new poignancy at the thought that the love he had struggled so hard to acknowledge might be snatched away from him.

At first, he had been determined to take Sybil

somewhere, anywhere they could be safe, but his wife, exhibiting that annoying rebelliousness of hers, had refused to run away. Simon, too, had advised him against leaving, warning of the vast reach of the Church beyond even the shores of Britain. Of course, it was easy for Simon to counsel compliance, for he was still convinced that nothing would come of the complaint. He claimed that nonappearance could only make matters worse, causing affront to the presiding bishop.

For his part, Robin didn't care to trust his future to the opinion of one of the least educated of his siblings, but he had received a communication from Geoffrey that had reassured him somewhat. Although claiming to know little of Welsh law, Geoff didn't see how a betrothal could supercede a marriage when the Church decreed that a woman should go willingly to her husband. Presumably, a baby could hardly be expected to make such a choice, let alone an informed one.

Still, the seriousness of the charge and the ramifications of a misjudgment made Robin's heart pound and his gut churn. He was a man of action, good with weapons and quick of mind and body, and he became more and more frustrated by his inability to act. For the first time in his life, he felt relatively powerless against his enemies, and he did not care for the sensation.

He grew so tense over the final few days that even Sybil's frequent searches for rashes, performed with plenty of salve, could not relax him. He knew, now, why he had fought so hard against falling in love, for it had the power to make a strong man weak, to strip him raw, aye, even to break him completely.

Yet when the fateful day dawned, Robin was gripped by a preternatural calm. Perhaps it bespoke his heritage from the rarely ruffled Earl of Campion, but he could not claim his father's skill at diplomacy. Indeed, part of his composure came from his certainty that no matter what the bishop might rule, no matter what anyone might say, Sybil belonged to him, and he would protect her with his life.

Robin had not shared the possibility of bloodshed with Simon, but he was glad his warrior brother was beside him. However, he might have wished for a little more quiet from his normally taciturn sibling, who was spouting his views to Bethia and Sybil as they rode toward the court.

"No cleric in his right mind is going to rule against the de Burghs, especially in something as minor as this," Simon asserted, and Robin winced at his description of the complaint. *Minor* was not exactly the word he would have used, but considering that the ecclesiastical cases receiving the most attention were those involving disputes over Church lands, he supposed the marriage of one couple was trifling in comparison.

"Not only is Campion one of the most powerful landowners in the country, but he contributes plenty to the Church's coffers," Simon said. "And he's hosted visits from some of those highest up in the hierarchy."

For once, Robin smiled as he recalled entertaining some of those men. "Remember that fat fellow who ate so much we thought he was going to pop?" he asked, cheered by Simon's guffaw.

"Just so!" Simon said. "They've eaten at his table and shared his hospitality. And if I know our father, he's already put a word in with these men that has filtered down to whoever is going to preside over this court, just in case that fellow has other ideas."

"You mean ideas that were bought and paid for," said Bethia, her voice rife with criticism.

"Are you saying the courts are corrupt?" Sybil asked.

Bethia sighed. "Perhaps not all, but in this case, I imagine that your relatives crossed someone's palm with coin in order to gain this hearing."

Sybil looked alarmed. "And what if they press more coin on the bishop?" she asked.

Simon snorted. "From what I've heard, they'll be needing that coin in their dispute with Edward, not for some nobody princess everyone else has forgotten."

Bethia made a noise of disapproval, and Simon glanced toward her. "What? Oh. Beg pardon, Sybil," he said, with a grunt. "And, anyway, even if he has taken a bribe, when he received word from his superior, whoever's in charge will adjust his thinking. Believe me, he'll dismiss the whole thing, especially after he's seen the witnesses," Simon said, with a rather evil-looking grin.

"What witnesses?" Sybil asked.

Simon smiled again, and Robin was glad someone was heartened by this whole wretched experience. "I'm guessing the de Burghs can muster up a few. Plus, the l'Estranges, being relatives of yours, will add credence to our position," Simon said.

"And just what is that position?" Sybil asked.

"That the Welsh have no claim on you. And, if things look bad, we can always declare that you two were betrothed long ago," Simon added.

Sybil blinked. "Are you saying that the de Burghs are planning to lie?"

Bethia glared at her husband. "Of course not! But I hardly think a few exaggerations would be bad, considering your opponents are murderers who will gladly perjure themselves in order to do more foul deeds."

"As knights, we have vowed to protect the weak, as well as all women," Simon said, gruffly. Then, a new, fell, light shone in his gray eyes. "And as de Burghs, we will do what it takes to protect our own."

Silently, Robin agreed. He couldn't vouch for anyone else, but he knew just what he was willing to do, and he faced the approach of the nunnery's gate with grim determination. The tall trees bobbed in the wind, as if in greeting, and Robin realized just how familiar the place had become to him. For Sybil especially, this visit marked an ill one to what had been her home for so many years. However, pleas relating to the episcopal laws were to be heard in the shire in question, and so the bishop had traveled here to preside over the case.

Apparently, they were among the last to arrive, for they could hardly press into the hall. Startled by the sight of so many people, Robin tightened his arm protectively around Sybil as he cursed such a spectacle. The nuns were there, of course, but others, too, apparently had come to gape at what didn't concern them. Already, Robin felt an animosity toward the judge who had allowed such idlers entrance.

"Here, now! I say, who are all these people?" A voice behind him echoed Robin's thoughts, and he turned in surprise to recognize the robes of a churchman, and, indeed, the bishop himself as the portly fellow who once had dined at Campion. In the years since that visit, he had not grown any smaller, and thus he was having great difficulty getting through the crowd. His companion, a tall, thin cleric, answered as Robin gaped.

"They've been lining up since dawn—nuns, servants, farm workers, villeins, villagers and servants, all in support of the couple."

"The couple?" the bishop echoed.

"Yes, my lord, the de Burghs. Lord Robin and Lady Sybil. Many are witnesses, as most of the nuns are, here to claim that the Lady Sybil was never betrothed to anyone, to their knowledge." He looked down at a piece of parchment in his hand. "All except one. I believe a nun named Maud is a witness for those lodging the complaint."

The bishop made a rumbling sound. "I've never seen anything like it in my life!" He squinted and pointed a pudgy finger near the front of the hall, where benches were lined up facing northward. "Why, that looks like a de Burgh there. Is that the boy?"

The cleric glanced at a group of cloaked figures. "No. Though I've only seen them all a few times, I do believe that is Lord Nicholas de Burgh. And Lord Reynold de Burgh. And Lord Geoffrey de Burgh." He paused to crane his neck, and Robin felt a warmth fill him that had nothing to do with the close confines of the hall.

Indeed, Robin hardly noticed when Simon and Bethia walked past him to take their places with the family. *His family.* This, he realized at last, was the real test of blood, for no matter where they might be in the wide world, each one of them could be counted upon to lend their aid and support.

"See, there is the Lord of Wessex. And isn't that the Earl of Campion himself, with his new lady?" the cleric asked. "'Tis said he rarely ventures beyond his stronghold of Campion Castle."

"I can see why," said the bishop, with a glance at Robin's new stepmother. "Quite the virile fellow, isn't he?"

"Apparently so, my lord," answered the cleric. "Of course, they are all here as witnesses for the defendants, Lord Robin and Lady Sybil, as are their wives, and, ah, yes, some relatives of Lady Sybil's, the Mistresses l'Estrange."

The bishop frowned, his forehead puckering. "And just who amongst all these people is here on the behalf of the complainant?" he asked.

The cleric looked down at his parchment. "Well, as I said, the nun Maud, and the man who filed the plea, a gentleman representing Lady Sybil's Welsh relations. I'm afraid I can't quite pronounce the name."

"Well, where is he?" the bishop asked.

The cleric surveyed the hall. "Why he was here not long ago. I saw him right after the de Burghs came in."

"Perhaps he thought better of taking on the entire family," the judge said in a dry tone.

The cleric turned round and round until he stopped to stare out one of the narrow windows. "Why, there he is!" the fellow exclaimed.

Robin, too, gazed out the window only to see a couple of fast-moving horses headed away from the nunnery.

"Why, where on earth do you suppose he is going?" the cleric asked the bishop with a puzzled frown.

The bishop did not appear one bit perplexed. "I'd say, my boy, that the man took one look at the de Burghs, turned tail and fled." With that pronouncement, he began to move determinedly through the crowd to stand at the front of the hall.

"My good people! Quiet please!" the bishop said, holding up his hands to call for order. A hush fell over the place at once as all leaned forward, eager for the proceedings to begin.

"Since the alleged betrothal in this case was contracted by the Welsh, and our good sovereign Edward is now at war with that country, and since those who put forward the suit have fled in the face of the might of the English, I hereby dismiss this complaint, now and forever, as baseless."

The entire hall erupted in a cheering that Robin would remember until the day he died. And suddenly, he and Sybil were jostled forward, to the head of the crowd, where the bishop himself welcomed them heartily, to the eruption of more cheers and shouts of goodwill. Among the well-wishers was the abbess herself, who congratulated them with a serene smile.

"I am well pleased, though I admit I had hoped for as much," she said.

"I am sorry I left so abruptly, without thanking you for all you and the nuns have done for me. You must have been shocked when you received my news," Sybil said.

"Oh, I wasn't a bit surprised to hear of your marriage. I have long thought you destined for a life outside these walls. And when you took such a... How shall I describe it? When you took such a sudden aversion to Lord de Burgh, I suspected something else might lie behind it,'' the abbess said, causing Sybil to blush.

''And when Lord de Burgh tried to discharge you from his association because he didn't trust himself with you, I deduced that the attraction was mutual,'' the abbess added.

Now Robin flushed as well, only too glad when any further commentary on his courtship was interrupted by Simon, who slapped him on the back so hard he nearly swallowed his tongue.

''Well, what did I tell you?'' Simon asked, with a smug smile.

''You were right,'' Robin admitted. ''And for once, I'm glad of it,'' he added, with an answering grin.

''So, we're all finished here? I think everyone would like to go to Baddersly to celebrate the verdict,'' Simon said.

Robin's gaze fell upon the remaining witness for the enemy, the only one in the room who looked decidedly displeased. ''Not quite,'' he said.

With grim intent, he approached the bishop, who seemed to be enjoying an animated conversation with Campion and his wife, especially Campion's wife. ''Excuse me,'' Robin said. ''But I see that one of those who would foment trouble between the de Burghs and the Church remains here, and I must point out to you, that as a member of this order, she is wholly untrustworthy,'' he said, inclining his head to where Maud glowered.

''Indeed, as coroner, I would like to lodge a formal complaint against this nun, who did consort with the men who murdered the nun Elisa and the woman

Gwerful, and who attacked my wife. I have a witness, a villager, perhaps more, who can place them together.''

With a frown, the bishop turned toward Maud. ''You there, what is your name?'' he asked.

''Maud, my lord,'' the nun answered, rising to her feet with what Robin supposed was an attempt at a conciliatory expression. To him, it looked more like the results of a bad case of indigestion.

''Maud, you have had a serious charge levied against you, that you consorted with murderers and kept information from the coroner investigating the case.''

Maud's considerable tail grew puffy indeed, but to no avail. She sputtered and shrieked, her deferential demeanor quickly replaced by her usual spiteful attitude, which did little to endear her to the bishop. Indeed, when Robin left, he was enjoying the prospect of Maud cloistered at a very remote location, where she would have little to do with her fellow nuns, let alone outsiders.

Personally, he had suggested a leper colony, but he knew he couldn't expect to get *everything* he desired.

Sybil had never heard so many loud voices in her life. Having been raised in the quiet of the nunnery, she was overwhelmed by the shouts erupting from more handsome men than she had ever seen together in one place. And the displays of affection astonished her, as well. These great knights, warriors all, slapped each other's backs, threw themselves into rough embraces and hugged their father without a qualm. The women were even more loving. Indeed, Sybil found it a bit difficult to watch her husband receive more than his share of hugs and kisses from the female contingent of the de Burgh family.

"I hope you've managed to settle this one down," a petite, dark-haired woman said. Sybil was having a hard time keeping everyone straight, but she thought it was Marion, who shook her head with a smile. "He was always up to such tricks! Why, once he filled my bed with chestnuts."

"Ha!" said one of the men, a tall, strapping fellow with gentle eyes. "You were lucky. I don't even want to tell you what he put in our beds!"

"And just what did he put in *your* bed?" purred a low voice, and Sybil turned to find a very handsome rogue eyeing her up and down.

Sybil eyed him right back. "Himself," she said, and everyone around them erupted with laughter.

"Very funny," said a familiar voice from behind her, and Sybil smiled up at *her* de Burgh, her husband, in truth. Not even the Church had dared to dispute this marriage of hers, conceived for her protection, but grounded in love. Yet she had only a moment to reflect upon the blissful state of her union before more congratulations were tendered.

This time, it was the earl himself who spoke with a benign nod. "Robin, 'tis well you have done for yourself," he said.

"I think so," Robin answered, but his ready grin quickly faded into a somber expression. "Thank you for your help, Father."

"No gratitude is necessary, for we could all do no less for you. I am just glad that all is well," Campion said.

"Is it?" Robin asked. "This latest effort has been

foiled, but what next? Will I always have to look over my shoulder lest some Welshman target my family?''

Campion shook his head. "No one would dare touch your wife now that she has the full force of the de Burghs behind her, as well as the support of the Church. Besides, her kinsmen have their hands full now. By all accounts, Edward raised a vast army on the borders and has marched in to subdue the rebellion. I suspect that this will be the end of the reign of the old princes, so you will be without a kingdom, Lady,'' Campion added, turning to Sybil.

Startled, Sybil loosed a laugh. "I make no claims of royalty, my lord,'' she said.

"Please, call me Campion since we are all family now,'' the earl urged, his oddly discerning gaze warm with welcome. And Sybil felt her heart fill to overflowing, for that simple word encompassed not only her own marriage, but all the men and women who milled about, laughing and talking, and the babies who would carry on the heritage of the de Burghs. Having gone from no relatives at all into the embrace of this wonderful clan was truly an embarrassment of riches, Sybil mused.

Robin, too, seemed to be contemplating his kindred, without his usual frown, for his feelings were clearly evident upon his handsome features. And the sentimental mood that had seized them both at this vast de Burgh reunion wasn't broken until the brother with the limp, Reynold, stepped forward to give Robin an arch look.

"I was just wondering, brother,'' he said, his tone wryly taunting, "whether you ever lifted the curse?''

Swiftly glancing at her husband, Sybil nearly burst

out laughing at the innocent expression he assumed as he feigned ignorance.

"Curse?" Robin said. "What curse?"

* * * * *

Travel to the British Isles
and behold the romance and
adventure within the pages of these
Harlequin Historicals® novels

ON SALE JANUARY 2002
MY LADY'S TRUST
by **Julia Justiss**
(Regency England, 1812)
A society lady fakes her own death and discovers
true love with an eligible earl!

DRAGON'S DOWER
by **Catherine Archer**
(Medieval England, 1200)
Book #1 of *The Brotherhood of the Dragon* series
By the king's decree a brave knight must marry
the daughter of his fiercest foe....

ON SALE FEBRUARY 2002
HIS LADY FAIR
by **Margo Maguire**
(Medieval England, 1429)
A world-weary spy becomes embroiled in intrigue—
and forbidden passion!

 Harlequin Historicals®
Historical Romantic Adventure!

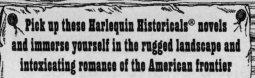

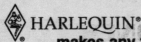

CALL THE ONES YOU LOVE OVER THE HOLIDAYS!

Save $25 off future book purchases when you buy any four Harlequin® or Silhouette® books in October, November and December 2001,

PLUS

receive a phone card good for 15 minutes of long-distance calls to anyone you want in North America!

WHAT AN INCREDIBLE DEAL!

Just fill out this form and attach 4 proofs of purchase (cash register receipts) from October, November and December 2001 books, and Harlequin Books will send you a coupon booklet worth a total savings of $25 off future purchases of Harlequin® and Silhouette® books, AND a 15-minute phone card to call the ones you love, anywhere in North America.

Please send this form, along with your cash register receipts as proofs of purchase, to:
In the USA: Harlequin Books, P.O. Box 9057, Buffalo, NY 14269-9057
In Canada: Harlequin Books, P.O. Box 622, Fort Erie, Ontario L2A 5X3
Cash register receipts must be dated no later than December 31, 2001.
Limit of 1 coupon booklet and phone card per household.
Please allow 4-6 weeks for delivery.

I accept your offer! Enclosed are 4 proofs of purchase.
Please send me my coupon booklet
and a 15-minute phone card:

Name: _____

Address: _____ City: _____

State/Prov.: _____ Zip/Postal Code: _____

Account Number (if available): _____

---

097 KJB DAGL
PHQ4013